PRAISE FOR *THE RAVEN ROOM*

"This story is gripping... With a cliffhanger ending, *The Raven Room* will leave readers wondering what will happen next."

—*RT Book Reviews*, 4 stars

"*The Raven Room* is really about the evolution of relationships, boundaries, and choices; and with Ana Medeiros providing plenty of insight into the complexities surrounding all three arenas, there's not only plenty of room for depth and detail in a novel that discusses control and domination; there's room for much more... Readers who enjoy complex stories with strong characterization and psychological depth will find *The Raven Room* a satisfyingly story of emotional turbulence."

—*Midwest Book Review*

"*The Raven Room* will have everything you could possibly want and more."

—*San Francisco Book Review*

SAVAGE BONDS

THE RAVEN ROOM TRILOGY
- book two -

ana medeiros

DIVERSIONBOOKS

Also by Ana Medeiros

The Raven Room

Diversion Books
A Division of Diversion Publishing Corp.
443 Park Avenue South, Suite 1008
New York, New York 10016
www.DiversionBooks.com

Copyright © 2017 by Ana Medeiros
All rights reserved, including the right to reproduce this book or portions
thereof in any form whatsoever.

This is a work of fiction. Names, characters, places and incidents either are the
product of the author's imagination or are used fictitiously. Any resemblance to
actual persons, living or dead, events or locales is entirely coincidental.

For more information, email info@diversionbooks.com

First Diversion Books edition December 2017.
Paperback ISBN: 978-1-68230-349-8
eBook ISBN: 978-1-68230-348-1

LSIDB/1710

To Teresa

PROLOGUE

"How do you know Tatiana Thompson?"

"I don't know who that is."

Julian Reeve still hadn't given the police any useful information, and he had yet to ask any questions. Based on her years of experience as a homicide detective, Pam found that unsettling. He might be able to put on a blank expression, but the dark circles under his eyes told her that he hadn't slept much during the seventy hours they had him in custody. His indifference was an act.

Soon, they would have to charge him or let him go. If she hoped to make sense of the events that occurred three days ago, and Julian's involvement, she had to act fast.

Pam slid a photograph in his direction. "Who is this woman?"

The image was of Julian and a woman surrounded by shelves and piles of used books. Julian covered the photograph with his palm and his fingertips touched the woman's face.

Julian's reaction caused Pam to stare at the photograph. He had his arm around her and the woman looked up at Julian while he faced the camera. They were both smiling. The photograph had captured one of those rare moments when two people felt genuinely happy; the type of feeling that can't be imitated or suppressed.

"Alana," Julian answered.

"Did you know Alana Stewart was a stolen identity?" Pam continued.

"No."

Detective Colton jumped in. "So you don't know the real name of the woman who called herself Alana Stewart?"

Colton had been assigned as Pam's partner less than a year ago.

She didn't despise him, but as the senior member of the team, she knew how his inexperience, and more often than not, his stupidity, hindered their performance.

"I met her at a coffee shop five months ago," Julian replied. "She introduced herself as Alana. I've always known her as Alana."

"Were you aware, throughout the course of your relationship, that she lived in a rented room at the New Jackson Hotel?" Pam had been the one who had told her stepdaughter, Meredith Dalton, where Alana lived. In turn, Meredith had shared that information with Julian, who Meredith had been sleeping with for the previous two years.

He nodded affirmatively.

"Did you know she had an identical twin sister?" she asked.

"I had no idea."

"Who's the woman at your condo the morning we arrived?" Pam hadn't expected to come face-to-face with someone who looked exactly like the dead woman in the morgue. Thrown off her game, she had made a series of mistakes. Luckily Colton hadn't picked up on her errors.

"Alana," Julian replied.

"That's not the woman we saw at your condo," Pam said. "Alana, the woman you've been having a relationship with, is dead. Murdered in her hotel room Friday night."

Julian's attorney interjected. "You have no proof that the woman who was in Dr. Reeve's apartment is not the same woman who appears with him in these photos."

"All the evidence suggests they are not the same person." Pam turned to Julian. "Where were you Friday night?"

"At home," he answered.

Colton, who had been standing with a coffee cup in hand, sat at the table. "The whole time?"

Pam saw Julian thinking.

"For most of it," he replied.

Pam leaned forward, closing the space between them. "Most of it?"

"Tell us the truth, Dr. Reeve, and we'll let—"

"Meredith was with me," Julian said, silencing Colton.

Regardless of his haggard appearance, he sounded confident—in full control of himself. It would be a mistake to ever underestimate this man, Pam thought.

"When was Meredith with you?" she asked.

"All night. Until the time you showed up in my condo."

Frustrated, Pam crossed her arms in front of her. She wanted to slam her fist into Julian's face. Meredith had given the same answer when Pam questioned her. Even though Meredith and Julian hadn't spoken since the morning Pam had brought him into the station, Meredith had successfully placed herself as Julian's alibi. Pam's gut feeling, which she trusted more than Meredith's version of events, told her both Julian and Meredith were lying.

"Recount to us the events of Friday night in chronological order," Pam demanded.

"Alana was supposed to come over to spend time with Meredith and I. When she didn't show up, we decided to drive to the hotel to look for her." Julian spoke as if what had happened didn't involve him. His voice sounded cold, indifferent. "We found her barely conscious, wandering down the street near North Jackson and South Sangamon."

Pam scowled. "And you didn't think to take her to the hospital? To call the cops?"

"She pleaded with us not to. She was afraid."

"What did you do after you picked her up?" Colton asked.

Pam held back a smirk. Even though he carried a badge and a gun, a man of Colton's stature rarely had the chance to wield power over someone like Julian Reeve. Colton's gloating attitude didn't escape Pam, but she let him revel in it.

"We brought her to my condo," Julian replied.

"It's clear Dr. Reeve had nothing to do with the other woman's death," his attorney intervened. Pam noticed the sweat stain on the collar of the man's twill shirt. While his client remained impassive, Jeff Davis—one of the best defense attorneys in Chicago—was showing signs of stress. "At the time the murder took place, he was with Meredith Dalton. You have no evidence against Dr. Reeve, otherwise the prosecutor would have pressed charges. Your time is almost up." He peeked at his wristwatch. "In ten minutes, to be exact."

Colton leaned back on his chair, coffee cup still in hand. "The prosecutor put forward a request to hold him for longer."

"Which the judge denied." Davis smiled, looking smug. "Ten minutes. Make it count."

Impatience took hold of Pam. She needed Reeve without an alibi, at the scene of the murder. With no hard proof of his involvement, he would slip through their fingers, and as soon as he stepped out of the police station, it would be much harder to get him back to where he now sat.

Pam opened a file folder and displayed a series of pictures in front of Julian. "I'll try to make this as straightforward as possible, Dr. Reeve." She pointed to the photograph she had shown him earlier. "This woman, with whom you have been having a relationship with for the last five months and who you say you met at a coffee shop, is dead—"

"The woman he's been having a relationship with was in his apartment when you brought him here," Davis interrupted.

Pam could see right through what Davis was doing—by declaring that the woman in Julian's apartment was the same one Julian had been romantically involved with, Davis was trying to clear his client of any connection to the victim.

"Alana was killed Friday night," Pam continued, undeterred. "She had an altercation with someone and died from blunt force trauma. Her brother-in-law identified her body, which means his wife, Tatiana Thompson"—Pam pointed to a blown up driver's license photograph of a female who looked just like the woman who had been using Alana Stewart's identity—"was the one in your condo that morning. According to what you just told us, the woman you knew as Alana failed to show up as planned, so you and Meredith went to look for her. When you did, you came across a battered woman, barely conscious, not far from the New Jackson Hotel. Believing she was the woman you knew as Alana, you brought her to your home. You didn't have a chance to ask who had hurt her. Is that what you're saying?"

"Wait." Julian's voice gained a tone of authority that incensed Pam. "Tatiana Thompson? What's her husband's name?"

"Steven Thompson. Do you know him?" Colton asked.

Julian blanched, then he started to drum his fingers on the tabletop.

Pam almost smiled. His inscrutable façade had started to crack.

"When we were at your condo that morning, why did Tatiana Thompson lead us to believe she was Alana, the woman you've been seeing? Can you explain that to us?" Colton continued.

"Because they're the same person," Davis reiterated.

Colton cursed out Davis under his breath. "When we find her we'll make sure to ask her."

"Find her?" Julian directed the question to Pam. "What happened to her?"

Colton replied instead. "According to Meredith, not long after we left your condo, Tatiana took off while Meredith was in the bathroom. She's missing. Any idea where she might be? We've got questions to ask her."

"Have you talked to Thompson? You saw the state she was in," Julian said. "He's the one who that did that to her. He almost killed her. What proof do you have that he didn't assault both women?" Julian pointed to his face. "He sought me out earlier that day and attacked me."

It didn't surprise Pam that Julian took the opportunity to incriminate Thompson. Had she been in his position, she would have done the same.

"Why did he attack you?" Colton asked.

"That's obvious," Davis jumped in. "He found out his wife is in a relationship with Dr. Reeve. Jealousy motivated Mr. Thompson to attack my client."

"Are you suggesting that this whole time your client has

been sleeping with Tatiana Thompson, who was pretending to be Alana?" Colton chuckled. "And that we have it wrong by thinking Alana was Sofia?"

Since being asked by Meredith months ago to find out more about Reeve, Pam had stumbled upon information that she knew he wanted to keep hidden. Now she had no other choice than to exploit it to get what she needed.

"Dr. Reeve, you're connected to both sisters." Pam pulled out three other photographs from the file folder. She put down a photograph of Julian when he was sixteen years old in the foster care system. She then placed one other photograph to the right and one to the left, leaving his photo in the center.

"Tatiana and Sofia were the twin daughters of Vadim and Olga Dulgorukova, your foster parents from the time you were fourteen until you were sixteen. Tatiana"—she pointed at the photograph on the left—"goes by Tatiana Thompson and is missing." She then pointed at the photograph on the right. "Sofia, who had been using Alana Stewart's identity, and with whom you were having a relationship, is dead." Pam stood up. "Do you really think we believe you're telling us everything you know?"

Julian didn't speak, but his shocked expression could either mean he hadn't known Alana's true identity or he didn't expect the police to have that information.

"You guys got nothing," Davis said. "Dr. Reeve has an alibi for the night of the murder. You have no evidence that he ever set foot in that hotel room." He grabbed the photograph that had been taken at Eliot's bookstore. "You have no way of proving that the woman in this photo with Dr. Reeve isn't Tatiana Thompson."

Pam glanced at her watch. She had five minutes left.

"The hotel room where Sofia Dulgorukova's body was discovered—where we found photos of your client with one of the twins—was registered under the name Alana Stewart," she said. "Her fingerprints are all over the room. Furthermore, Sofia's driver's license and passport were found hidden under the mattress. It's clear to anyone with half a brain that Sofia Dulgorukova was the one pretending to be Alana Stewart."

"That's all circumstantial." Davis stood up, tapped Julian's shoulder, and made a gesture for him to get to his feet. "Without Tatiana to tell her side of the story you're shit out of luck. And, even if you do find her, she will tell you what I already know—Dr. Reeve is innocent of any crime."

"We'll find her and we'll see if that's the case," Pam said.

"Anyone could have been in that hotel room with Sofia Dulgorukova," Davis continued. "Anyone could have killed her. Let's not forget she was living at the New Jackson Hotel, which is basically a flophouse."

Pam wouldn't bend. "Exactly. The New Jackson isn't a safe place. She knew the person who killed her. She let them into her room. It wasn't just anyone. It was someone she trusted."

"Do you have proof that the door was locked?" Davis asked. "How was she found?"

Pam met Davis's eyes. He knew the answer. He just wanted to hear her say it.

"The door of her room was wide open," Colton replied. "Another guest walked by and saw her naked on the bed."

As he waited for Julian to follow him, Davis smirked at Pam. "Good luck solving this one."

CHAPTER 1

"We had to let him go."

"Had to?" Thompson asked.

Faint from lack of sleep, Pam sat on one of the tall stools by the kitchen counter. The clock on the wall read two thirty in the morning. She had been awake for well over twenty-four hours.

Lately, she was waking up in the middle of the night, her heart racing, her mind plunged into confusion. With her eyes wide open, the darkness around her prolonged her feeling of turmoil, and suddenly, she would be struck by racing thoughts of all the cases she had been unable to solve—and the ones still demanding her attention. But one case always stood out. During those panic-filled moments, her instinct would tell her to reach for the man lying beside her, but before her hand found his body, she remembered that she didn't want to accept the comfort that this man, her husband, readily offered her.

And now there was another dead woman.

"Reeve didn't kill Sofia," she replied. "And there's no good evidence to suggest that he did it."

Thompson sat down next to her. His bloodshot eyes revealed that he felt as worn out as she did.

"He might not be the one who killed her, but he knows where my wife is," he said. "That's all I care about. Finding Tatiana."

"Finding your wife is not my main concern."

"Hasn't it crossed your mind that Tatiana might have witnessed what happened to her sister? Finding Tatiana should be your main concern."

"I've been to Reeve's condo with a search warrant. I've visited Meredith at her place. I talked to her housemate. I've visited Reeve's adoptive mom. The woman is senile, but I showed a photo of Tatiana to her live-in caregiver. No one has seen her. It has been a week. Maybe Tatiana *did* sneak out when Meredith was in the bathroom."

"Are you trying to convince me? Or yourself? You said Tatiana was covered in cuts and bruises. She could barely hold herself up. Where would she go?"

"Would they help her?" she asked.

"Who?"

"You know who." She paced in front of Thompson. If she remained seated, she wouldn't find the energy to leave his home before dawn.

"I've asked around. No one has seen or heard from Tatiana."

"Was that wise?"

"There are people I can trust within the organization."

"Don't be naïve, Steven. Your access to the club has been suspended because of your fight with Reeve. You're not one of them."

"Neither is Tatiana."

"Her ties are stronger than yours."

"I'm the one with the money. That's all they care about."

"Every single person in that organization is only in it for the money?"

Thompson nodded. "Those I've met."

"Tatiana has something you'll never have, and it can be worth just as much as all the money you have in the bank."

Thompson eyed her with disgust. "Don't be crass, Pamela. It's not your style."

Hearing her full name made her grind her teeth. It reminded her of a time long gone, and she didn't want to be faced with such memories.

"Be careful, Steven. I understand you want to find Tatiana, but you don't want to get killed in the process."

Pam hadn't been inside Thompson's home before Tatiana's disappearance. Now, as she stood in his kitchen, she looked for traces of his wife. But she saw no pictures and no personal objects that provided an insight into Tatiana's life. Not even proof that she ever lived there.

"Nothing will happen to me," Thompson said. "I know what's important to them and I won't stand in their way."

"Helping me is standing in their way."

"That's my problem. Not yours."

"You still haven't told me why you beat your wife within an inch of her life. As soon as I saw her I knew it had been you."

"How many times do I need to say to you that I wasn't the one who left Tatiana in that state?"

"That's hard to swallow."

"I thought, of all people, you'd believe me."

"Because you've never lied to me?" Pam asked.

"Because you know me."

"That's my point." She walked up to the fridge. Several clippings from magazines around the world, featuring libraries, were pinned to it and stood out amidst the spotless kitchen. "Reeve incriminated you. He also pointed out that you came to him earlier in the day and hit him."

"Did he also say how it happened? Where it happened?"

"Of course not. Reeve isn't stupid. He knows he can't bring up The Raven Room. Especially during a murder investigation." Pam noticed some of the clippings had an aged, yellow tinge to them. "Do you have a library?" she asked.

"Sure, upstairs."

"I want to see it."

Thompson took her to the second floor and then up a second set of stairs to the attic.

"This is an impressive collection." Pam approached one of the rows of shelves that ran along the periphery of the room, from the floor all the way up to the slanted ceiling. "I didn't know you were into books."

"They're Tatiana's. I rarely come up here."

Pam pulled a book from the shelf. As she leafed through it, she noticed a black marker line on the bottom, outside of the pages. She returned the book to the shelf and picked up another one. Four out of the five books she looked at had the same black marker line.

"I'd never admit this to Reeve, or to his attorney, but we have no proof that your wife isn't the one Reeve has been seeing."

"Tatiana isn't fucking Reeve. When he tried to have her leave the club with him, I misunderstood what was happening. I got angry and I slapped her. I regret that."

"Right. You slapped your wife but someone else beat her. All in the space of a couple of hours."

"When you saw Tatiana that morning, and you asked her who had done that to her, did she say it was me?"

"She didn't say anyone's name. But she knows about you and me. She doesn't trust me."

"You should have brought her home."

"I was protecting you. If I took her in, she'd reveal that you were the one who assaulted her, and there'd be nothing I could do to stop you from getting arrested."

"Don't blame me for your stupidity. Keeping me away from the police's eye assures I can still help you in your investigation. You left Tatiana in that condo and you took Reeve with you to protect your interests, Pamela."

"How is bringing a serial killer to justice protecting my interests?"

Thompson chuckled. He sounded bitter. "It won't hurt your career."

"Do you have any idea what will happen when—"

"We've known each other for twenty-nine years," he interrupted. "Nothing is more important to you than your career. Not even Meredith, who you claim to love. Let's be honest, she'll be the one who'll suffer the most when the truth comes out."

"Now you're concerned for Meredith?"

"She knows where Tatiana is. She was the last person to see her."

"Didn't you hear me? I've talked to her. She doesn't know."

"And you believe her?" Thompson asked.

"Why would Meredith lie about anything involving your wife? She would need a reason to do so."

"Reeve is her reason. You need to show her the video."

"And then what? You don't know Meredith. She wouldn't stay silent. She would ask questions—"

"Of course she would. But it would also compel her to reveal where Tatiana is and to stop pursuing the idea of writing an article on The Raven Room."

"You haven't mentioned the article to anyone, have you? I shared that with you because—"

"You trust me. I'm aware. I don't have to explain to you why it'll be a problem if people find out about the article, do I?"

"Meredith is impetuous. She gets an idea in her head and she goes for it. No matter what. But she's also fickle. One day she wants one thing; the next, something else. I'm hoping she's already moved on."

"She's been sleeping with Reeve for over two years. She doesn't sound fickle. Hasn't Meredith asked why you hate him? She knows you've been keeping secrets; she's suspicious. Also, she's been going to the club, don't you think sooner or later she'll—"

Pam cut him off. "No."

"Look, I want to find my wife and you want justice," Thompson continued. "That brings both of us to Tatiana. And if we show the video to Meredith, we'll *have* Tatiana. Why are you refusing to see that?"

"Leave Meredith out of this. She's my concern, not yours. Don't go near her, do you understand?"

"I'm the one who has the video. If I decide to show it to her, you can't stop me."

Pam rushed to Thompson, raising her hand to strike him but he caught it midair.

"Do it, Pamela, and I'll hit you right back."

She pulled her hand away and walked out of the attic.

Thompson followed her as she made her way back downstairs. "Have you reopened the four cases?"

"Not yet."

"Why not?"

"I have to look into a couple of things…I'll let you know."

"I'm thinking I'm going to pay Reeve a visit."

Pam spun around. "Don't approach him."

"He's keeping Tatiana from me."

"I doubt he's holding her against her will."

"I love my wife. Regardless of whom she fucks. Or I fuck, for that matter."

Thompson's words were meant to wound her but she refused to allow it. "You were so sure Tatiana wasn't involved with him."

Thompson's expression hardened.

"Steven, you might love your wife, but she doesn't love you back. She's afraid of you."

Pam left Thompson's house. Glancing at her phone, she saw she had two missed calls from her husband. Without hesitation, she put her phone back in her pocket.

All of a sudden, she felt like she was being watched. She scanned her surroundings as she crossed the street—the several parked cars appeared to be empty. With no sign of pedestrians or passing cars, the street looked deserted. She didn't fear for her safety—she knew how to defend herself—but she locked all the doors as soon as she entered her car. Before she drove away she decided that, instead of heading home, she would go straight to the station.

• • •

Thompson heard a noise behind him as he stood by his stove, boiling kettle in hand, ready to make himself a cup of tea.

"Let me guess, you came back to explain why you haven't reopened the cases?"

20

He turned around and almost dropped the kettle when he found himself face-to-face with someone other than Pam.

"How did you get into my home?"

The Asian man in the suit smiled.

"The front door was unlocked." He sat down on the kitchen stool. Before he continued, he placed a gun on the counter. "It hasn't been that long since we saw each other, has it?"

"What do you want?"

"It appears that some of our employees—our women—are being killed. That's not good. Not only because we need them, but also because their deaths have, it seems, sparked some talk."

Thompson started to speak, but the man cut him off. "Our business operates best when no one is asking questions or looking in our direction. Everyone, including you, prefers it that way. Anything that threatens our anonymity has to be taken care of. You're a businessman yourself, Thompson. You understand."

"You still haven't told me what you want."

"I want you to talk."

"Listen, I don't know who sent you or what you were told, but I know nothing about any dead women."

"Should I have this conversation with your detective friend? She left your place in quite a rush just a few moments ago. What were you two talking about?"

Without taking his eyes from the man, Thompson's hand shook as he set the kettle down on the stove.

"You and Pamela Sung met in your first year of college," the man said. "She was your girlfriend for a while, wasn't she? Five years. Long time."

"How do you know that?"

"You proposed to her on Christmas Day with the ring you bought with the money from the sale of your beloved Shelby Cobra. You refused to buy it with your family's money. You wanted the ring to have a special meaning to both of you. But she turned you down, and then broke up with you. I like that you have remained friends. It shows you know how not to hold a grudge."

Thompson turned and tried to run. Before he could do so, the man grabbed him, pushed him to the ground, and pinned his arm behind his back. With skill born from experience, the man twisted Thompson's arm further, breaking it with an audible crack. Thompson screamed out in pain.

The man returned to his seat by the kitchen island. He ran his hands through his shoulder-length hair, then tugged on the sleeves of his dress shirt, adjusting the silver cufflinks. "Get up and make me a cup of tea."

Gasping for air, his eyes filled with tears. Thompson moaned as he rolled over and held his injured arm close to his chest.

"I said get up."

Thompson struggled to get back on his feet.

"I like chamomile," the man continued. "You have it, right? Who doesn't have chamomile tea?"

Thompson finally managed to stand. He failed to pour the boiling water inside a mug and spilled it on the counter. The water dripped onto his bare feet. After a couple of tries, he succeeded at filling the mug halfway. As he reached for a tea bag, he dropped the box of tea. Using the counter for support, he kneeled down, his whole body trembling. He staggered as he stood up again and placed the tea mug in front of the man.

"It needs to steep a bit longer." The man held the tea mug in one hand and the gun in the other. "But that's OK. Our conversation has only started. How is Tatiana doing?"

Thompson held on to the kitchen counter. He struggled to breathe through the pain of his broken arm.

"When I heard about the death of Tatiana's twin, I remembered a conversation she and I had years ago. She told me that when she was a kid, she thought her and her twin, because they had been born at the same time, had to die at the same time. Don't know why, but that story stayed with me." The man blew on his hot tea. "I always liked Tatiana."

"Fuck you." Sweat dripped down Thompson's temples.

"Your wife is under Reeve's protection. Which I doubt is news to you. But that protection only stops you and the police from getting to her. Not us. Now it's up to you, if we do or don't take her from him." The man took sip of his tea. "How does it feel to hold your wife's life in your hands?"

"Just tell me what you want me to do."

"Who is killing our women?"

Thompson grimaced. "If I tell you what I know, will you help me see my wife?"

"We don't get involved in marital quarrels."

"Do you promise not to hurt Tatiana?"

"If I'm pleased with what I hear, we won't hurt your wife. What Reeve does, though? We can't make any promises."

CHAPTER 2

"What do you want?"

Meredith stood in the open doorway, blocking Pam's entrance into Julian's condo.

"I need to speak to Reeve. If you tell me he's not here, I'll just come back," Pam replied.

"You spoke with him three days ago, when you were here with your search warrant."

"I need to speak to him," Pam insisted.

"It's nine o'clock at night."

"Reeve is a busy man. Want to make sure I catch him."

Meredith heard the sarcasm in Pam's voice and had to stop herself from cursing. Without a warrant, she wasn't legally obliged to allow Pam inside Julian's home, but sending her away wouldn't stop Pam from harassing them.

As Pam entered the spacious living room, Meredith noticed her stepmother's attention gravitate toward the large windows. The curtains were pulled back and, from that height, the Chicago skyline stood too striking for anyone to ignore.

"Wonder how it must feel to stand here, night after night," Pam said. "A whole city at your feet."

Meredith did not join Pam at the window.

"You're angry at me for doing my job, Meredith. Which, in turn, is motivating you to do and say things that will only cause you harm. I've told you this before—you shouldn't be here."

"And you shouldn't be working this case. You and I are related. I told that to your sergeant when I was at the station but for some reason, which I can't fathom, it's made no difference."

24

Her stepmother didn't hesitate. "Get me Reeve."

Closing her hands in tight fists, Meredith turned around to go find Julian.

When she discovered him fully dressed, lying on his bed, she exhaled with relief.

"Pam's here. She wants to speak to you."

Julian didn't move. She grabbed his arm and shook him a couple times. "Julian, did you hear me? Pam's here. We can't leave her alone for too long. She'll start looking around the condo. Get up."

"I can't," he said, still not moving.

"You must." She started to pull him out of bed. "Have you been drinking? What are you on?"

Julian propped himself onto his elbow, his hand covering his eyes. "I've already answered all her questions."

"And you'll do it all over again. Just stick to our story. In the last week, since you were released from jail, neither of us has seen or heard from Tatiana."

"She doesn't believe us."

"I know her. If you refuse to speak to her, she'll do anything necessary to convince the judge to grant a new search warrant."

Julian sat on the edge of the bed. His head hung between his knees. "I'm going to be sick."

He vomited on the floor.

"Jesus Christ, Julian." Meredith went into the en suite bathroom and came out with a wet cloth. She passed it to him. "Obstruction of justice can land someone in prison for three years. I lied for you. I'm not going to let both our lives get fucked because you can't pull yourself together. Go out there and deal with whatever Pam throws at you."

Julian managed to get to the living room, and when Meredith sat down beside him on the couch, the reality of his unkempt appearance hit her—he wore a vomit-stained t-shirt and wrinkled, threadbare sweatpants. With his greasy hair and heavy beard, he barely resembled the man she knew.

Julian reached for her hand and laced his fingers through hers.

"Both you and Meredith have told me what happened the day we took you in for questioning, Dr. Reeve. You've assured me time and again that you're unaware of Tatiana's whereabouts," Pam began, only to be met with Julian's stony silence.

"We told you the truth," Meredith replied. "We've got no idea where she is. She took off."

Pam gestured toward the living room entrance. "I'm sure you haven't forgotten the state Tatiana was in. She was injured. When she showed up in that hallway, she was naked and could barely stand. I have to ask myself where would she find the strength, let alone the clothes, to make her way out of here."

"She had her clothes from the night before, the ones she had been wearing when we found her." Meredith had rehearsed her answers.

Pam turned to Julian. "And she didn't have a chance to tell you what happened? Who did that to her?"

"Her husband did it. I told you this at the station," he replied.

"We need to find Tatiana," Pam emphasized, ignoring Julian's answer.

He sat so still that Meredith wondered if he had heard Pam. She gave his fingers a little squeeze. A few seconds went by with no reaction from Julian.

"Did Sofia ever mention anyone who you think might have wanted to hurt her?" Pam continued.

"If you don't have anything new to ask me, don't bother coming around," Julian's said in a harsh tone.

For the last week, Meredith had lived in a mix of exhaustion, fear, and unanswered questions. And she couldn't even begin to grasp the complexity of Julian's emotional state. How does one feel after losing so much?

"Would it be OK if I did a quick walkthrough of your home?" Pam asked. "Just to be sure we didn't miss anything from our search?"

"Detective Sung, the only walking you'll be doing in my home is back to the front door. I will not give you permission to invade my life more than you already have. I'd like you to leave."

Pam didn't seem bothered by Julian's animosity.

"Am I still a suspect?" he asked.

"We are, at least at this point, dealing with two separate cases—a missing person and a homicide. You're a person of interest in both of them."

Pam had started to move toward the foyer when she stopped and turned around. "One more thing," she said, hands in her coat pockets. "Since we haven't been able to track down any other relatives, Mr. Thompson has offered to pay for Sofia's funeral. I'd say that's more than considerate. But maybe you'd want to pay for it instead, seeing as Tatiana and Sofia are the closest thing you've ever had to siblings?"

Meredith had seen Pam's blank expression before. It was the same vacuous look Pam relied on when she knew she had struck a nerve and wanted to savor the other person's suffering.

Julian didn't hide his anger. "Get. Out."

"Next time I knock on your door," Pam glanced at Meredith, "she won't be standing by you."

CHAPTER 3

Her blood covered Julian's chest.

She used it to draw on his skin. Her fingertips moved smoothly at a slow, taunting pace. She drew a line over his stomach and continued past his navel. Aroused, Julian moaned when she closed her hand on his erection.

The room they were in was small. No noise broke in or out of it, and Julian's loud, short gasps sounded almost painful. The thought that he might have lost grip on reality crossed his mind, but as fast as the notion formed, it disappeared.

The sensation of her lips made Julian's hips shoot off the bed into her eager mouth. With his eyes closed, he ran his fingers through her hair. It was so straight that they slid easily from the roots to the ends. He did it again. And again.

He couldn't convince himself she was who he needed her to be. Her hair felt too straight, too sleek, and not long enough. The next time he slid his fingers through her hair, instead of a gentle caress, he closed his hand on her nape and, without care, pulled her face close to his.

That's when Julian finally dared to open his eyes.

As soon as he did, he knew he shouldn't be there. The same disgust he felt for himself he suddenly felt toward her. He couldn't control the sensation of boundless shame.

Julian sat up on the bed and pushed her into the mattress. As he reached for the knife, he lifted her hair away from her neck. She didn't fight him. Her pliant body welcomed his touch. Straddling her, he stared at her naked breasts. Awash with the lighting's red hue, her pale skin turned luminescent. It begged him to do what he hungered for.

He brought the tip of the blade to the base of her neck and she cried out when he pressed it firmly into her flesh.

Julian smiled, but he didn't know why. He felt no joy.

Only what came next was better than this moment. He moved the blade in a curved line, almost meeting her shoulder and, before he lifted it from her flesh, blood starting to seep out of the long cut.

The sight of it hypnotized him.

But this time, it didn't feel enough. Maybe never again would it be enough. Reaching for the small bag on the night table, he poured the white powder into a small pile between her breasts. With the short straw that they both used earlier that night, he inhaled it up his nose. The rush seized him. He threw his head back and chuckled with euphoria. He didn't recognize his own laughter, and that only made him laugh harder.

Her blood seeped into what was left of the powder on her torso. He mixed the two with the tip of his finger and then he rubbed it into his gums. The metallic taste of her blood with the chalky texture of the powder should have made him gag, but it only made his whole body yearn for more.

He grabbed the small glass vial by the bed and, using the eyedropper that came with it, placed one drop of his favorite hallucinogenic under his tongue.

Julian began to hear crying sounds. Aroused, not knowing if the cries came from him or her, he surrendered to the wave of desire growing within him. He grabbed the knife and stroked her sides with the blade.

Julian only realized he had cut her again when deep red blotches appeared on the linen sheets. Wanting to absorb her blood with his own body, Julian pressed his palms to the cuts. Her skin became slippery and he couldn't get a good hold on her. Sweat dripped from his forehead into his eyes but the sting of it didn't stop him. He stared down—his favorite moment—and saw his fingers crossed with her blood.

Julian caressed her stomach; her skin was now stained red. He couldn't stop. He continued, spreading her blood onto her shoulders and arms. Nestled between her legs, his need to orgasm became undeniable. His palm and fingers moved in a closed fist along his cock. As he guided himself into her, the sight of his blood-slicked hand wrapped tightly around his member sent a rush of desire up his spine. He didn't remember having a more powerful erection. He began to move in and out of her with a force that pushed her against the headboard. His release came fast—almost immediate.

Julian refused to wait for his body to recover. As he got off the bed on unsteady legs, he stumbled and ended up colliding into the wall. That didn't deter him. He hurried to put on his clothes and was so frantic that he almost ripped his dress shirt trying to get his hands through the sleeves. He left the room without looking back.

Covering his eyes, Julian moved down the narrow corridor. He felt as if people were determined to walk into him. He cursed, forcing his way through the crowd.

By the time he sat behind the wheel of his car, he wanted to run back to The Raven Room. He turned the key in the ignition and the sound of the engine coming to life made him cover his ears. Everything around him appeared to be too bright and extremely loud. He turned the AC on full blast. He saw red confetti blowing out of the vents, and opened his mouth and let the small flecks of paper land on his tongue. They instantly dissolved with a bitter taste. He tried to get rid of it by rubbing his fingers over his tongue but it only made the acrid flavor worse.

Julian buried his face in his hands and cried.

CHAPTER 4

"This one is different."

Pam sat doubled over scattered pictures and police reports strewed across her desk. She had downed seven cups of bad drip coffee in the span of two hours and its effects were finally kicking in—she felt both exhausted and restless.

She heard a knock and raised her eyes to the door, wondering who was idiotic enough to bother her so late in the day. When she saw Colton's head peek in, she resisted throwing her empty coffee mug at him.

"I have the toxicology report you were asking about," he said.

She rubbed her temples trying to stave off a crippling headache. "Why wasn't the toxicology report in the case folder?"

"You're asking me?" Colton dropped the report on her desk. "I'm not a file clerk."

"Sit down."

He sighed and eased himself down onto the empty chair by her desk. "What's this about?"

Pam leafed through the toxicology report. "Sofia Dulgorukova's murder."

"We were both at the crime scene. I know what you know, which isn't much."

"That's the problem. If you knew more than me we might actually get somewhere."

"I don't know much about her murder, but I know plenty about her," Colton said. "She's a slut who ended up living in a dump, giving away blow jobs in a used bookstore. She had no business sense, which is the only thing that can make me respect a woman who would choose to live her life like that."

"Keep your piggish thoughts to yourself. They're terrifying."

He began to stand. "Doesn't sound like you need me here so, if you don't mind, I'm gonna jet…"

"Stop." Pam interrupted him. "I do need you here."

"Why?"

"Sit your ass back down.

"This better be good."

"I need you to tail Julian Reeve. Everywhere he goes, you go. If he doesn't leave his house for three days, you don't step out of your car for three days."

Colton almost jumped off his chair. "That shouldn't be my frigging job. Put an officer on him. There are more useful ways for me to spend my time."

"Your job is whatever I tell you it is. How long have you been doing this, huh? Six months? You've a lot of dues to pay, Colton. Just be happy I'm not telling you to go pick up my lunch."

"How's tailing Reeve any different?"

"You're working a case. That's how it's different. Pay attention to his routine. The places he goes. Who he's with. I want a full description of every female that goes within ten feet of him. He knows where Tatiana Thompson is and we need to find her."

Colton nodded.

"Make sure he doesn't see you. No one can know about this. Not even here at the station. This stays between you and me."

"Why can't anyone know?"

"Just do what I tell you."

"Since when do we keep secrets around here?"

"We're not keeping secrets. We're protecting our case. I need you on this with me. Aren't you my partner?"

"Listen, Sung, you like having me as your partner as much as I like having you as mine. We'll never be part of the same circle jerk. But I'll be your obedient errand boy if I, in return, get something I want."

"Careful, Colton. I'm not a woman you want to bargain with."

"If I have to stew in my fucking car for the next couple of weeks I'll take my chances."

"Let me guess, working beats on the North Side is looking damn good and you want me to put in a word so a transfer can happen."

He appeared surprised, perhaps even downright insulted, by what she had just said.

"This is where I want to be. No beats on the North Side for me," he replied.

"Then what the fuck do you want?"

"More vacation time."

"More vacation time?" she repeated, as if he had just spoken in a foreign language she couldn't fully comprehend.

"When I started I was promised two weeks. Now the sergeant is saying I only get one. See, that doesn't work for me. I want my two weeks."

"And you want me to talk to him."

"You've got sway around here. If anyone can get me my vacation time, it's you."

"I'll talk to the man. Can't promise anything, though. In the meantime, you work hard as a dog. No whining."

"Not even a growl."

"So, what the hell are you waiting for?" Pam pointed at the door of her office. "Go do your job."

"This will be another wild goose chase, just like when we searched his condo. Reeve is fucking loaded and motherfuckers like that don't go down—guilty or not."

"That's the thing, you ever meet a psychologist or a professor who can afford to live in a place like that?"

Colton paused at Pam's comment. She saw that he was starting to think about Reeve the way she needed him to.

He was almost out the door when Pam called out to him. "Are you sure more vacation time is really what you want?"

Colton's expression changed and he chuckled. "Oh, don't you worry, Sung, I know a dime piece who will make every second of that extra week be more valuable than a lifetime in Reeve's posh condo."

CHAPTER 5

I really need to buy an umbrella, Meredith thought to herself as she walked down South Ellis Avenue in Chatham. Instead of taking the subway to 79th Street like the last time she made her way to that part of town, she had decided to drive. But after circling around the block for several minutes in search of a spot, she had given up and parked in a lot a couple of streets away. Although it had poured earlier, it was only drizzling now and she toyed with the idea of slowing down, lighting a cigarette, and putting her Burberry showerproof trench coat to good use. As she recalled how much time she had spent that morning fighting with her hair straightener, her need for nicotine became less urgent.

Suddenly, her skin prickled with awareness. She glanced over her shoulder, expecting to find eyes on her, but the street remained empty of people. In recent weeks, as soon as she stepped out of her home, she struggled with the suspicion that she was being followed. It might be the police attempting to find Tatiana, or it might be someone connected to The Raven Room.

She slid her hand into her pocket and closed her fingers around the necklace she had found in Julian's drawer. She needed proof the necklace didn't belong to Lena, the woman whose death had wrongly been ruled an accidental overdose.

To ask Julian where the necklace had come from seemed pointless. He could tell her whatever he wanted and she wouldn't be able to challenge him, but Samantha Williams would tell her if the necklace she possessed belonged to her late friend.

Meredith climbed the steps to the porch and knocked on the door. She had tried calling Samantha a couple times, but she hadn't been able to get a hold of her. She knocked again, louder. No noise came from inside of the house and the blinds were drawn. Beginning to worry that she might be out of luck, she knocked one more time.

A couple of teenagers with cigarettes burning between their lips tinkered with an old boom box on the porch of the neighboring house. She caught them eyeing her.

"Hey," she called out. "Have you guys seen Mrs. Williams?"

"She moved," one of them replied.

Meredith cursed under her breath. "Where?"

He shrugged. "Don't know."

"How long ago did she move?"

"Couple months, maybe."

She noticed the pile of old junk mail in the corner and realized she should have visited sooner. Without Samantha, she wouldn't find the answers she needed.

The rain started to come down harder again and Meredith, putting her hands back in her pockets, felt the cross necklace brush against her knuckles. The little energy she had left vanished and disappointment took hold of her. Too tired to rush back to her car, she lit a cigarette and inhaled the soothing smoke into her lungs.

An hour later, Meredith parked her car on her street in Wicker Park, not far from her apartment. As she walked, she sensed someone was watching her.

She had just turned the key on the lock of her front door when a change in the air made all the hairs on the back of her neck stand up. She turned around quickly and gasped when she saw a figure standing only a few feet behind her.

"Calm down, it's me." Pam took a step forward. The light above the door now reached her face. "You're not answering your phone."

"So you decided to scare me half to death?"

"I don't remember you ever being this jumpy."

"What do you want, Pam?"

"Can we go for a walk?"

"It's raining. I'm tired."

"Let's go grab a coffee."

"Why?"

"Meredith, please." Pam rubbed her eyes with her fingers. "I'm not here on police business."

"Then why?"

"To talk. As your stepmom."

"You must think I'm an idiot."

"Can we go somewhere?" Pam insisted.

"Fine. But you're driving."

As they made their way north on Oakley Avenue, Meredith kept shifting her gaze between the back and side windows.

"Is everything OK?" Pam asked.

"Uh-huh."

"Are you sure?"

"Did you send your lackeys after me?"

Pam frowned. "What are you talking about?"

"Hoping I'll lead them to Tatiana?"

"I don't have anyone following you, Meredith."

She didn't know if she believed her.

They ended up at Mystic Muffin, a small coffee shop near Logan Square subway station with checkered tablecloths and a collection of dying plants by the window.

The man behind the counter handed them their coffee, before returning to his spot by the door, newspaper in hand.

Sitting back on her wobbly chair, Meredith felt nauseated. "What's that smell?"

"Bleach. John uses it to wash the floor. You'll get used to it. Soon, you won't be able to smell it anymore."

"John?"

Pam tilted her head toward the man reading the newspaper.

"You must come here often," Meredith said.

"Years now."

Meredith's physical discomfort added to her agitation. She wished she had declined Pam's invitation and just stayed home.

"How well did you know Sofia?"

Meredith held her coffee cup in front of her face. She hoped the smell of black coffee would mask the scent of bleach. "I thought you weren't on police business."

"Just tell me."

"I never met Sofia. Julian has been in a relationship with Tatiana Thompson. That's the woman I know."

Pam sighed. "Really?"

Julian's attorney had made it clear—it worked to Julian's benefit if the police couldn't prove which of the twins Julian had been having a relationship with. Meredith figured her stepmother knew she was backing the story, not because Meredith believed it, but because she was determined to protect Julian.

"Yes, Tatiana Thompson."

"Fine. Assuming we're talking about the same person, how well did you know her?"

"You've asked me that before and I've answered."

Pam leaned forward, her elbows on the tabletop. "Were you two intimate?"

"Oh, I see." Meredith chuckled. "Don't look so uncomfortable."

"Have sex with whomever you want. I don't care. Were you two intimate?"

"Yes."

"While at the club, did you talk to Tatiana?" Pam continued.

"No, I did not. Why do you want to know if I had sex with Tatiana or if I spoke with her at the club?"

"You have no idea the amount of pressure I'm under."

Meredith took a sip of her coffee. It tasted bitter and she made a face as she forced herself to swallow it.

"Why would Tatiana steal some dead woman's identity and use it to find a job and rent a room at the New Jackson?" Pam added. "How would she be able to keep this double life a secret from her husband?"

"Is Sofia's death somehow connected to The Raven Room?" Up until this moment, the idea that the club was involved in what happened to Sofia had just been a lingering suspicion in the back of Meredith's mind.

"There are things I can't tell you. If you know where Tatiana is—"

"I don't," Meredith said, interrupting her. "The club hasn't come up at all during this investigation. Why is that? If we're going to be honest with one another, it's time to admit that the club is being protected."

"I can't discuss the investigation with you."

"That's always your excuse. You've already told me things you shouldn't have. The fact that you're not looking into the club makes me question you and your integrity as a cop."

"My job is everything to me, Meredith."

"Then why didn't you arrest Tatiana at Julian's condo that morning? She stole someone else's identity." Meredith made sure to reiterate that it was Tatiana who had committed identity fraud. "You had told me, weeks prior, you were going to arrest the woman passing as Alana."

"I said she was using a stolen identity. I never told you the police were looking for her or that I was going to arrest her. I'm a homicide detective. At the time, it wasn't my problem."

"You led me to believe it was. You knew I thought the police were after her."

"You came to that conclusion on your own."

"Are you listening to yourself?" Meredith spoke loudly enough to catch John's attention. He raised his eyes from the newspaper.

"Keep your voice down," Pam ordered under her breath.

"You're a cop. If you tell me someone is wanted for identity theft—a federal offense—I'm going to assume the police are looking to arrest them. How did you find out Alana wasn't really Alana?"

"When you approached me and told me about a woman named Alana who worked at Bucket O'Blood, I got them to give me a list of their employees. Alana Stewart was on it. I did a background check, and that's when I found out that Alana Stewart was dead and that her Social Security number was being used. I showed a picture of the real Alana Stewart to the bookstore owner and he confirmed she wasn't the woman who worked there."

"Did you know she was one of the Dulgorukova twins the day you met me at the diner?" Meredith asked.

"No. I had no idea until the night of the murder. When I got to the New Jackson, I found the pictures of her and Julian, but I still didn't know her real name. It wasn't until we found her ID with the name Sofia Dulgorukova hidden under the mattress. Then, there were her fingerprints all over the room."

"How do you know they weren't Tatiana's fingerprints? They're identical twins."

"No two sets of fingerprints are exactly the same," Pam explained. "Not even identical twins."

"Well, did you find any of Tatiana's fingerprints in the room?"

"We did. We found Tatiana's fingerprints as well. And her purse with her ID."

Meredith could tell that didn't sit well with her stepmother. It helped Davis's theory that Tatiana had been the one renting the room at the New Jackson Hotel while maintaining a relationship with Julian.

"Pam, at this point, what can you prove?"

"I can prove that Tatiana was in her sister's hotel room. And, considering the condition and location she was found in—badly beaten and near the New Jackson—I'm quite sure Tatiana knows who murdered her sister."

"Let's suppose Tatiana happened to witness her sister's murder. Do you really think if Julian killed her sister that Tatiana would have taken shelter with him?" Meredith asked. "Where was Thompson that night?"

With her jaw set, Pam didn't reply.

"Tell me, why didn't you arrest Tatiana that morning? You had a homicide on your hands and, as you said, she's a legitimate witness. Instead, you walked out with Julian and left her with me. Why?"

"I fucked up, Meredith. OK? I should have arrested her, but I was shocked to find her alive. I had come for Julian, and that's who I wanted to speak to."

"I don't buy it. Why?"

Pam threw her head back and sighed. "I guess I felt for her."

"You felt for her?" Meredith didn't see her stepmother as the type of person who would allow her emotions to interfere with her job.

"You know what I mean." Pam chugged down half of her coffee. "When Colton and I arrived at Reeve's condo I was convinced the murdered woman was Sofia. Then this woman, who looks just like someone who is supposed to be dead, shows up. I had no idea we were dealing with identical twins. Or that they were the two girls I had read about in Reeve's file."

"Neither did Julian or I."

"Her marks and bruises were a man's handiwork. Women don't beat each other like that. I couldn't bring myself to arrest her right then and there…she looked like a victim, not a criminal."

The weight of their exchange lingered in the silence between them.

"I don't know where she is," Meredith finally said.

"Has she contacted you?"

"She knows you and I are related. I'd be the last person she would contact."

"How about Reeve? They have a shared history. She'd turn to him and he'd help her."

"You've seen him. He's broken. He can barely get out of bed much less help anyone. Have you checked with Thompson?"

"We've searched his house." Pam shook her head. "Nothing."

"Thompson could have—"

"What's with your obsession with Thompson, anyway? Do you know something I don't?"

"I could say the same about you and Julian."

"Please tell me you've given up on the idea of writing a story on The Raven Room and Reeve."

Meredith refused to answer.

"Please Meredith, you're the closest thing I have to a daughter. What I do and say is with the intent to protect you. Always remember that."

She sounded sincere, but Meredith couldn't let go of the feeling that her stepmother might be lying.

Chapter 6

"You keep giving me strange looks," Isaac grinned.

"I'm sorry." Meredith tucked her hair behind her ear. "I had imagined you to look different, that's all."

Trying to hide her blush, she reached for her rum cocktail and took a long sip. "When we spoke on the phone your voice made you sound older. What are you, thirty?" She saw the expression of amusement on Isaac's face and covered her eyes with her hand. "I'll stop talking. I shouldn't have asked your age."

Isaac laughed. "I'm thirty-five. And please don't stop talking. I can't remember the last time I've had this much fun with someone." He swallowed his drink. "Maybe I should invest in a more erudite, grown-up look. Something that better matches how I sound."

Meredith eyed his dark jeans and faded denim shirt, with the sleeves rolled up to his elbows. "I blame it on your accent. I pictured you as a bald, potbellied sixty-year-old British man."

It was Isaac's turn to almost choke on his drink. He continued to laugh. "You just can't help yourself, can you?"

After an exchange of e-mails that extended several weeks, Meredith had reluctantly agreed to meet with Isaac Croswell, the managing editor of Features at the *Chicago Tribune*. When he had suggested they meet at Lost Lake, a tiki bar on the border of Avondale and Logan Square, she should have realized that her assumptions of the man were off.

She had wanted to impress him with her intelligence and journalistic talent but now, as she sat across from him, she wished she had worn her new Chloé summer dress and fussed a bit longer with her hair and makeup. Perhaps she would feel more confident.

Instead, she had picked a boring white dress shirt and black skirt that, she thought, made her look like her father's secretary. It was the first time she'd tried to impress a man without relying on her sexuality, and she felt awkward, unworldly, and dull.

Isaac caught her staring at him. "What now?" he asked, grinning.

"Oh, God, I'm usually way more socially adept than this. I can't tell you."

"You must."

"I must be more socially adept, or I must tell you what I was thinking?"

"Both."

Meredith sat up straighter in her chair. If she were to embarrass herself even further, she would do it with her head held high. "I'm curious, where are you from?"

"I thought we had established I sound like a bald, potbellied sixty-year-old British man."

Meredith rubbed her forehead with her palm. It had been a while since she had felt this way in the presence of a man. "I know, but—"

Isaac didn't let her continue. "What you really want to know is what's my ethnicity."

"No," Meredith was quick to reply. Isaac raised an eyebrow in response and she knew it was obvious she was lying. "OK, maybe…" Her cheeks felt like they were on fire. "It's not that it matters at all and I don't want you to—"

"Meredith, I get—"

"I shouldn't have mentioned it," she jumped in, now being the one to interrupt. "I don't know what's wrong—"

"Meredith." Isaac rested his hand on her arm and gave it a little squeeze. "It's OK. I know you meant nothing by it."

She moved her arm from under his hand and reached for her glass. She wasn't a big drinker but she found comfort in alcohol when nervous.

"I'm half Nigerian thanks to my dad and a quarter British and a quarter Chinese thanks to my mom."

"Before you moved here, did you always live in the UK?"

"I think I've lived in over ten countries. I was born in South Africa but because my parents were both professors, we traveled a lot. I've called Chicago home since I've moved here after doing my Masters at City, University of London." Isaac rested his elbows on the table, his eyes not leaving Meredith's face. "Does that answer all your questions?"

"Not quite. Where does the name Croswell come from? I like the sound of it."

"I go by my mom's maiden name."

"Why?"

"People wouldn't get past the second syllable of my dad's last name."

"Please tell me."

Isaac shook his head. "That's a hard-earned secret."

"What do I have to do to earn it?" As soon as she spoke, Meredith wished she could take back the question.

She read the answer in the look on his face. Had he been another man, she would have seized his blatant expression of desire and turned it into a no-strings-attached night of pleasure and fun. But that wasn't what she wanted out of Isaac Croswell, so all she did was smile.

"I'm happy you agreed to meet. When I didn't hear from you after my first e-mail I thought I might be pushing my luck by e-mailing you a second time," Isaac said. "In your reply, you told me that you're no longer interested in publishing the piece on The Raven Room. Does agreeing to meet with me here tonight mean you've changed your mind?"

"I'm afraid not." Meredith was pleased the conversation had reverted back to what had brought them together in the first place. "I agreed to meet you tonight to tell you in person."

"Why?"

"You're a successful journalist. I admire your career and I didn't want to pass the chance—"

"I meant, why don't you want to publish the piece?" Isaac cut her off.

"I haven't even written the piece. Just done some research."

"You'll have time. I didn't expect you to be handing it in right away."

"Mr. Croswell, a lot has happened since I first told Professor Harris about my interest in writing that story."

"I can take you walking away from me, but I can't take you calling me Mr. Croswell."

"OK, Isaac, I cannot express how appreciative I am of the opportunity to work with you but—" Meredith paused, taking a deep breath. "I can't do it."

"Forgive me for prying—why, Meredith?"

He was tenacious. She appreciated that trait in people.

"Tell me, what would you say?"

She frowned. "Excuse me?"

"If you wrote the piece, what would you say?"

"Say? I don't understand."

"What would you want to tell your readers?"

Meredith was quiet as she circled the rim of her glass with her fingertip. "The truth about The Raven Room."

"And what's the truth? C'mon, I want to hear you pitch your piece to me."

Isaac's genuine enthusiasm almost succeeded in rekindling her own, but she promised herself she wouldn't betray Julian.

"I don't have proof to back up my suspicions," she finally said.

"I can help you find the proof. What are your suspicions?"

Meredith met Isaac's dark eyes. "Corruption, trafficking, murder. Those are my suspicions. Can you help me find proof for that?"

"If that's what's going on, then yes, I can help you."

"What if there's a possibility of you or me getting hurt?"

"When Harris told me about your idea to write an investigative piece on The Raven Room I was thrilled." Isaac lowered his voice. "Over six years ago, when I started my job at the *Tribune*, I was young and needed to assure my boss that hiring me was the best decision he ever made. I was slaving away at my desk until ten at night, seven days a week, and I became somewhat friendly with this journalist who was there before I arrived every morning and was still there when I left every night. I heard he wrote about finance, but he never spoke to anyone and, if you asked around, you wouldn't find a single person who knew how long he had been working there. The man had created his own office—four walls, taller than me, of stacked crates filled with newspapers around his desk. He had a 1960s TV on his desk that didn't work. He was eccentric, to say the least. His name was Owen Glendon."

"He and I started chatting, usually when it was just the two of us in the office. I remember one evening there was this awful snow storm and I decided to just work through the night rather than deal with the hassle of getting home," Isaac continued. "That's when he told me about this members-only underground club called The Raven Room."

Isaac locked eyes with Meredith. "Before that, I had never heard about such a place. And I hadn't heard anything since, until you. During our chat I remember Glendon saying that since its inception, only the city's most powerful people had access to The Raven Room. Glendon had three journals filled with research notes on the club, all of which he showed me."

Meredith was stunned. "Why was he researching the club?"

"He didn't say. I'm assuming to write about it."

"But he never did?"

"Four years ago, Glendon stopped coming to work. I've no idea what happened to him."

"Did he retire?"

"As I told you, I have no idea. He was somewhat unstable. Who knows what happened to him. Hell, he could have packed his bags and moved to Florida to wrestle crocodiles."

Meredith raised an eyebrow.

"You never know. Sometimes people surprise you." He smiled at her incredulous expression. "After Glendon abandoned us to pursue his dreams, his files ended up in boxes in my office. They wanted me to see if there was anything in there I might need. To me, they just looked like piles of loose sheets of paper with illegible writing on it, so I threw everything in storage and never looked at it again."

"Do you have his Raven Room journals?"

"I might. They could be in one of those boxes. If you decide to write the piece and the journals are there, they're all yours."

"Can I have them regardless?"

Isaac pretended to be offended. "You're a horrible negotiator."

"I don't want to negotiate with you."

"Because you'll lose?"

"No." She ran her hands through her hair and hoped her frustration wasn't obvious. "I wouldn't be shocked if your coworker's disappearance had something to do with his research."

The comment didn't seem to surprise him. "But that's exactly it, Meredith. The Raven Room is a once in a lifetime story. This is your chance to write a piece that will show Chicago what the one percent of this city are up to when no one's looking."

She considered Isaac's response.

"If people connected to the club have been killed, that's even more of a reason for you to write this bloody piece," he added.

She chuckled, softening her expression. "You know, I say The Raven Room is connected to the death of a woman and then you say bloody piece," she paused, suddenly feeling foolish. "Forget about it."

"After all these years, even though I still have an accent, I speak like an American 98 percent of the time. But, once in a while, a word or two escapes me and the timing is always flawless. And, when I say flawless, I mean that ironically."

"So, you're not afraid of what might happen to you or your career if you publish my piece?"

"I have never shied away from a little danger. It keeps the blood flowing, you know? Keeps me young," he replied, his tone playful.

The approachable, energetic quality of his demeanor enthralled Meredith. "I highly doubt danger is what's been helping you keep your good looks."

"Be careful, I might start thinking you want to shag me," he said, winking.

"Don't take it personally. I want to *shag* most people."

Isaac's laughter proved to be contagious as Meredith found herself laughing with him.

"I'm confident you and I will work beautifully together."

"I wasn't aware I had agreed to working with you at all," she replied.

"Meredith, you want to write this piece. That's clear. You're just dealing with a case of cold feet, which is perfectly normal. If you weren't nervous I'd be concerned. It would mean you weren't taking this as seriously as you should."

"So you're hoping to warm up my cold feet?"

"With any luck, not only your feet."

Meredith wasn't sure how to act now that she realized she was openly flirting with Isaac and he was reciprocating. Their banter felt natural. Maybe besides their professional interests, the desire to cross the line of propriety was something else they had in common. Meredith was surprised by Isaac's straightforward nature but she pretended to be more shocked than she was. "Are you flirting with me?"

"We're flirting with each other."

"Are you married? Engaged? In a relationship?"

"I'm happily divorced. Yourself?"

"Happily single." She closed her eyes and gave her head a quick shake, as if she was trying to wake herself up. "I'm sorry, should we be discussing this?"

"Don't be so American, Meredith. Maybe I can teach you to have a more laissez-faire attitude."

It was time for Meredith to focus on what brought them

together and mention the main reason why she had decided not to write the piece. "See, if it was only about me, I'd go forward with the story on The Raven Room. But it's not. It involves someone else, someone important to me, and I won't let them down."

"The man who took you to the club?" Isaac watched her closely. "You're choosing him over the piece."

"Disappointed?"

"It's personal for you. Nothing I say will change your mind."

She shook her head, confirming his suspicion.

"Is he worth it?" he asked.

"Our friendship is."

The chatter and music around them made it easy for them to sit together in silence. Meredith felt relieved she had been honest with Isaac.

He raised his glass and smiled. "I respect your decision, Meredith."

She reached for her glass and they toasted. "Thank you, Isaac."

They kept their eyes on each other as they finished their drinks.

"What are you thinking?" Meredith asked, surprised by how quickly her body came alive under his stare. She didn't dare move.

"How lucky I am to have your number."

CHAPTER 7

Julian sat across from a woman he despised.

She looked much older than a woman in her thirties. Although she was a natural blonde, at some point she had decided to go even blonder. Her brittle and wet-looking curls, a sign of too much styling product, had the yellow tinge of a bad peroxide job. She was once overweight, and now her skin hung loosely around her body as if it were slowly melting away from her frame. With a complexion still plagued by acne, her face appeared swollen, or perhaps, Julian thought, it had failed to keep up with the rest of her shrinking body. She reminded him of Sofia and Tatiana's mother, Olga Dulgorukova.

Every time she moved, a strong odor of stale cigarettes mixed with cheap hair product hit him. He tried to take sparse, shallow sips of air. He wished they were not trapped in a small room on the seventh floor of the hospital, where the windows were permanently shut.

"Lily, do you want to tell your mom what you told me the last time we met?" He shifted his attention to the girl who sat without speaking at the other end of the couch.

Lily looked at Julian, an expression of unease was etched on her face. He didn't know if her feelings were as obvious to her mother as they were to him, but he smiled at her, encouraging her to speak.

Lily didn't reply and Julian didn't rush her. He continued to sit and kept the blank notepad in his hands. His shallow breathing started to make him feel lightheaded.

When he heard Lily's mother make an attempt to say something, he raised his hand and nodded to Lily, making sure she understood he would not allow her mother to interject.

"I don't want to go back there. I can't," she finally said, her voice timid but clear.

"What do you mean, you can't?" A deep furrow marked her mother's forehead. "That's your home. He's your dad."

"He's drunk all the time," Lily continued in the same tone.

"Does he hit you? Does he scream at you?"

Lily lowered her eyes to her lap and started to pick at the white bandage on her wrist.

"See? I know—"

"Please, Mrs. Hamilton, let's give Lily time to answer your question."

Julian leaned forward on his chair, toward Lily. "It's OK, you can take as long as you want. Your mother and I will wait."

"Dr. Reeve, you might have all afternoon, but I've got to get back to work. I know my daughter. She's playing games."

Julian felt on the verge of losing his restraint. Because Lily was the only person who mattered in that room, he emptied his mind and filled it with thoughts of her. He had to concentrate on Lily and not on her mother.

"Mrs. Hamilton, we're here for your daughter. There's time." He wondered where his affable tone had come from and if he should be shocked or happy about the extent to which he could pretend.

She crossed her arms over her chest and rolled her eyes at her daughter. "Go ahead."

"Why can't I come live with you?" Lily asked.

"We talked about this before. Your stepdad and I are moving to North Carolina so he can be near his kids. Now is not a good time for you to come live with us. Maybe in a few months, when we get settled."

"You're leaving me here with him."

"He's your dad," her mother said. "He's dealing with some stuff but he loves you. He'll take good care of you."

Lily now picked at the white bandage on her other wrist.

"How do you feel about your mom's move to North Carolina?" Julian asked her. "And you can be honest. No one here will be upset with you for being honest. We want to know how you're feeling."

"I don't want her to go."

"Why?" he pressed, hearing despair in Lily's voice—she was trying not to cry. Julian realized that the whole time Lily had been his patient—they had been having weekly sessions for well over a year—he had never seen her cry.

"Because I know she won't come back. I know she won't ask me to come live with her. She's going to forget all about me. I don't like living with her either but it's better than living with my dad." She turned to look at her mother. "Please let me come with you. I'll do better. I'll eat and I won't try to hurt myself ever again. I promise."

"Stop lying. You're saying all of this so you can get what you want. For the last two years all I've done is deal with your crap and I've had enough, Lily. It doesn't matter what I say or do, we always end up here, in this goddamn hospital, dealing with these goddamn doctors that can't fix anything. Now is your dad's turn. It's time you were his problem, not mine. You're staying in Chicago and that's the end of it."

Lily shut her eyes tight. The cut on her left wrist had opened up and the bandage turned bright red. "Please, I don't want to live with him."

"That's too bad."

Hearing her mother's response, Julian rested the notepad on the table near him and stood up. He couldn't bear it a minute longer. "Lily, I'm going to ask one of the nurses to have a quick look at your wrist and, while they do that, your mother and I will continue to chat. We'll both be here waiting for you when you're done."

Julian walked Lily out of the room. Seeing the lack of concern on Mrs. Hamilton's face as he reentered, he knew the conversation he was about to have might mark the end of his career at Lurie Hospital.

"You're in a rush, aren't you?" Rage made it hard for him to speak. "So, I'll be as straightforward as I can. You're not a fit mother and Lily shouldn't be in your care. But if you refuse to have her live with you, she won't be staying with your ex-husband. He's an alcoholic with a criminal record. Lily will be placed in foster care. Being in the system is hard for any child; in most cases it defines the rest of their lives. Your daughter is a thirteen-year-old girl who suffers from an eating disorder and who recently tried to commit suicide. I know, without a doubt, that she will be dead within a year. Is that what you want for your daughter, Mrs. Hamilton?"

"You don't know anything, Doctor." She sat on the edge of the couch and pointed her index finger at Julian. "What have you done for my daughter? Instead of getting better she keeps getting worse. You're not helping her."

"I'm doing a hell of lot more for Lily than you ever have." The professional tone vanished and now he sounded openly hostile. He remembered the numerous times he had wanted to tell her how Lily's mental state stemmed from her parenting but he had been silenced by his position as a psychologist. Now he no longer cared about the consequences of his words.

"You've made up your mind," he continued, speaking louder. "You don't want to help your daughter. You want her gone, out of your life, and if she happens to die then better for you. That way you don't have to deal with her problems ever again. I imagine you wish it hadn't been her stepfather who found her bleeding to death in the bathroom. Would you even have called 9-1-1?"

"Are you saying I want my daughter dead?"

"If that hasn't become clear then you're stupider than I thought."

"Fuck you, asshole." She stood up with her purse under her arm. "I've been putting up with your smug face all this time because of Lily. I'm done. You think you're better than me? Well, you're not. My daughter is staying here in Chicago with her dad and if she ends up in foster care so be it. She's tough. She'll be fine."

"Get out." Julian left his chair and, if she hadn't moved past him as soon as he had opened the door, he would have dragged her out of the room.

He slammed the door behind her and pressed both hands against it. Convinced he would be soon out of a job, he let his head hang forward as he heard her cursing and shouting down the hall. Instead of fear, Julian felt relief. He shouldn't continue to do his job if he couldn't help someone like Lily.

• • •

Less than two hours later, Julian sat in the office of Dr. Bruno Rodriguez, the head of the psychiatry department. Julian had been throwing his books inside a cardboard box when he received the call.

"I've started to pack my things," Julian said to the man behind the large desk that was littered with papers.

"In a tidy-up mode are you, Dr. Reeve? Because, if you're looking for part-time work as a maid, I could use your services, as you can see." He grabbed some folders off his desk and then let them fall, not paying attention to where they landed.

"I'm resigning. Saves you the trouble of firing me."

"I'm glad you realize what happened earlier today between you and Mrs. Hamilton is unacceptable."

"Yes, it's unacceptable, but I don't regret it. I wish I had said more."

"You know what else is unacceptable?" Dr. Rodriguez reached inside one of the desk drawers and pulled out a cigarette. Julian had heard rumors that Rodriguez kept a pack of cigarettes in his desk, a memento from when he was a chain-smoker, and every time he embarked on a long conversation with one of his doctors, he pulled out a cigarette and held it between his fingers with the expertise of a veteran.

Julian didn't understand why the cigarette had made an appearance. Their arguments about Julian's methods as a psychologist were ongoing and, Julian imagined, if anyone would be happy to see him leave the hospital as fast as he could it would be Rodriguez. But he didn't seem happy at all. Instead, Rodriguez appeared to be waiting for an answer to his question.

"That I waited this long to resign?" Julian's words lacked irony. He felt defeated.

"No." Rodriguez still held the cigarette between his fingers. "That my best doctor thinks he can just pack up and go."

Julian didn't know how to respond.

"You never thought you would hear me say that, did you?" Rodriguez's austere expression broke into a smirk. "Well, neither did I."

Julian chose to remain silent.

"I don't like you," Rodriguez continued. "But you're great at what you do, which makes my personal opinion of you irrelevant. I want you to take some time to resolve whatever it is you have going on in your life. And once you're done, I want you back here."

"What happened earlier had nothing to do with my personal life." As soon as the words left his mouth, Julian knew he had replied too fast. He sounded defensive.

"I don't know how you have managed not to fuck up until today but I know a floundering man when I see one. Get your act together, then, come back. A personal leave is my way of saying thank you for caring as much as you do. But I won't be thanking you ever again."

Julian rose from his chair but then hesitated. He sat down again. "Lily, my patient, will go into foster care. She won't survive. What can we do?"

"Dr. Reeve, the foster system is there to catch kids failed by their families. When the system fails them, the best thing we can do is to let them go so we can help the kids who still have a chance. We invest our time, energy, and resources where they can be the most effective. Happy endings. Everyone likes happy endings, right Dr. Reeve?"

At that moment he didn't care that Rodriguez had offered him an opportunity to save his job at the hospital or, more than that, an opportunity to save the career he had worked so hard to build. In his mind, Julian saw himself beating Rodriguez to a pulp. But such reaction would get him arrested and subsequently bring even more police scrutiny into his life. For that reason alone, Julian didn't act on his violent urge.

As he stood up, he knocked down a large pile of papers that teetered on the edge of the desk. If Rodriguez saw it as a premeditated act to challenge him, Julian didn't care.

After he left Rodriguez's office, Julian went to finish packing up his things. Whether he faced personal leave or resignation, he didn't want to abandon his collection of psychology books. He felt attached to them. He tossed the last couple in the box and reached for the only picture in his office—a framed photograph of him and Hazel the day he had obtained his GED. The expression of pride in Hazel's eyes as he held the diploma in front of him made Julian pause. That had been a rare happy day for both of them.

He drove across town toward Hazel's house with Odetta's music playing on the car stereo. Odetta's sorrowful voice forced him to acknowledge how lost he felt. When he caught himself dialing Meredith's number, he ended the call before she had the chance to answer. He cursed, frustrated by his instinct to reach out to her.

By the time he arrived at Hazel's it had started to rain. He sat with her on the front porch to watch the summer storm.

"How are you feeling?"

Hazel looked up at him and her expression didn't change. Not a hint of recognition in her eyes. "Who are you?"

Julian almost told her the truth but, fearing an angry reaction, decided to choose the safe answer. "I'm a friend of your son, Julian. Do you remember Julian?"

"Of course I remember Julian. I'm his mother. A mother never forgets."

He tried to smile but failed. "I spoke with him recently."

"Why doesn't he come visit me anymore? I wait for him but then he never comes."

"He's going through a tough time. He doesn't want you to worry."

"What kind of trouble is he in now? Is he in jail?" Now Hazel sounded frantic.

"He's not in jail." Julian wrapped an arm around her shoulders. "No problems with the police." Not absolutely true, but he needed to reassure her. "It's Sofia...she's..."

For him, Alana would always be his lover with an unwavering adoration for used books, mint chocolate chip ice cream, and cold, gloomy winter days. Alana was the one who had been killed. Sofia remained an eight-year-old child to whom he had been an older brother. But Alana's death meant he would never again see that young girl. Now he mourned the death of a person with two separate identities and to each one he had given a different part of himself.

"Sofia died," he said.

Hazel didn't offer him any words in return.

"I spent twenty-three years wishing I could see her and Tatiana, speak to them and now..." Julian's voice wavered. "She reminded me of them but I never thought, never believed—"

"Who is Sofia?"

Hazel's question discouraged him but it didn't silence him. "Sofia Dulgorukova, one of the twins. Do you remember them?"

"The Russian girls?"

Julian nodded and, in response, she caressed his hair. Unsure of how to react, he stood still. He didn't remember her showing him a physical gesture of affection before. In the weight of her hand on the back of his head Julian felt for the first time the love he knew Hazel had for him.

The noise of a car parking in front of Hazel's house got their attention. As soon as Julian saw the tall woman in the two-piece suit he tried to regain his composure.

Earlier, as he was leaving the hospital, he had called Kimberly Simmons, a social worker he trusted. When Julian had started his first year at Lurie, Kimberly had already been working within the system for twenty years. She was well past the age of retirement and every time they crossed paths, she told Julian she would be retiring the next year.

"I can't linger," she said as she sat down. She glanced at Hazel, who stared at the rain. "Sorry dear, how are you doing?"

Hazel ignored Kimberly's question.

"It takes her a while to warm up to people she doesn't interact with often," Julian said.

"I've known your mom even from before I met you. I know who we're dealing with. But let's talk about why you called me. How long will you be away? I need you at Lurie."

"There's this girl, Lily Hamilton. She's going into care. I know that sometimes you take in some kids. I need you to take in this one."

"I can't. I stopped doing that."

"Please Kimberly, she's in bad shape. I e-mailed you her file, have you had a chance to look at it?"

"I have, and that's why I can't take her. She needs a lot of help and I already have dozens of kids who need me. I'm spread so thin I can't even tell you. I can't offer her the support she needs." Kimberly shook her head. "I can't be her foster mom in good conscience."

"Listen, I know how much you have on your plate. That's why it's hard for me to ask this of you, but whatever you give her will be, without a doubt, better than she's going to get anywhere else. The families who are willing to take in a kid like her won't be enough. What do you think will happen when she goes to live in a house that's bursting at the seams with foster kids? Or worse, a group home? You won't be alone in this. While I'm away she's going to continue to receive treatment at Lurie. I won't leave you high and dry. I'll help you with whatever you need. I'll help you deal with Lily."

Kimberly gave him a hard look. "If that girl kills herself under my care I'll never forgive you."

"It won't happen."

"You can't promise me that and you know it. These kids are ticking bombs."

"I have no one else to turn to."

"How come you got this involved? It's not like you haven't dealt with kids like her before. Kids way more troubled."

Julian had anticipated the question but hoped Kimberly wouldn't ask it. Seeing how much he sought from her, he didn't want to lie, but he also didn't want to explain himself.

"I recently lost someone close to me. I can't lose anyone else." He left unsaid his need to do for Lily what he failed to do for Sofia.

"Of course it goes beyond Lily." Kimberly didn't sound happy but her voice carried no criticism. "It's like they say, you're trying to save yourself by saving the kid."

"We all have that one kid we can't shake off." He looked at Hazel. He had been that child for her.

"Sadly," Kimberly added.

Julian didn't know much about Kimberly's personal life, but he gathered from the expression on her face that she had also experienced it.

"It's important no one knows I reached out to you. Lily's mother and I had a disagreement. She's choosing to walk away from her daughter, but if she suspects I had anything to do with arranging her placement she's going to cause problems. This has to stay between you and I."

"I'm agreeing to help this kid out. I'm in all the way. That woman has no idea what she has coming her way if she tries to fuck with me." Kimberly gave Julian a glimpse of the dedication that made her such a great social worker. "How did you get hard-ass Rodriguez to agree to give you time off?"

"I didn't. It was his idea. I still don't know if I'll go back."

"I guess after all these years you two were bound to come to a head. I'll take Lily in but you have to promise me that you'll return to Lurie."

"That's a hard bargain, Kimberly."

"Come back when you're ready."

Rodriguez had said the same thing. "I'll do my best."

"I'll start working on Lily's case," she said, already halfway down the porch steps. "Nice to see you, Hazel."

Not waiting for a response, she got into her rusty 1993 white Honda Accord and drove away under the pouring rain.

"Julian?"

He wondered if Hazel's calling him by his name meant this was one of the brief but valued moments when she regained her lucidity.

He squeezed her hand. "I'm right here."

"Who died?"

Her recognizing him made it harder for Julian to speak about it. "Sofia. One of the Dulgorukova twins."

"I remember her. How about Tatiana?"

Regardless of what he might want to share, protecting Hazel remained more important. "I don't know."

Hazel went silent and Julian wondered if he had lost her again. Minutes went by.

"Tell Tatiana I wouldn't mind seeing her," Hazel said. "Tell her that it's safe. Tell her that Julian is gone."

• • •

Julian left Hazel's home well past midnight and drove straight to The Raven Room. As he entered the club and made his way toward the lower level, he had the unnerving feeling that time stood still. Once inside, it was impossible to tell if it was day or night. He knew this intentional, unchanging atmosphere lulled the club members into a dreamlike state where they would eventually succumb to everything the club had to offer.

The usual seductive jazz and blues music had been replaced by the psychedelic rock melodies of Pink Floyd for the club's Alternative Night—an event that took place every other month. The soft, deep red lighting had vanished. Kaleidoscopic lights gave the illusion that all the surfaces, furniture, and people were being showered with slow-moving, oversized, colorful glitter.

Glad he wasn't under the effect of drugs, Julian squinted, trying to regain his bearings amidst the loud music and disorienting lighting. He was about to enter the long corridor with red walls when he saw someone he recognized—the man who smoked the black dragon cigars. The two of them stared each other down until the man smirked. Julian turned his back on him.

Focusing on his reason for being there, Julian's heart beat faster as he approached the last door on the left. He stood, head bowed down, eyes closed. He took a deep breath and turned the doorknob.

"You're here." Those were the first words that came out of Julian's mouth as soon as he saw the woman on the bed. He felt relieved.

"Didn't you ask for me?"

"I did…" Julian sat on the chair in the corner of the room. "What happened last time?"

She laughed, rolling into her stomach. "I'm not sure. We were pretty fucked up."

"I thought I had killed you."

"Did you enjoy it?"

The room was too warm. Julian felt the heat of the nearby candles on his skin.

The woman kneeled at his feet. She brought a mirror closer to him. "It's a new designer mix. Premium quality."

He saw the powder on the mirror. "I'm not doing it with you. Not tonight."

Holding a short straw in her other hand, she smiled. "Please."

"That's not why I'm here."

"Don't be like that," she pleaded, bringing the mirror to Julian's face. "Just one rail."

Aware that he wouldn't be able to stop at just one line, Julian threw the mirror against the wall. The woman made a high-pitched noise as she crawled across the hardwood floor toward the shattered mirror.

"How could you?" she whispered, picking up a shard of the mirror.

Julian knew he should be moved by what he saw—her naked, on her knees, crying—but he saw too much of himself in her to feel compassion.

She crawled back to him. "You have to do something for me. You have to." She placed the shard on his palm, begging as she held onto his hand. "You have to."

Remaining at his feet, she guided his hand to her naked breast. "Cut me. You know that's what you want."

Feeling the shard between his fingers, Julian stared at her breasts.

"You can't say no. I know you," she whispered.

With blood roaring in his ears, Julian ran the back of his hand across her breast. He wanted to touch all of her. Not tenderly, as he did now, but with the ruthlessness he had been born with.

"I know you," she repeated, her eyes wide.

Julian slid from the chair and met her on the floor. He closed his mouth on her breast and she let her head fall back. He sucked on her nipple and didn't stop until she started to moan. That was when he moved away from her. "I can't…"

"Call me by the name you always use. The name you like," she said in earnest, fondling him over his suit pants. "C'mon, say it."

He closed his eyes, hoping he was strong enough to fend off the blunt desire growing in him. She unbuckled his belt, unzipped his pants, and reached inside of his underwear. The name formed in his throat and Julian felt shame.

"Say it," she demanded, stroking his bare flesh.

With every muscle in his body as tense and hard as his member in her hand, Julian held the piece of the broken mirror tightly between his fingers. His lips moved from her forehead to her temple. "Tatia." The name escaped his lips, almost a whimper.

"Again."

"Tatia," he whispered as his mouth met hers. "Tatia," he repeated, breaking the kiss. She tightened her hold on him and he groaned in response.

"Cut me," she said, her breathing shallow.

Julian lowered his head to her breast and the sharp edge of the mirror followed the light caress of his lips. She held her breath and didn't move. Even before he had lifted the piece of mirror from her flesh, bright red blood seeped from the cut. He watched, entranced as it dripped over her ribcage and down her stomach.

With her free hand she smeared it on her skin. "More. Cut me more."

His eyes traveled to her face and the realization of what he was doing to her jolted him. He fell back toward the chair. "I want to leave," he uttered, his hands unsteady.

"That's not what your cock is telling me." She moved her hand along his erection and Julian's body involuntarily swayed forward, craving what she offered. "Fuck me the way you love. Hard. Until I scream for you to stop."

Julian pushed her away from him. He stood up, fumbling with his zipper.

"Are you running away again?"

The candles cast large, dancing shadows on her body. She rested her bloodstained fingers on his lips and, with his back against the wall, Julian felt breathless.

"I came here tonight to make sure you're OK." His lips rubbed against her wet fingertips as he spoke. He was close to hyperventilating.

She shook her head. "That's not why you're here."

Julian ignored her, making his way toward the door. She wrapped her arms around him from behind, stopping him.

"Don't leave."

"Let me go."

"No!" She tightened her hold on him.

Seizing her wrists, he pulled her away from him. She stumbled and caught herself on the opposite wall. "You'll come back. You always do."

She laughed as Julian left the room.

CHAPTER 8

Meredith couldn't get over the feeling that the woman standing in front of her wasn't the woman she had known as Alana. She shuddered at the eeriness of it.

"Here you go." She passed Tatiana the large bags she carried. "Groceries. All stuff you can eat."

"Even if I wasn't a vegan I'd starve. The fridge and the cupboards are empty."

"There's a new cell phone and a prepaid card in there too."

"You'll find two hundred bucks on the kitchen counter. This time you really should take it. It's Julian's money. He won't miss it."

Meredith ignored Tatiana's sardonic comment. "How is he?"

Tatiana raised an eyebrow.

"Tell me," Meredith insisted.

"He sleeps all day. It's the benzos."

"Where is he getting them from?"

"Any doctor."

"He needs help."

"You have no idea."

"What are we going to do?"

Tatiana examined the black underwear that Meredith had brought in the bag. She tossed them back in. "We? *You* help him."

"Why are you two angry at each other?"

"He's not angry with me." Tatiana sounded bored with their conversation. "He's angry with Sofia for lying to him. Since he can't lash out at her, I'm the next best thing."

"Listen, Alana, I can't—" Meredith stopped herself as soon as she realized she had addressed Tatiana by the wrong name. "I'm sorry. You look and sound exactly like her…I still think I'm talking to your sister. It's disconcerting."

Tatiana didn't appear to be taken aback by Meredith's remark. "If she and I stood side by side you'd see a few differences."

"Do you know why she didn't tell Julian who she was?"

Tatiana's defensive demeanor vanished. She now looked sorrowful. "Does it matter? She's gone. Her mistake was getting tangled up with him."

"Where is he?"

"Check his bedroom. He rarely comes out. He stopped teaching…is he even still working at Lurie?"

Meredith didn't bother responding. In the last few weeks, she had learned that Tatiana didn't ask questions because she wanted answers. She used it as a passive aggressive way to slip a disapproving comment into the conversation.

Meredith walked down the hall, wary of what she might be faced with. Cautiously, she opened Julian's bedroom door.

The sight filled her with dismay. Drawn curtains blocked out the sunlight and discarded sheets covered the floor. Julian lay asleep naked on the bare mattress, on his stomach, his arms and legs spread out. Meredith entered and kneeled by the side of the bed. Memories of their time together the previous June brought tears to her eyes. They had spent many mornings in that bed, her head lying on his chest. She hadn't realized it at the time, but she had been happy and she figured if Julian had ever felt the same way with her, it would have been then.

"Julian, can you hear me? You need to get up."

She waited for a reaction, but he didn't stir. There was no change in the steady cadence of his breathing.

"Julian? C'mon, get up. You can't continue like this. Julian?" She shook him but he didn't move. "Julian?"

"Don't worry, he'll wake up eventually."

Tatiana watched them from the door.

"I don't know what to do." Meredith rested her forehead on Julian's temple.

"There's nothing for you to do. He needs to sleep it off."

"What's going to happen when he does? He'll wake up and take more benzos?"

"Probably."

Meredith faced her. "You don't want to help him? Fine. But I took you to my place after the police left; I hid you from everyone, including my roommate. I took care of you. When it was safe, I was the one who brought you back here." Meredith knew she sounded desperate. "Now I need you to do something; I need you to help me get Julian through your sister's death."

"You want *me* to help him?"

"You're stronger than him." Meredith truly believed that. Tatiana exuded a resilience she had never encountered before.

"That's asking for a lot."

"I'm asking you for what I need."

Tatiana sat on the edge of the bed, not far from Julian. She went silent, and Meredith didn't rush to continue speaking. She wouldn't give Tatiana the opportunity to evade her request.

"I'll help you," Tatiana said. "He doesn't deserve it, though. I hope you know that."

"You blame him for your sister's death."

"I blame Julian for everything."

The resentment in Tatiana's voice made Meredith lean closer to Julian, as if to shield him from her. "He never understood what Sofia was afraid of, but he tried to protect her regardless. He's doing the same for you. He's protecting you from your husband. Do you recognize that?"

Meredith expected Tatiana to further attack Julian, but she didn't. Tatiana's silence drove her to press for answers. "Why did you make my stepmom and her partner think you were your sister? You still haven't explained why you did it."

"I guess I figured if Julian thought I was Sofia he would be more inclined to help me."

"You didn't think he would figure it out?"

Tatiana shrugged. "It was worth a shot."

"And you'd be okay with doing that?"

"I did it, didn't I?"

Tatiana's feelings became clear to Meredith and it unnerved her. "Why do you hate him?"

"I don't hate him. For you everything's either love or hate. Nothing else."

"If that were true I wouldn't be here."

"What has Julian told you about me and my sister, about the past?"

"He said that he got placed with your family and when he spoke up about your father, your parents said he was the one sexually abusing Sofia." Meredith remembered what Pam once told her about Olga Dulgorukova's death. "Do you believe Julian shot your mom, is that why?"

"I don't have to believe anything. I was there. I saw Sofia shoot my mom."

"So Julian didn't do it."

"That's what I just said. My parents were sick people. I'll be forever grateful to my sister for shooting my cunt of a mother. They should have never been allowed to keep their own daughters, much less take on foster kids."

Meredith recalled Julian only briefly mentioning Olga Dulgorukova.

"You and Sofia were eight-year-olds...you didn't want your mom dead."

Tatiana looked genuinely repulsed. "No, of course not. We never dreamt of seeing our mom having her brains blown out. I still have nightmares where she's on the floor, a piece of her head missing, blood everywhere."

"You spoke like you were happy about it."

"No, not happy. Relieved. When abuse is all you live day after day, year after year, something weird happens. You start to feel a kind of fear that grows in the pit of your stomach and then spreads through your whole body. Like heat waves rolling over you. You can't run, though. It's like you become a trapped animal. And you don't care what happens. You just need it to happen. You just need something, anything, to happen so the fear can stop."

Tatiana started to braid her own hair, and just like Meredith had seen her do several times before, Tatiana undid the braid as soon as it was done and restarted braiding it. Her nervous habit endeared her to Meredith.

"At first I thought you were just a privileged girl," Tatiana said. "But that's not all you are. You might not be able to relate to what I told you, but you can understand how Sofia and I might have mixed feelings about our mom's death."

Meredith watched Tatiana run her hand along Julian's back. While it appeared absentminded, her touch remained purposely tender.

"What did your mom do?" Meredith asked.

"When Julian came to us, he was a fourteen-year-old cutter, hooked on crack. My mom picked up on his weakness pretty fast. She'd give him money for his fix in exchange for him doing whatever she wanted."

"Whatever she wanted?"

"They fucked. Often. I knew about it because she liked to have me there. She would tell him—*go get Tatiana*—and he would never say no to her. He would bring me into bed with them." Tatiana stared at Julian's body. "I can still hear the sounds she'd make when he was inside of her."

Meredith desperately wanted Tatiana to say something that would break the heavy silence in the room, but at the same time, she was afraid of what that might be.

"When they were done, she never gave him the money directly. My mom would give it to me and then I would pass it to him. He also never said no to the money. After she got what she wanted she'd leave us alone and I'd watch him cut himself." Tatiana touched Julian's tattooed arm. "If it wasn't for all this ink, his arm wouldn't look so pretty, that's for sure." Tatiana traced the raised scars with her fingertips. "He used to cut his ankles too. Have you ever looked at his ankles?"

Meredith shook her head in response. She didn't want to look.

"He didn't tell anyone what my mom did because he thought Sofia, his favorite, was safe from all of it," Tatiana continued. "But I told my sister what was happening. I had to tell someone. Besides Julian, she was the only one I trusted. Then Julian found out my dad was sexually abusing Sofia. At the time, I didn't believe her when she described what he had been doing to her, but when I got older I started to."

Meredith tried not to reveal how affected she felt by Tatiana's words. She doubted Tatiana wanted her sympathy. "Why?"

"Because believing my sister was the right thing to do."

A question formed in her mind and, even though the answer had the power to crush her, Meredith had to ask. "Did Julian ever touch you?"

"For two years he never once tried to stop my mom from forcing me to watch them together. Julian was like my big brother, but having me there, with them, put sex where it shouldn't have been. I wish he had touched me—raped me. Then I could just hate him. But he didn't. So, while I blame him for not standing up to my mom, I know he was just a kid, too."

Meredith wanted to reach out to Tatiana, hold her hand, offer her some comfort, but she couldn't get herself to move.

"Nothing hurt as much as when I heard Julian tell Social Services what my dad was doing to Sofia. By protecting her, it felt like Julian loved her more than he loved me. That he loved her more than he loved crack. And if Julian loved something or someone more than he loved crack, then it for sure was real love."

Beneath her brash demeanor, Tatiana was sorrowful. Now Meredith understood the reasons why.

"Today, I'm aware that he was young, with no family—an addict that saw fucking my mom as the only way for him to get what he needed," Tatiana continued. "Sometimes I feel like I'm eight years old again though. That's when things get messy...my feelings toward Julian change. One minute they're ugly, the next they're beautiful. But they're always strong."

"I…" Meredith swallowed hard. "I don't know if this is what I should be saying, but I'm sorry. I'm sorry for what happened to you."

"You should get the hell away from here, Meredith. Away from Julian and away from me."

"I can't."

"What's stopping you?"

Her knees had started to ache from kneeling for so long but still she did not move. "Should I hate Julian?"

"They're your feelings. Own them. If you want to hate him, then hate him. If you want to love him, love him. I won't judge you for it."

"I lied to the police. I wasn't always with Julian. Did you see who killed your sister?"

Tatiana slid from the bed to the floor and sat beside Meredith.

"You have scars all over your body from that night," Meredith added. "Did your husband have anything to do with Sofia's death?"

"Drop it, Meredith. I'm not doing this now. I can't."

"Julian won't tell me anything about The Raven Room," Meredith persisted. "One of the times I was there, I had a chance to explore it and ended up on my way to the lower level. I came across this man—security, I think. If it hadn't been for Julian showing up, I don't know what would have happened. What's The Raven Room all about, Tatiana? Is it drugs? Sex trafficking? You go to the club. You must know."

"There's nothing I can tell you."

"A woman, Lena Rusu, was found dead—murdered by an overdose of heroin. She went to the club, I'm sure. Her death is connected to The Raven Room. And so is Sofia's."

Tatiana faced Meredith. "How did you find out about this Lena?"

"My stepmom."

"You need to be careful, Meredith. It's not a safe time for any of us."

She didn't need Tatiana to tell her that. "How did you first learn about the club? Through your husband?"

"I'm not ready to talk about it," Tatiana replied.

"It's important—"

"Stop, Meredith. Just stop. Please."

The pain in Tatiana's voice made Meredith pause. She felt a pang of guilt. "I don't mean to be so pushy. It's just who I am. All of this is horrible. I can't even imagine what I'd do if I was in your situation."

"You'd do what I'm doing. Survive. There's nothing else to do. We're pretty much strangers, and even though you don't owe me anything, you've been the one here for me." She reached for Meredith's hand and kissed the middle of her palm. "Thank you."

Meredith didn't pull away. "When Julian told me about you and Sofia I hoped the three of you would reconnect again one day and I'd have a chance to meet you both. I just wish it was different...and Sofia was still here with us."

"Did you like her?"

Meredith heard the anticipation in Tatiana's voice.

"Almost everything I know about her I learned through Julian. I only met her once. She was kind to me."

Tatiana smiled.

When she first saw Tatiana at The Raven Room, Meredith had been attracted to her. That feeling hadn't changed. She yearned to kiss Tatiana and, in that moment, Meredith wanted nothing more than to share her intention—despite the uncertainty of Tatiana's response clawing at her stomach.

"What would you say if I told you I wanted to kiss you?" Meredith asked, bravely.

Tatiana's fingertips brushed Meredith's chin. "I'd say please."

Meredith leaned forward and touched Tatiana's lips with hers. She didn't rush into the kiss and neither did Tatiana. Their mouths parted slightly and Meredith felt Tatiana's warm breath on her face. In that moment, there was a promise of everything Meredith could ever desire, and she suspected she was about to do something she would either cherish forever or deeply regret. Their lips came together and their kiss remained unhurried. Tatiana didn't demand more than she received, and Meredith, with her eyes closed, lost herself in the moment. She savored the sensation of pleasure that slowly spread through her body.

Meredith covered Tatiana's face with small kisses. She enjoyed the feeling of Tatiana's makeup free skin on her lips.

"Tell me, Meredith, on your way here, what did the air outside smell like?"

Meredith buried her nose in Tatiana's hair. The familiar fragrance of Julian's shampoo suddenly filled her senses. She was glad that she had brought a bottle of a different brand of shampoo for Tatiana.

"It's that only time of year when, if sunshine had a scent, you would be able to smell it."

"Tell me more," Tatiana pleaded.

"There's this little bakery at the corner of North Oakley and West Shakespeare, in Bucktown. Sometimes, on Sunday mornings in the summer, I wake up early and go for a walk in the park across from the bakery. There's almost no one around—no people, no dogs. I take off my shoes and I sink my toes into the grass and feel the damp dirt beneath them…the smell of warm breakfast buns—all butter and sugar—hangs in the air." Meredith wrapped her arms around Tatiana. "Maybe, one Sunday morning we can go together."

Tatiana hid her face on the curve of Meredith's neck. "Maybe."

CHAPTER 9

"What's so interesting outside?"

Meredith pressed her fingertips to the glass. She pretended to catch the raindrops running down the other side of the window. She couldn't tell Isaac that she hoped to spot whoever it was that might be following her. "The rain. I hate the cold but I love the rain."

"I hate both." Isaac rested his napkin on the table. "Six months of harrowing weather and now this. It's quite the letdown. At least it's warm outside."

Isaac had texted her a few days ago asking her about her week. They had sporadically communicated since then, a mix of friendly banter peppered with flirtatious comments.

She had reciprocated his advances, but getting involved with Isaac was an unwelcomed distraction. Meredith wished they had met months ago, before Sofia's death.

"Perhaps I'm feeling this way because I haven't come up with a good enough story idea to rival The Raven Room." She shouldn't have said that, she realized. It would be foolish of her to diminish her value as a journalist in Isaac's eyes. "But I've been pitching smaller articles to a couple of magazines." A lie. She hadn't thought of writing anything else besides her piece on the club.

"The Raven Room is a hell of a story. One of a kind. But you can come up with a sex tips article worthy of Cosmo, I'm sure."

She wondered if Isaac's words were an attempt at flirting with her, or if he wanted her to regret her decision to not move ahead with the piece.

"You're right," she said, matter of fact. "There's nothing that I can't do."

Isaac smiled. "Never thought otherwise."

She glanced at her watch. They had been having lunch for two hours. "Are you heading back to the office?"

"I should. But I don't want to." They left the restaurant as Isaac spoke, and while he put on his jacket, Meredith looked up and down the sidewalk. There were cars parked on the opposite side of the street and the high number of pedestrians made it hard for her to notice anyone suspicious. The chances of her being harmed in broad daylight, while surrounded by people, were slim, but she still felt uneasy.

"Meredith?"

She faced Isaac. "I'm sorry, what did you say?"

"What are your plans for this afternoon?"

"I have a seminar." She searched inside her purse for her cigarettes. She had been smoking a pack a day and, while she wasn't proud of her vice, they did help her calm down.

"This is me, shamelessly stepping into the role of the bad influencer, but why don't you skip it?"

She found the cigarette pack empty and a curse escaped her lips. She had smoked her last one before lunch. "Skip it?" she repeated.

"Yeah, let's spend the rest of the afternoon together." Isaac opened his umbrella and Meredith leaned closer to him, taking shelter from the rain. "I'd rather spend the rest of the day with you than answer e-mails and sit in a boardroom, pretending to listen to what my coworkers are saying."

Meredith didn't need to be persuaded. Her studies had become a burden instead of a priority. "With this weather where would we go?" Isaac's grin made Meredith pause. "No, we're not going to your place or mine." She couldn't keep a straight face. "Not yet."

"Do you mean not yet as in, right now, or not yet as in, today?"

Cars drove past them, the sound of rubber tires on the wet pavement muffled their laugher.

"What if I turn out to be shitty in bed?" she teased.

"I can't tell if you're joking or being serious."

Meredith laughed harder at his appalled expression. "What if I'm serious?"

"Impossible. You're smart, sexy, beautiful, and—"

"I can be all of those things and still under-deliver."

"I disagree. Good sex is everything but just sex."

She reached for the zipper of his jacket and unzipped it halfway. Meredith pressed her face to his chest. He didn't wear cologne and she breathed in his clean scent. She tilted her head up and her lips touched the base of his neck, right above the collar of his shirt. His skin felt warm.

He lowered his lips to her ear. "Right now, I'll go anywhere with you."

Meredith felt safe, hiding under Isaac's large umbrella. She didn't want to move away from him. But if she didn't, they would kiss and she would need to find out if his sheets smelled as clean as he did.

"There's this coffee shop in Wicker Park where you can play old videogames." She pulled back from him. "They have Mortal Kombat. My favorite. Are you up to getting destroyed?"

"I'll love every minute of it."

Twenty-five minutes later they sat at on a small, frayed couch, playing Super Nintendo.

"I won!" Meredith said, clapping her hands.

"I let you win."

All the triumph vanished. She grew serious. "You did?"

Isaac's somber expression cracked. "No, I'm fucking with you. You destroyed me fair and square." He leaned closer to her. "Look around you. What do you see?"

Meredith gave the other occupied couches a sweeping glance. "Geeks?"

"Terrified geeks. You're like their virtual reality dream girl in the flesh, they don't know how to act."

Laughing, she sank into the cushions, her body nestling against Isaac's. Neither of them made an attempt to move away.

It started to get dark outside, and Meredith wondered if she should leave. Every time she thought about how her every move might be tracked, she felt fear. She didn't want to be alone.

"There's this opening coming up at the newspaper for an administrative assistant. Would you be interested?"

She scowled at Isaac.

"Don't worry, you wouldn't be reporting to me," he clarified.

"I have no plans to join the pink ghetto of admin work. Ask me if I'm interested when you have an editorial position available."

"OK. You said you have other story ideas. I can connect you with people in the industry. It'll give you an opportunity to pitch the new material."

She knew she needed to come up with new challenges and continue to work on her career. But a part of her didn't want to. By abandoning her piece on The Raven Room, Meredith felt like an accomplice in the murder of two women.

Suddenly, it became clear to her—with access to The Raven Room and more knowledge on the murdered women than the police, she found herself in the perfect position to uncover who had killed them. She might not tell Chicagoans about The Raven Room, but by gathering evidence and passing it on to Pam, who could conduct a legal investigation and make an arrest, she could see justice for both Lena and Sofia.

"What are you smiling about?"

"I just realized—"

The sound of her phone ringing interrupted her. She knew who was calling before she even answered it. She had saved Julian's number under a different ringtone.

"It's me."

Hearing Tatiana's voice surprised her. "Why are you calling me from his phone? What's going on?"

"Julian. He locked himself in his office. He hasn't come out since yesterday."

"Why didn't you call me sooner?"

"Are you coming over?"

Tatiana sounded worried, and that alone frightened Meredith. "I'm on my way." She hung up and faced Isaac. "I need to go. There's something I need to deal with."

Isaac didn't hide his disappointment.

"This was the most fun I've had in a long time," she said when they were outside of the coffee shop.

"You sound sincere."

His words caught her by surprise. "Unlike everything else I said all afternoon?"

Isaac started to speak but then stopped himself. He went quiet.

"Text me when you're done," he finally said. "I'm having dinner with two journalist friends visiting from New York. I'd love to introduce you to them."

The prospect of making new contacts excited Meredith, but her concern over Julian dampened her delight.

She felt Isaac's stare as she walked away and flagged down a taxi.

• • •

As soon as Meredith entered Julian's condo, she came face-to-face with Tatiana.

"Has he spoken to you?" Meredith asked, knocking on the locked office door. She waited for Julian to respond.

Tatiana approached her. "What if he hurt himself?"

Meredith remembered the other time she had stood by a locked door, calling out to Julian, demanding to be allowed inside. He had eventually relented, and the state she had found him in had shocked her. She had never contemplated what might have happened to Julian if she had walked away that night, but as she banged her fists on his office door, she feared he might have carried out what she had prevented him from doing then.

"Listen, Julian, I'm out here with Tatiana. If you don't speak to us, I'll call 9-1-1. There will be cops all over this place again. This time, I can't sneak Tatiana out of your condo without being seen." Meredith rested her forehead on the door. "Please don't make me do this."

"You have to call 9-1-1," Tatiana said.

Meredith looked up at her, conflicted.

"If you don't, I will," Tatiana insisted.

She saw true fear in Tatiana's eyes, and that enraged Meredith. "Julian," she said as she slammed her fists on the door with renewed urgency. "This isn't just about you. You lost someone you loved? So did Tatiana." Meredith kicked the door forcefully. "I'm making sacrifices for you. I'm choosing you over everything else in my life." The more she spoke the angrier she felt. "Don't you dare choose your grief over us."

Tatiana took hold of her arm, stopping Meredith from her continued assault on the door. "Call 9-1-1."

Meredith ignored her and continued to shout Julian's name. Her shouting came to an abrupt stop when Tatiana started walking away.

"Wait! Where are you going?"

"I'm calling for help."

Before she could take another step, Meredith rushed in front of Tatiana. "No."

"All the pills he takes…what if he's dying in there?"

Meredith's growing anxiety, together with the pain of her throbbing hands, left her lost for words. She refused to accept the fact that Tatiana might be right.

"You don't want to have someone's death on your conscience. Especially someone you love." Tatiana reached for Meredith's purse and took her phone from inside. "Call 9-1-1."

Tatiana tried to pass her the phone but Meredith didn't take it.

"I have enough time to get out of here before the cops and the ambulance arrive," Tatiana continued. "I'll be fine." She pushed the phone at Meredith. "Do it."

"Don't."

Julian's voice, coming from the other side of the door, made them both jump.

"Open up," Meredith said, her hand turning the doorknob. "Let me in."

Julian unlocked the door and Meredith pushed inside. Tatiana showed no intention of following her, but she looked relieved.

Meredith suppressed a gasp as she faced Julian. It had been just a couple of days since the last time she had seen him, but while he had looked grief-stricken right after Sofia's death, he now looked frail. She didn't know how to react. Of all the emotions coursing through her, one stood out—pity. That wasn't how she wanted to feel toward Julian.

Deciding not to approach him, Meredith stood with her arms crossed and her back pressed against the wall. "Do you want to talk?"

"There's nothing to say." His eyes bored into her. "You don't want to be here. I can see it."

She wasn't going to challenge him. In fact, she'd rather be spending time with Isaac and his journalist friends. "I'm here, regardless," she replied.

"Let me be, Meredith."

She saw the pill bottles on the desk. "I know what Olga asked of you."

Julian stared at her wide-eyed. "How—" His shocked expression morphed into guilt. "Tatiana?"

"Yes, she told me."

"Do you expect me to deny it?"

"I just want you to know I'm aware of what Olga did."

Julian lashed out. "Yeah, I had sex with Olga countless times during those two years, and I can't remember a single time when Tatiana wasn't there with us."

With Julian visibly upset, Meredith tried to rein in her emotions—she didn't want to say anything she might later regret—but when she spoke, her voice carried a hint of recrimination. "Why didn't you tell me?"

"I'm glad I didn't. Otherwise, your stepmom would know that, too. Maybe she does now?"

"That's not fair, Julian."

"Fair? You lied to me! You betrayed my trust. I thought we—" Julian's voice cracked and silence filled the room. "It doesn't matter."

"How about what I've done for you since then? Everything I'm risking for you? I'm on your side, Julian."

"Having you on my side means nothing to me now."

It was as if Julian had struck her. "You're saying that to hurt me. You know what's really getting to you? That I betrayed you, and even though you wish you didn't, you need me. You needed me to say I was with you that whole night. You need me to help you hide Tatiana. I'm the only one you have."

"I can't stand your selfless act. It's not who you are."

"Do you think you're the only one who's angry?" Despite her ire, Meredith didn't raise her voice. "Sofia is dead and Tatiana is here, with no other place where she can hide and no one else she can rely on. And what do you do? You get hooked on prescription pills. You lock yourself up for days, with complete disregard for everyone else."

"Meredith—"

"I'm afraid you'll take too many of those pills and never wake up." As she spoke, she realized her anger sprung from the fear of losing Julian. Suddenly, all her frustration vanished and in its place, she felt sadness.

"I don't want to hurt myself."

"You don't?"

"No. I just want to stop feeling, remembering. All of it."

"I understand why you didn't tell me." Meredith wanted to go up to Julian, wrap her arms around him, let him know that she would protect him from everything and everyone, but she feared he would rebuff her. If that happened, neither of them would forget it.

Julian sat on a chair and buried his face in his hands. Putting her fear aside, Meredith took a step forward to go up to him, but

Julian didn't give her that chance. He stood abruptly and stalked to the window with his back to her.

"We're angry and disappointed with each other. Where do we go from here, Meredith?" he asked, sounding as lost as she felt.

"I was angry but not anymore. And I've never been disappointed with you," she replied. "Will you stop taking the benzos, will you do that for me?"

Julian turned around and in his eyes she saw that he couldn't.

CHAPTER 10

Meredith cursed the heavy traffic the entire trip to West Garfield Park. She hated summer storms. Leaving her car on an empty side street, she jumped out and braved the pouring rain. It was a warm day, and even though she was soaking wet, her body felt clammy from the humidity. She ran up a set of rotting wooden steps that led onto a slanted porch, and rang the doorbell. As soon as the door opened, she stepped inside.

"Took you long enough."

Meredith kicked her feet out of her soaked flats. "I swear, no one in this city knows how to drive in the rain."

Colton sighed. "Babe, tell me you didn't drive your shiny Beamer here."

She disliked that he called her babe, but at least he didn't call her baby—that, she wouldn't be able to stomach. "It's the only car I own so, yeah, I kind of did."

"Don't complain if it gets stolen."

She looked down at her bare feet with a mix of weariness and yearning. "Do you have hot chocolate?" she asked, abruptly.

"What?"

"Hot chocolate, you know, hot milk mixed with chocolate."

"No, I don't. And it's June. Why would you want that?" Colton reached out and closed his arms around her. "I know a much better way to warm you up. Can't wait to make your pussy as wet as the rest of you."

She smiled up at him. "Who says it isn't already?"

"You're all fired up. I love it," he said, peeling her wet hair away from her neck.

As soon as he pressed his lips to hers, Meredith intensified the kiss, coiling her tongue around his. Her sexual encounters with Colton were crude, forthright, and devoid of sensual eroticism. The primitiveness of it all helped her stay connected to her emotions. She needed the pleasure Colton gave her.

Colton backed Meredith up the stairs, toward his bedroom. But that wasn't what Meredith wanted. She lowered herself on the carpeted steps, pulling him down on top of her. Sliding her hands under Colton's t-shirt, she pressed her nails into the skin of his upper chest. She scratched him all the way to his stomach. He grunted against her mouth.

"Fuck! That hurt. You're so fucking crazy, babe. So fucking crazy." He took hold of her hands and pinning them over her head against the steps.

"Right here. I want it right here," she replied, arching her back. "On the stairs."

"You really make it hard for a guy to treat you right."

"You treat me right when you give me what I want."

"And what's that? My cock pounding your ass? Me coming all over your face? Me choking you? Biting you?"

"C'mon, don't say you don't want it, too."

"Of course I want it, babe. I love it."

"Then what are you waiting for?" With her hands still pinned over her head she rubbed her crotch against his, feeling his erection. "If you wait any longer you'll come in your pants."

Colton licked her collarbone. He let go of her wrists and, flipping her around, unzipped her jeans. He pulled them down—along with her underwear—to her ankles. With both knees spread wide on one of the steps, Meredith pressed her torso against the carpet. She felt him rub her from front to back, coating her with her own arousal. His finger entered her but he stopped at the first knuckle.

"I need to get a condom."

"No. Just stick it in my ass."

She glanced at him over her shoulder and saw that Colton had one hand on her and the other gripping his erection. She opened her legs wider and leaned back, bringing her body closer toward him.

"Spit on your cock."

Colton grinned. "Damn babe, how much porn do you watch?"

"I'm just classy like that."

Meredith pressed her forehead to the edge of the step. With his thighs under hers, she felt him entering her. "Make it hurt," she whispered.

She closed her eyes tightly and bit her lower lip. Just as she had requested, he didn't take any time for her comfort and, before she could catch her breath, he was all the way inside of her.

With his arm around her waist, he pressed her back tightly against his chest and his fingers started to stroke her. "Jesus, babe, your ass. Fuck!" he shouted.

They were both panting and, between the pain and the pleasure, she became aware of Colton sucking the flesh of her neck between his lips. He kept his mouth on the spot for a long time and, at some point, she felt his teeth joining his lips on her neck. He had marked her, and that only aroused Meredith more.

"Come for me, babe. C'mon, your ass clamping down on my cock. C'mon. I know you're close." His laborious breathing almost drowned his words.

He no longer touched her with his fingers and she was moaning, her whole body pulsating with pleasure and pain.

"Can you feel that?" He punctuated his question with a powerful jab of his hips. She cried out. "Can you feel my balls slapping your pussy as I shove my cock deep in your ass?"

"Yes," she replied, clawing the carpet.

"I don't fucking hear you."

Colton moved once more and Meredith whimpered. "Yes! I can feel you!"

His body tensed up and shuddered against hers. There wasn't

much more she could do than just feel his orgasm roll through him. She wasn't going anywhere until he pulled out.

"Jesus, babe." He sounded breathless.

Meredith winced when he left her body. She was about to move when his hand closed on her hip. "Stay like that. I want to watch it drip out of you."

She did as she was told. When Colton was done getting an eyeful of her with her legs spread wide, jeans and underwear tangled around her ankles, bent over the steps of his staircase, she got dressed and followed him to the kitchen.

Colton got a beer from the fridge. "You want one?"

"I'm good."

He leaned against the kitchen counter, beer in hand. "I'll pick up hot chocolate next time I'm at the grocery store."

"No need. Tell me, what's going on with the investigation?"

While she no longer planned to publish the article, she needed to uncover who had murdered both Lena and Sofia and, for that, she had to stay on top of any new developments.

"Fuck, babe, if your stepmom finds out—"

"She won't. How many times do I have to tell you that you can trust me? Pam doesn't give a fuck about you or your career. But I can help you make sense of this case and get recognized for it. What do you have to lose?"

"My career."

"I won't let that happen."

"Sung has me following Reeve. She doesn't want anyone to know that. She asked me to keep my mouth shut. If she were to find out that I'm with you and not keeping an eye on him she'd have my ass."

"Does she have someone following me as well?"

"Not that I know of."

She had both expected and wanted him to answer yes. "Are you sure?"

"Yeah."

Meredith cursed under her breath. "Did she say why she doesn't want anyone at the station to know you're following Julian?"

"Something about the need to protect the case. But she must think I'm stupid if she believes, even for a second, that I buy that. Who would she be protecting the case from, anyway? There has to be another reason."

"Maybe she doesn't want anyone to know because she shouldn't be having you follow him. She's trying to protect herself, not the case."

"Does Reeve know where Tatiana Thompson is?" Colton asked. "Your stepmom's hoping he'll take us to her."

"That's bullshit. Do you really think Tatiana is still in Chicago? I bet she's far away by now."

Colton reached toward the folder on the counter and slid it toward Meredith. "Here is the file on Lena Rusu and photos from Sofia's crime scene. You still haven't told me why you wanted to look at it."

Meredith didn't waste time going through the folder. A photograph of Lena against faded floral sheets jumped at her. She put it aside as she searched for Sofia's photograph. When she came across it, her breath caught in her chest. She laid it beside Lena's. "Lena was found naked on the bed, right?" She tapped the photograph with her nail. "Look at how she's lying down."

Colton's face inched closer to it. "Okay…"

"Now look at Sofia." She pointed at the photograph. "What do you see?"

Colton frowned. Shortly after, he raised his eyes to Meredith. "Why are they in the same position?"

"Exactly. It can't be a coincidence."

"Are you saying these two deaths are related? Lena's was ruled an accidental overdose."

"It wasn't accidental. She was murdered." Meredith had no doubt.

"Did you suspect this? If you did, why and how?"

Meredith recalled the conversation she had overheard while

Pam was on the phone, how she had recognized The Raven Room's scent on the file folder that Pam—after working Lena's crime scene—had given her. To reveal to Colton the existence of the club seemed unwise.

"I remember you mentioning Lena had been found naked on her bed," she replied. "Then there were the photos of Sofia from the crime scene, the ones Pam showed me the morning you both came to Julian's condo. Made me think I needed to have a look at Lena's photos as well. Also, both Lena and Sofia have an Eastern European background and similar body types." Meredith held both photographs in her hand. "You can't deny that we have something here. Has Sofia's toxicology report come back yet?" Meredith needed to know if Sofia had any drugs in her system when she was killed.

"I haven't looked at it. Gave it to Sung."

"What do you mean, you gave it to my stepmother? You gave it to her without looking at the results first?"

"I was in a rush. I'll look at it tomorrow."

Meredith stopped herself from cursing. She would make a better detective than Colton.

"There were no signs of drugs in Sofia's hotel room," he added.

"Were there any in Lena's apartment?"

"I don't think so. Not that I remember."

"Lena didn't shoot up heroin somewhere else, manage to get to her apartment, undress, and get into bed," Meredith said. "It makes no sense. She was either killed in her apartment or she died somewhere else and someone brought her body back to her place, removed her clothes, and displayed her like that on the bed."

"We had no reason to believe that Lena's death was a homicide. And Sofia died from a blow to the head."

"Let's go over what we know so far," Meredith said, resolve in her voice. "Sofia was in her room at the New Jackson Hotel. Someone knocked on the door. If I was Sofia, I'd only open the door to someone I knew. Not a stranger."

"We don't know if the door was locked."

"Was there sign of forced entry?"

"No."

"Sofia would lock her door," Meredith added. "It's the New Jackson we're talking about."

"She had bruises on her arms."

Meredith pondered this. "So she opened the door, got into an argument, struggled and, somehow, got a hit to the head that killed her."

"There was a suitcase in the middle of the room, toppled over a few feet in front of the nightstand. The edge of the nightstand is cheap, compressed wood, and along the edge of it there was a dent. This is how I imagine it: she was pushed back, tripped over the suitcase, and hit her head on the nightstand." Colton snapped his fingers. "Bang. She's dead."

"Did she die immediately?"

"According to the autopsy. But whoever killed her undressed her and put her on the bed." He glanced at Lena's photograph. "And laid her out the same way as that one. If their deaths are linked, finding Tatiana Thompson might give us answers about both murders. She must know what happened. That's probably why she's hiding. Maybe whoever killed Sofia beat Tatiana up."

"Steven Thompson was the one who beat Tatiana."

"Did she tell you that?"

"Yes, before she took off. The fucker is abusive. Can you find out if Thompson was in town around the time Lena was killed?"

"Sure, that's not a problem. Do you think it was him?"

"It doesn't hurt to look into it."

"Did you know that two years ago Tatiana disappeared? Thompson filed a missing person's report but then, out of nowhere, two months later she reappeared. They called it a misunderstanding. You say her husband was the one who beat her that night. I'd bet money it wasn't the first time and, two years ago, when he filed the missing person's report, she had run away from him. But for Thompson to involve the police means he must have been sure she wouldn't open her mouth. Or, that even if she did, the police wouldn't touch him." Colton appeared pleased with himself for coming up with a credible answer. "It would explain why your stepmom, when it comes this investigation, is putting all the heat on Reeve. Maybe she can't touch Thompson."

Meredith gave Colton a concerned look.

"If I'm right about Sung and Thompson, we'll never get him for beating up his wife," Colton continued. "And we'd better hope he had nothing to do with her sister's death because he'll probably get away with that, too."

Meredith didn't want to agree with Colton, but he might be right. Pam hadn't wanted Meredith to write the piece on the club, and throughout the investigation she had yet to officially bring up The Raven Room. The thought that Pam might be protecting someone like Thompson, or the club itself, scared Meredith.

"Also, it's been almost a month since Sofia's murder."

"So?" she asked.

"Listen, I want to make an arrest. I'm sick and tired of having your stepmom look at me like I'm an idiot. She's all over this case and if I can get a leg up on her I'll be seen as her equal partner. I hate to say it, but Sofia's case has gone cold. What do we have?" Colton threw the empty bottle in the garbage bin. "Useless fucking theories that won't mean shit. I heard they're going to finally shut down the New Jackson. Soon, the place will be a boutique hotel or condos for rich people. No one will care or want to hear about anything that happened there."

"The police might not be able to prove who killed Sofia, but I need to know who did it. At least that."

"Knowing who killed her, without seeing them brought to justice? That'll drive you crazy. Why would you want that?"

Because I'll know that Julian is innocent, Meredith admitted to herself. To her, the certainty that Julian hadn't harmed either Sofia or Lena was as important as the police arresting the killer.

"Still no footage from the security cameras at the hotel?" she asked.

"They weren't working, so we won't be getting anything."

"How about the shops nearby? Maybe their security cameras will show who walked by, who entered the hotel."

"Are you sure Reeve was with you all night? He never left the condo?" Colton lit a cigarette. Without asking, he gave Meredith one and passed her the lighter.

Both Colton and Pam had asked her that question right after Sofia's death. She had lied to the police then and would continue to do so. Admitting to deception now would not benefit her or Julian.

"Yes, we were together all night," she replied, cigarette in hand.

"What were you guys doing?"

"Fucking. What else?"

"And you're OK with that?"

She raised an eyebrow.

"Being with a guy that just wants to fuck you?" he clarified.

Meredith remained impassive but the disapproval in Colton's voice made it hard for her not to react. At that moment, as she stood in Colton's kitchen, wearing damp clothes and smoking a cigarette that failed to mollify her, she wanted to walk out of his home and never speak to him again. But she couldn't. She needed him.

"I love it. I get off on it," she replied. "And that scares you."

"It confuses me."

Meredith threw her head back and blew a cloud of cigarette smoke toward the ceiling. "That's your problem, not mine."

"Your stepmom said something that got me thinking, Reeve's lifestyle. How can he afford it? And please don't tell me he works hard. It means shit. Hard work doesn't make you rich."

"So now you're looking at his bank account too?"

"Everything. Him and Thompson are two motherfuckers cut from the same cloth."

At least she and Colton agreed on something. "I don't like Thompson either."

He wrapped his arms around her waist. Meredith continued to hold her burning cigarette.

"Stay the night. I want to make you come again and again, babe, just like you did on the stairs."

She hadn't had an orgasm, but she didn't want him to know that. It wasn't that she hadn't enjoyed it—she had. But what had taken place on the stairs had not been about pleasure. It had been about her making sure Colton would never say no to her.

• • •

Colton stepped out of the pitch-black bedroom and Meredith heard the water running in the bathroom. She grabbed her phone from the nightstand and called Julian. He answered at the second ring.

"Hey. Listen, I can't talk long. The police have someone following you." Meredith pressed her face against the mattress, waiting for his reply.

"Where are you?" he asked, his voice as low as hers.

"At some guy's place…in his bed. But he's coming back, so I should hang up."

Another pause. Meredith was about to end the call when Julian spoke. "Are you going back to sleep?"

"No…"

"Don't hang up."

Meredith waited for him to continue.

"I want to hear you."

With Colton approaching the bedroom, she placed the phone face down on the nightstand, closer to the bed this time.

Colton joined her in bed and started to caress her body. While she held on to him, kissed his skin and moaned against his lips, he wasn't the man she thought of as she experienced the pleasure that had eluded her all night long.

CHAPTER 11

"What's going on, M? You've stopped coming to the house. I never see you anymore."

Meredith raised her eyes from her salad and faced her father. "I've been busy."

"How are your studies?"

"Fine."

"I'm glad you called and suggested lunch."

"I thought you would like that." Meredith needed to learn more about Thompson, and since her father has talked about him in the past, she figured she'd start there.

"You're not being your usual cheerful self. Things are not fine."

"Everything is fine," she insisted.

"When I asked Pam if she had seen you, she brushed it off. Sounds to me like you two had another argument. We both only want the best for you. We care about you."

"She's not my mother."

"She's obviously not your mother, and no one is saying she is, but Pam has been part of your life since you were sixteen. Don't dismiss her contribution to who you are today."

Meredith didn't want to get into a conversation with her father about Pam. She needed to placate him. "I might have hated Pam when I first met her, but I was a teenager. I would have hated any woman. You're right, sometimes we fight, but it's nothing serious. Pam and I are fine. Believe me."

"A friend of mine mentioned he saw you having drinks with Isaac Croswell. Are you two dating?"

Meredith almost dropped her fork. "You know Isaac?"

SAVAGE BONDS

"Socially. Chicago can be a small city."

"He never mentioned you to me."

"I'm assuming he was distracted."

"By what?"

"I'm your father, don't make me spell it out to you."

"We're not sleeping together if that's what you're trying to get at."

"Who you choose or don't choose to have sex with is up to you. I've never gotten involved in that aspect of your life and I'm not going to start now. All I can hope is that your choices prove that I'm a good father and that I raised you well."

"I never accused you of not being a good father. You're certainly better than most."

Meredith put a fork filled with spinach in her mouth, forcing herself to chew. She wondered why she had ordered the salad when there were several other items on the menu she'd rather eat. She hated salad. It was messy and by the end of it she would still be hungry.

"Are you still planning to move to France once you're done with your Masters?" he asked.

"You don't think it's a good idea?"

"On the contrary, I believe it's exactly what you need. The next chapter in your life. I can help you get settled."

"Are you saying you'll pay for it?"

"You're my only child and living in Paris will make you happy. I will do anything in my power to make that happen. I'm not spoiling you. I'm helping you achieve your dream."

Meredith smiled. "An apartment in the Sixth Arrondissement?"

Samuel smiled back at her. "You remind me of your mother. She also loved Paris, and that was her favorite neighborhood. We used to visit the city twice a year before you were born. It reminded her of St. Petersburg. She was permanently homesick."

"And then I came along and ruined everything."

"That's not true, M. We wanted you very much. And after you

were born we continued to take you everywhere we went. You were just too young to remember, that's all."

"You two always sounded too perfect. There had to be something wrong with you guys. I don't know anyone who has happily married parents."

"Pam and I are happily married."

"You're happily married because you're both always working. You live separate lives. She's obsessed with her murder cases and you, I don't know"—she played with a piece of cucumber on the edge of her plate—"lock away as many people as possible, I guess."

"Both Pam and I love this city. We have dedicated our careers to it, and everything we do is to protect the ideals we believe in. Our strong love for Chicago is what brought us together and one of the reasons our marriage works. We have common goals."

Meredith saw this as the perfect opportunity to shift the conversation. "That reminds me, I just read an article about Steven Thompson. It jumped out at me because you, Pam, and I once had a conversation about him and Mayor Matheson. Do you guys know Thompson?"

"What was the article about?"

Meredith took a long sip of her water so she could buy herself time to come up with an answer. "Something about the city," she replied, making herself sound nonchalant.

"Steven was the one who introduced Pam and I," Samuel chuckled. "I always said I owed him one."

Meredith was sure her jaw had just touched the tabletop.

"But we aren't friends. If you recall, Pam is not his biggest fan."

"You met Pam through Thompson?" She couldn't believe it.

"They went to college together. He introduced us at a fundraiser."

"How about Thompson's wife? Do you know her?"

"We frequent the same circles. I've seen her a few times but we've never been formally introduced. Why do you ask?"

Meredith hoped she wouldn't end up spitting up organic leafy greens all over the pristine white tablecloth. Conveniently, Pam hadn't mentioned her connection to Thompson.

"You look upset, M."

"I find it surprising that Pam and Thompson have known each other since college, that's all."

"Why?"

"Because he's—" Meredith stopped herself mid-sentence. It was best not to mention the details of Sofia's murder and Tatiana's presumed disappearance with her father. She didn't want the discussion to lead to Julian. Instead, she came up with another answer. "I got the impression that Thompson comes from money and Pam had—how should I put it—a more humble background."

"She grew up in Albany Park."

"I guess that makes her from the right side of town."

"What is that supposed to mean?"

"C'mon, you raised me in a bubble. We still live in one. You don't mingle with anyone that doesn't belong in your world, so I never really understood how you and Pam came to be. But if she's from Albany Park and she went to college with someone like Thompson, she's not the rough-around-the-edges, South Side homicide detective that she pretends to be. It explains things."

Her father sighed, resting his fork in his plate. "You told me you and Pam were on good terms but that's clearly not the case. What can I do to fix whatever is going on between the two of you?"

"She's a lying bitch. Can you fix that?"

"Meredith, stop it." Samuel kept his voice low but his tone was stern. "I won't have you talk about her like that. She's my wife and your stepmother. You are going to sit down and have a conversation like two adults. Can you come by the house tonight?"

"I can't. Got things to do."

"Cancel whatever you have going on. We're having a family meeting."

"A family meeting? What the hell are we? The Brady Bunch?" She removed the napkin draped over her lap and placed it on the table. "I'm not coming."

"You and Pam are working out this nonsense tonight or you can kiss the apartment in the Sixth Arrondissement goodbye. What's it going to be, Meredith?"

"Are you serious?"

"It's your choice. I'm tired of the two women in my life acting like immature schoolgirls. You can't have everything you want and not at least make an effort to give back to your family."

"Why is it on me to fix it? Have you told Pam she has to play nice or you're going to take away the swanky lifestyle she'd never be able to afford on her own?"

"I don't talk to my wife as if she were my twenty-three-year-old daughter. We've had conversations and she's aware of how important it is for me that the two of you are on good terms."

Meredith wanted to smash all the dishes laid out between them but she knew that such emotional display would only make her look like an idiot. She needed to harness all her self-control and use it to act rationally. She reached for her purse and stood up.

"Thanks for meeting me for lunch." Before she turned to leave, she faced her father. "I'll live in Paris. Without your help."

● ● ●

"Are you sure you didn't know that Pam and Thompson went to college together? That he introduced her to my father?"

Tatiana shook her head. "I wish I did. You can't trust your stepmom, Meredith. Her or anyone else."

After her disastrous lunch with her father, Meredith had sought out Tatiana's company. She wanted to find out more about the relationship between her stepmother and Tatiana's husband. Pam was investigating a murder that somehow involved Thompson and she had said multiple times that she disliked the man. But was it possible Pam was protecting him, and did he have anything to do with her hatred toward Julian?

Meredith lay on Tatiana's bed. "I wonder if she's aware that your husband goes to The Raven Room."

"If she does, it's because Steven couldn't keep his mouth shut. My sister was the only person I ever told I had a membership and I wish—"

Meredith sat up. "You have a membership?"

"Didn't you see me at the club?"

"I assumed you had access to it because of your husband."

"He has a membership too, but I got mine first. It's because of me that he got involved with The Raven Room."

"If you wanted to, would you be able to get in?"

"Sure, why not?"

"Do you ever think about going back?"

"I've never met anyone who has managed to walk away. That place takes hold of you." Tatiana's serious expression broke into a smile. "It's a mix of prohibition bordello with opium den atmosphere."

"Julian said that what Thompson did to you at the club cost him his membership…would it be safe if you visited The Raven Room?"

"Nothing happens to me there that I haven't consented to. Same with you or anyone else."

"What if you and I went together? Could we?"

"When?"

"Tonight?"

Before Tatiana could reply, she continued. "How long has it been since you've been outside? A month and a half, two months?" If Meredith was to learn more about the murders, she needed to go back to the club, but she didn't want to share her true motivation with Tatiana. "Don't you want to get out of this condo? Go somewhere? The Raven Room is the perfect place. We'll have fun together, without having to worry about your husband or the police."

"Six weeks. It's been six weeks since I've been outside."

"Listen, I'll go back to my place and borrow a dress and pair of high heels from my roommate for you. You two aren't the same size, but close enough. I also have this black wig I wore to a

Halloween party a couple of years ago. I'll drive back here, drop off everything, and while you're getting ready I'll head to the club." Meredith knew she was being followed, either by the police or someone else. It would be safer for Tatiana if they traveled separately. "You can take a cab there. You'll look very different. No one will know it's you. We'll meet at the check-in area of the club."

Tatiana continued to face the ceiling. When Meredith thought she had decided to ignore her, she spoke. "As long as on our way back here we get to stop in the cemetery to visit my sister's grave."

Meredith didn't hesitate. "Let's do it."

"Julian can't know."

"Is it because I shouldn't go to the club without him? I've always been there as his guest."

"If you've been at least once it means you've been vetted. After that, you can get in as a guest of any member."

"Where is he now?" Meredith asked.

"Not home."

"What if we run into him at The Raven Room?"

"We won't."

Tatiana spoke with such certainty that Meredith believed her.

• • •

Two hours later, Tatiana met Meredith by the check-in area of the club. Relief over having reached their destination without any trouble coursed through Meredith, and on impulse, she kissed Tatiana.

"I like the way you kiss," Tatiana said as she caressed Meredith's neck. "Like you don't have a care in the world."

"There's only one thing missing." Meredith pulled out her Chanel lipstick from inside her purse. She applied it to Tatiana's lips and when she was happy with the result she took a step back to admire Tatiana. Wearing a black bob wig, a short red dress, and six-inch heels, Tatiana had lost her soft, ingénue appearance. She looked like a woman Meredith should be intimidated by. "You're beautiful," she whispered to Tatiana.

Tatiana turned to the check-in desk and passed the security guard her phone and Meredith's. Next, she pressed her thumb to a small glass surface by the reception desk. When Meredith didn't follow her through the main door, Tatiana appeared confused. "What are you waiting for?"

"Don't you need your membership card?"

"You mean my key?" Tatiana chuckled. "That's just theatrics. All they really need is my fingerprint."

As they entered the club, Meredith smiled inwardly—she had missed The Raven Room. But the nostalgic feeling quickly disappeared and she stiffened. She remembered the club might be the reason behind the deaths of two women.

Tatiana left to use the bathroom, and Meredith lingered on the main floor, surrounded by a crowd too at ease to allow her to continue to feel apprehensive. Bodies brushed against her. The usual curtness that came with that type of anonymous contact, which she had experienced at concerts and nightclubs, wasn't there. The touch of soft fabric, bare arms touching her uncovered skin, the physical awareness with which the people around her moved, all made her feel attuned to her own body.

She saw Tatiana talking to a well-dressed Asian man with shoulder-length hair. In his three-piece suit, he didn't blend in. He reminded her of the security guards she had come face-to-face with when she had tried to sneak into the lower level. But he didn't wear all black, and as far as she could tell, he didn't wear an earpiece either.

By the time she reached Tatiana, the man had walked away.

"Who was that?" she asked.

"An old acquaintance." Tatiana adjusted her wig, running her fingers through the short bangs. "Let's go. I need to drink something strong."

They had just sat at the bar when Meredith spotted Ben, the bartender.

"I was wondering when I'd get to see you again. Where's Julian?" he asked.

Meredith pondered over her response. She didn't know how much she should trust Ben. She held Tatiana's hand. "He's not here tonight. I came with someone else."

As Ben took in the faded scars on Tatiana's body, Meredith felt Tatiana tense up beside her.

"What can I get you?" he asked.

Even without words, Tatiana's displeasure toward Ben became evident. Awkwardness settled between the three of them and Meredith, mustering a grin, tried to dissipate it. "Bulleit on the rocks."

Tatiana's demeanor remained cold. "Mint Julep. Add both to my account."

"I need your key."

Tatiana made a sound of disgust. "Jesus, Ben, spare us. Straight up alcohol with no bullshit will do."

"It's the rules."

"I don't have my key with me, and I know you can add it to my account." She tilted her head toward Meredith. "Do it for our beautiful friend here."

"I can't—"

"Go ahead, Ben."

The same man Meredith had seen speaking to Tatiana arrived at the bar. He gave a silent nod to Ben, who responded by preparing their drinks.

Tatiana didn't turn to face him and the man's eyes lingered on the curve of her neck, his stare as intimate as a caress. Tatiana let go of Meredith's hand.

"Aren't you going to introduce me to your girlfriend?" he asked.

Meredith reached for the drink Ben had placed in front of her. She took a long sip.

"Vincent, Meredith; Meredith, Vincent."

Vincent extended his hand to her, seemingly not bothered by Tatiana's hurried introduction. "Pleasure to meet you, Meredith."

"Likewise." Meredith gave him a firm handshake. "How do you and Tatiana know each other?"

All his attention was now on her. "The club."

Meredith waited for Vincent to elaborate, but suddenly, he stepped away from the bar.

"I'll see you both around."

Meredith watched Vincent walk away. He carried himself with effortless authority—the type of man that didn't answer to anyone.

"An old acquaintance, huh? Who is he really?" Meredith asked Tatiana quietly. The background music drowned their voices, but part of her felt that Vincent could still hear their conversation.

"Someone you might want to fuck but not fuck with."

"How did you two meet?"

"I used to work here."

Meredith's eyes widened.

"Not as a sex worker."

"I didn't—"

"Don't lie, Meredith; it's written all over your face. You're not as open-minded as you pretend to be, do you know that?" Tatiana chugged half of her drink. "I had Ben's job."

For a short second, Meredith thought that Tatiana might be kidding. "How come? And you and Julian never saw each other?"

"I stopped bartending before Julian showed up. By then, I had my own membership. It was easy to avoid him. He always stayed downstairs. Until the day he brought you with him. That's why he saw me. I guess I have you to thank for bringing us back together."

"It wasn't me who brought you two together again. It was your sister."

"I guess you could say that."

"How did you get a bartending job here? Do all employees have a membership as well?" Meredith asked.

"Employees don't have memberships. And I can't tell you how I ended up working here. That's against the rules."

"The same way it's against the rules to buy alcohol without your key."

"Some rules, like that one, are there to make you feel like you belong to an exclusive club. They're meaningless. Others are there to keep you alive. Those rules, Meredith, should not be ignored."

"Does Vincent work for the club?"

"Sort of."

"I was expecting a yes or no answer."

"'Sort of' is the most honest answer I can give you."

Tatiana absently traced the marks on her arms.

"I tried finding a dress with long sleeves." It sounded almost like an apology, Meredith realized.

"Do you think they're ugly?" While the question implied vulnerability, Tatiana's voice carried no such emotion.

Meredith recalled Ben's reaction to Tatiana's scars. "People might think they're unpleasant."

"For some people here, they make me captivating." Tatiana chuckled, but Meredith was unable to do the same. "I've become priceless."

At that moment, Ben replaced their empty glasses with new drinks, and even though he didn't say it, Meredith knew they came with compliments from Vincent.

"I've only been here a few times but I never saw anything that I wasn't, in a way, expecting to see at any sex club," she said to Tatiana. "Which makes me believe that the people who might find you priceless dwell in other areas of the club; perhaps the lower level?"

"I can't take you down there."

Tatiana's firm answer didn't deter Meredith. "Why not? Is it because I'm not allowed?"

"Yes. And even if I could, I wouldn't."

"What are your reasons not to?"

Tatiana turned on her seat, toward Meredith. "Dive into BDSM, explore some safe, sane, and consensual fetishes. If that's not your thing, the club still has plenty to offer. Three floors of it. They were designed for people like you. Healthy, fun, exciting. You'll meet some amazing men and woman along the way. I guarantee you."

"The young woman I told you about, Lena, she—"

"It's called The Raven Room," Tatiana interrupted.

"Excuse me?"

"The lower level. That's where the name of the club comes from. There's no harm in you knowing that. Don't ask me why that name, though. I sincerely don't know."

"Both Lena and Sofia ended up dead because of this place. I can't prove it yet but I know that's the truth. I also know that this club killed your sister."

"What do you want me to do? Call your stepmom?"

The bitterness in Tatiana's voice warned Meredith that they were about to fall into an argument.

"I'll be back." With her drink in hand, Meredith left the bar and made her way upstairs. She needed a few minutes to herself.

As Meredith reached the second floor, she stopped by the banister. The unique scent she had come to love filled her senses. She remembered the first time she had visited the club with Julian. She had felt welcomed, at ease. Such strong sense of belonging had been a new emotion for her. She didn't want to feel at home in a place associated with murder, but she had to be honest with herself—she loved The Raven Room.

"You look unhappy."

Startled by Vincent's sudden appearance, Meredith took a step back.

"You can see your girlfriend from here."

Meredith followed Vincent's gaze. Tatiana still sat by the bar.

"She looks even more unhappy than you do."

Vincent was right. Tatiana looked like she was crying as she slouched on her stool, her elbows resting on the counter, with her head tipped forward.

"Did Tatiana tell you how we came to know each other?" Vincent asked.

"Are you trying to find out how much I know about the club?"

"I'm trying to find out how much you know about me."

Meredith instinctively leaned away, toward the banister. The nervousness she felt in Vincent's presence made her overlook her fear of heights. The wooden handrail, which now supported her weight, gave slightly under her. She suppressed a gasp.

"You're a journalism graduate student at the University of Chicago. How do you like it?"

"Who told you that?" she asked, still holding the handrail. She didn't have to look at her hand to see that her knuckles had turned white.

"Julian Reeve."

"You two are friends?"

A naked couple to their left started having sex against the wall. Neither she nor Vincent paid them any attention.

"It's on your guest file," he replied.

"So you're an employee?"

Vincent smirked. "Exactly. What do you think of The Raven Room?"

His question sounded innocent enough, but Meredith worried it carried a double meaning.

"Sex, money, and power. Aren't those the things everyone wants?"

"The more often you come to the club, the less sex you'll end up having. At least here," he said.

Meredith took in his flawless white teeth, his smooth skin, and his well-groomed black hair. Human beings were not supposed to look so unmarred.

"Too much choice?" she asked.

He tilted his head in the direction of the couple. "Not enough clothes."

She frowned, confused.

"Fully naked people are hardly ever sexy."

Meredith chuckled at his words.

"You should visit the room on the top floor." He pointed toward the staircase that would lead her upstairs and his silver cufflinks caught the light. "It's known as the Black Dragon."

Meredith remembered a conversation she had had months ago

with a woman named Nina. She had drawn a floor plan of the club on a mirror with her red lipstick. She had mentioned that each room at the club was named after an animal and she had pointed out that particular room—the only one with a door, walls, and ceiling painted black. Meredith had yet to go in.

She finished her drink. Her throat felt dry. She couldn't shake the feeling that, somehow, Vincent was leading her into a trap.

"I have no interest in the upper floor." Meredith walked by him, heading downstairs. "Come talk to me when you'r ready to take me to the area of the club that I really want to go to—the original Raven Room."

Despite her sense of foreboding, when she glanced at him over her shoulder and found him smiling at her, Meredith caught herself smiling back.

CHAPTER 12

"This is a bad idea."

"Calm down, Meredith."

"What if we get caught? What if someone calls the cops? We should just go back to Julian's." She followed Tatiana, who walked a few feet ahead of her. "I can't believe I let you talk me into breaking into a cemetery in the middle of the night."

"That was our deal. Club first, cemetery second." Tatiana stopped walking and faced Meredith. "You really need to calm down. You're making me anxious. Why can't you understand that visiting my sister's grave is important to me? I understood that visiting the club was important to you."

"Yes, but now that I'm here I can see that this is a bad idea. What if we get caught?"

"You were gone for a while. Did you fuck him?"

"Who?" Meredith asked, confused.

"Vincent."

She didn't understand why Tatiana would think she would. "Of course not."

"It's a sex club. Don't act like that's the most outrageous question someone has ever asked you."

"I didn't. We spoke, but that was it."

"Did he come up to you? What did you two talk about?"

"He asked me how my studies were coming along. He said he got the information from my guest profile. Is that possible?"

"Did you believe him?"

"I don't know. Why can't you just tell me who he is?"

Tatiana started to go through the contents of the clutch purse hanging from her wrist. Meredith watched her put something in her mouth and swallow it.

"What are you doing?"

"Taking a benzo. Snatched a few from Julian. I'd be a wreck without it."

Meredith shook her head in disapproval.

"I'm not like him. I only take them when I'm in a really bad place," Tatiana said.

In an attempt to reduce her own agitation, Meredith lit a cigarette. Tatiana asked her for one and Meredith passed her the whole pack. They stood, side by side, two burning red specks in the dark.

"Now, can we focus on finding my sister's grave?" Tatiana held the shoes in one hand and the cigarette in the other. "This dress is killing me. Tugs in all the wrong places."

Throwing away what was left of her cigarette, Meredith threaded her arm through Tatiana's, pulling her close. She guided her toward a grave two rows away from the path they were on.

"We're here," Meredith said.

"I can't see anything."

Meredith and Pam had been the only two people who attended Sofia's funeral, so she had a clear memory of the grave's location. She used the screen of her phone to illuminate the headstone.

"Who paid for her funeral? For everything?" Tatiana asked.

"Your husband was going to but Julian wouldn't allow it. He took care of it."

"Did Julian attend?"

Before she had left for the cemetery that day, Tatiana had been in bed, dazed from a high dose of painkillers, and Julian had been sitting in front of the window of his bedroom, staring at the Chicago skyline. The tallest buildings were lost in the morning fog. When Meredith had returned hours later from burying Sofia, Julian had yet to move. She had tried to find the words to console him, but none had felt right.

"He didn't," Meredith replied.

They sat on the grass, and Meredith removed her jacket and draped it over herself and Tatiana.

"*I remember.*" Meredith read out loud the words on the headstone. Julian had been the one who had arranged it so she knew the phrase had come from him. "Do you know what it means?" she asked.

Tatiana didn't reply.

"Tell me something about Sofia. Anything."

Tatiana's silence, together with the stillness of their surroundings, unsettled Meredith.

"She was a great storyteller," Tatiana said. "When we were sent to live with our aunt in Lawrence, after everything we went through, I started to have really bad nightmares. I'd wake up and cry for hours. But then, she would hide under the covers with me and come up with stories that would go on and on. It always worked. I'd calm down and fall asleep. I wish we had never stopped being that close."

"What happened?" Being an only child, Meredith couldn't speak from experience, but she always imagined that if she had siblings, they would always remain best friends.

"She wanted to get as far away as possible. I didn't. As soon as we turned eighteen she left for Russia. I returned to Chicago. Both of us knew she wasn't planning to come back so it was an awkward goodbye. Like we were pretending we were going to see each other soon." Tatiana rested her head on Meredith's shoulder. "When she called me saying she was back in Chicago I was shocked. I had barely heard from her in the last twelve years. But I was also happy. My twin sister was back."

"How did Sofia end up at the New Jackson? The place is close to being condemned. Why wouldn't she stay with you?"

"When she called me she was already living there and I didn't ask her if she wanted to stay with me. I thought she would be better off away from me and Steven. We were going through a really rough patch. Vicious arguments."

No one, including Tatiana, knew why Sofia had arrived in the city eight months ago. Meredith had found out, through Colton, that Sofia had boarded a flight in Moscow, destined to Chicago, with one stop in London's Heathrow Airport. Not one person from her life back in Russia had come forward inquiring about Sofia. At least not yet.

"How did you meet your husband?" Meredith asked.

"I was waitressing at this restaurant; I was nineteen. We got married a year after that."

"The police said two years ago he filed a missing person's report for you. What happened?"

Tatiana leaned forward and caressed the dirt on Sofia's grave. "I got pregnant. I didn't tell Steven, and I went ahead and had an abortion. He found out. He was so angry. I think more than angry, he was hurt. He felt betrayed."

"So you left him?"

"He hit me so hard he cracked several of my ribs." The sound of Tatiana's voice dropped a notch. "I loved him, but after that I couldn't stay with him. I hadn't worked since we got married. I had become a lady of leisure with a monthly allowance from my husband. So I took a chunk of his money, as much as I could get my hands on, and left."

"But you went back to him."

"I was living in San Francisco when one morning he showed up at my doorstep. I asked how he found out where I was staying but he refused to tell me. I got the sense he'd find me anywhere I went." Tatiana grabbed a handful of dirt and held it between her hands. "He apologized. I apologized. At that point we had been married for seven years. We thought we could get over what had happened."

Tatiana had left her wig in the car, and Meredith kissed her hair. "Knowing what he did to you the night your sister died, I assume you were wrong."

"It was over for us a long time ago. The fights, the broken furniture, the bruises…it kept getting worse and worse. He couldn't let me go, and I was too afraid to pack up and leave like I'd done before." Tatiana pressed her hands tighter together and some of the dirt fell on her lap. "Steven had access to my bank account. He knew exactly how much I spent and saved. I had tried to find a job before, but Steven said he could give me in a day what I'd make in a month at any job I was qualified to do."

Meredith's hatred toward Thompson intensified.

"I wanted to have my own money, put all of it aside so I could leave him," Tatiana continued. "I wanted a new life that didn't give him the chance to find me. That's all I wanted, Meredith. To be free from Steven."

"He hit you from the beginning of your marriage, didn't he?"

"He'd slap me when we had bad arguments. It got worse after he found out I had the abortion."

Tatiana opened her hands and the remaining dirt fell on her lap. It had rained earlier, and Meredith smelled the dampness coming from all around them. She didn't care her dress was getting wet from sitting on the ground.

"I really fucked up, Meredith. Big time. I have nothing. Now that my sister is gone I don't have anyone either. Every day I wake up and I wonder if it will be the day that Julian kicks me out of his place."

"I remember the way Julian looked at you the first time he saw you at the club," Meredith said. "You don't have to worry about him throwing you out. It'll be your decision when you leave."

"Julian's not that predictable."

They got quiet and Meredith tried to pick up on the sound of the traffic from the road. There were so deep inside the cemetery she couldn't hear it.

"Or that honorable," Tatiana added.

"If he threw you out I'd be there for you."

"You can't protect me the way Julian can."

Meredith wanted to ask her why, but Tatiana continued. "I remember the first time I saw him at The Raven Room. It was still early in the evening, not many people were around. As I walked through the main floor, toward the staircase, I heard a laugh. There wasn't anything special about it, it was just a laugh, but it made me look toward the bar. I saw this tall man in a dark suit, dressed like almost any other man at the club, talking to Ben. His wavy black hair, the way his body was leaning on the counter, I don't know… grabbed my attention for a second too long. I went to the bar and, even though there were a few people between us, I managed to get a good look at him. Then he laughed again and I thought: it's him. It's Reeve. How did that junky motherfucker end up looking like a million bucks?"

"Did you tell your husband about him?"

"I did. Big mistake. He hates Julian."

"Because of what happened between you, Julian, and your mom?"

"You'd think, right? But no. Other than my husband, Julian is the only other man I've ever loved. That bothers Steven."

Meredith hadn't expected such a confession. Julian reserved his most honorable feelings toward Sofia and Tatiana, and it felt right to Meredith that he was as important to Tatiana as she was to him.

"Your husband is bothered by the power that Julian has over you," Meredith said. "That's something your husband wants to have just for himself."

"Both of them have hurt me so much."

Meredith hugged Tatiana tighter.

"Steven wasn't the one who killed Sofia," Tatiana whispered into Meredith's ear.

"How—"

"I need you to know that," Tatiana continued. "It's important to me that you do."

Tatiana rubbed her dirty palms on her dress and got to her feet. She was halfway down the main path before Meredith realized Tatiana had decided it was time for them to leave.

CHAPTER 13

"Why did you go?"

Julian followed Tatiana into the guest room. She started to undress as if she didn't care that he stood right beside her, clad only in a pair of sweatpants.

"Do you have any idea what could have happened?" His stare traveled from her muddy feet and over her wrinkled dress, ending on her messy hair. Whatever makeup she'd had on earlier was now gone.

After several attempts to unzip the back of her dress, Tatiana sat on the bed. "Are we really going to do this now?"

"Do what? Have a conversation about you going to The Raven Room and taking Meredith with you?"

"That didn't take long." She faced him for the first time since she had returned to the condo. "Who told you?"

"How can you be so reckless?"

Tatiana started to fight with the zipper again and Julian, both frustrated and impatient, moved toward her. As soon she felt his hands on her back, she pulled away.

"Don't touch me." She lifted her feet into the bed, smearing mud onto the white duvet cover.

"You're filthy. Where are have you been?"

Tatiana ignored him.

"Where'd all the dirt come from?"

She refused to answer.

"Have you taken a good look at yourself?" He caught himself screaming at her, but didn't try to stop. "You're here in my home, covered in dirt, dressed in borrowed clothes, with no friends, no money, no place to go. Hiding from the police and your husband. You've run out of options. I'm it. I'm the end of the road for you. So when I tell you going to The Raven Room is a bad idea, you listen." Julian closed his hands on the back of her dress and pulled hard. "You need me Tatiana, so you do what I tell you."

The zipper finally came undone and so did the dress. Tatiana didn't react to the sound of fabric tearing. Julian, with brusque but purposeful movements, tore off her clothes.

Grabbing Tatiana by the arm, he took her to the bathroom and dragged her to the shower. As he turned on the water, he let go of her and she lowered herself to her knees on the tiles. Julian crouched by her, hot water falling on both of them. With her forehead almost resting on the shower floor, her hair clung to her. For the first time since the night he had found her on the street, he saw her naked body.

He admired her scars to their smallest detail. With no symmetry to them, they stood out—small and large—scattered on her pale skin. While he abhorred what they represented, they only made him want to touch her more.

Julian dug his nails into his palms. He refused to succumb to the urge to run his fingers along the discolored lines on her shoulders.

As he turned his back on Tatiana, she slammed her fists into him. She wasn't strong enough to harm him but her reaction startled him.

She hit him again. "This is all your fault. Everything has always been your fault."

He took hold of her wrists and pressed her against the bathroom wall, forcing her to cease her attack on him.

"My sister is dead." She tried to break free from his hold. "She's dead because of you."

Julian flinched at her words.

She kicked out, and he pressed his body to hers, making it impossible for her to strike him again.

"Look at me." Tatiana demanded. "Are you afraid you'll see her in me? Or do I remind you of what you did?"

When Julian didn't comply, she bit his naked chest. He cried out in pain. He continued to hold her wrists with one hand and got her mouth away from him by gripping her chin with the other.

"Steven killed Sofia," she blurted out. "He's the one who killed my sister."

"Why…" Julian's voice cracked. "How do you know that?"

"I was there," she paused, swallowing hard. "But I got away. If he finds me, I'm afraid of what he'll do to me."

"Why did he kill her?"

She attempted to break free but he held her more forcefully.

"Tell me!"

"You!" She shouted. "He killed her because of you!"

Words failed Julian.

"Steven knows who you are," she continued. "I had told him about the years you lived with us when we were kids. I told him everything. When you came up to me at The Raven Room, he thought I had gotten involved with you."

"Why did he think you'd do that?"

She had gone very still, no longer struggling against him. "He didn't believe me when I said I'd never fuck you. After security kicked you out of the club, I thought he'd kill me."

"He almost did," he whispered more to himself than to her. Tatiana's bruises had been some of the worst Julian had ever seen.

"I tried to make him understand it was Sofia. Not me. Steven wanted to ask her himself so we went to the New Jackson Hotel."

"Why did he care if she and I were involved?"

"He didn't. He hit me again in front of her. She tried to get him off me. She tried to protect me. He pushed her."

Tears ran down her face, over his fingers, and that made Julian let go of her chin. He didn't want to feel her tears on his skin.

"It gave me a chance to run out," she said.

Julian pictured Sofia's lifeless body. He squeezed his eyes shut to make the image disappear.

"Have you told anyone else?" he asked.

Tatiana shook her head.

"Don't tell Meredith. Do you understand?"

"I'd never do that."

His chest throbbed where she had bit him and Julian didn't know if it was blood or water from her wet hair that dripped down his stomach.

"How do I know you're not making this up to incriminate your husband?" he asked.

"Steven hit me in front of you. When you thought I was Sofia, you had no hesitations believing he was a man capable of violence. Now, because it's me telling you he killed Sofia, you have doubt."

It didn't matter to Julian that it had been Tatiana and not Sofia whom he had seen Thompson hit. He loathed Thompson just the same.

"I've thought about getting a gun," Tatiana said. "Taking a taxi to our house, ringing the doorbell, and then, when he opens the door, shooting him right between the eyes. Straightforward justice."

The scenario Tatiana described brought Julian pleasure. He wanted Thompson dead.

"Steven won't get locked up for what he did to my sister." When she pressed her face to Julian's neck he didn't stop her. But instead of biting him once more, she kissed him. Her gesture, absent of eroticism, brought him unexpected comfort. "I know too much. He'll never let me go."

"He won't hurt you again."

She wrapped her arms around his waist. "The police don't care what I have to say about Sofia's murder. Steven has friends there." She held Julian tighter. "If the police find me or if Steven does, it's the same thing. They'll make me disappear."

He didn't hug her back. "You're right. I'm the reason Sofia is dead. Ever since the beginning, I've always been bad for both of you. If you stay here, near me, it won't end well."

Tatiana didn't let go of him. "I've been surviving men my whole life. I've survived you once before. I'll do it again."

CHAPTER 14

Julian opened the top dresser drawer and found it empty. He walked into his en suite bathroom and went through all the drawers of the vanity. Many of the useless grooming products he had accumulated through the years ended up scattered on the floor. When he realized he had misplaced what he was looking for, he raked his hands through his hair forcefully. He hadn't slept in two days and the only way he would be able to fall asleep was if he knew that, when he did, there would be no dreams.

He rushed through the silent condo. The overbearing gray sky peeked through the curtains. Having lost his sense of time, he glanced at the bright green numbers on the stove. He came to a dead stop when he saw it was four o'clock in the afternoon. Filled with a new resolve, Julian went straight to the guest room at the opposite end of the condo. He didn't bother to knock. He slammed the door open and walked up to Tatiana, who was lying on the bed.

"Have you seen my pills?" he asked, his voice not hiding the panic he felt.

"I threw them out."

He felt his stomach drop. "You did what?"

"You heard me."

"Where did you put them?"

"Down the toilet."

"How dare you go through my things? I need those pills!"

"That excuse won't work on me."

"You don't understand." His voice carried a pragmatic tone.

He felt desperate enough to try reason with Tatiana. "I can't just stop. The withdrawal symptoms will make me sick."

"I'm helping you the only way I know how. Might not be the best way, but if it gets you to think with a clear head again then it's good enough."

Before Julian could respond, the sound of a bell ringing echoed through the condo.

"Stay here," he said. "If you hear anyone come toward the bedroom, hide."

He closed the door behind him and went to find out why the concierge had called. It was Grace, stopping by with the boys. He couldn't turn them away.

"What happened to your phone?" Grace asked as soon as he let her in. "I was worried. I've been trying to get a hold of you all day."

"You have?" Julian didn't even know where his phone was.

"You should get a landline."

Julian watched as Grace carried the twins, and several bags, to his living room. He didn't understand why she always showed up carrying the twins in her arms.

"Don't you have a stroller?" he asked, concerned she would drop them. He took one of the boys from her. "They're getting too big for you to carry them both by yourself."

"It's broken and I haven't had the time to go buy a new one."

Julian didn't know if he was holding Seth or Eli and because he didn't want Grace to know he couldn't tell them apart, he hoped she would call one of them by name.

"You don't look too good," she continued. "How have you been holding up?"

I feel unhinged and I don't know what to do, Julian thought. Instead he said, "Don't worry about me."

"Anything you need. Anything at all, you let me know, OK? Pete won't tell me why he isn't talking to you, but he's worried too."

Julian didn't want to discuss what had happened between Peter and him.

"What's got him so upset?" Grace asked.

"I'd rather not get into it, but please believe me when I say it has nothing to do with you and the boys." He tried to smile and failed. "Men being stupid."

Peter knew more than Julian wanted him to about the night Sofia had died. If Peter ever decided to speak to the police, Julian would be in trouble. He had decided that as long as Peter remained silent, he could stay angry forever.

"How are things between the two of you?" he asked.

"Better, actually." Grace smiled. "And it has somewhat to do with why I'm here today. I need to ask you for a huge favor. With everything you've got going on, I feel awful asking but you're the only person I can rely on on such short notice."

"Stop rambling and tell me what you need."

"Pete and I have decided to open up our marriage. Give it a go and see what happens. We both have dates tonight, and our babysitter just canceled on us. I'm hoping you can watch Seth and Eli for a few hours."

"You guys are trying an open marriage?"

"Yes, you know, we have both agreed we can see other people as long—"

"I know what an open marriage is, Grace. Seeing the state your relationship is in, I'm surprised you guys chose to go that route."

"You don't think it's a good idea?"

Julian didn't want to discuss Grace and Peter's marriage when he couldn't make sense of the signals his body sent him. One second he needed to sit down, the next to walk around. The words coming from Grace's mouth sounded too fast to him, and he struggled to concentrate. "Can we talk about this later?"

"This is important to me, Julian."

He looked at the boy in his arms—he had to push through his discomfort. "With all honesty? No, I think it's an awful idea. Why did you agree to it?"

"The open marriage was my idea, not his."

"Is that what you really want, Grace?"

"For the first time since I got pregnant, I'm feeling sexy and beautiful and desired. Why wouldn't I want that?"

Julian sat down on the couch. All of his energy went into maintaining his conversation with Grace. He worried he would collapse while holding one of the boys. "Of course you should want that. But if you have to sleep with other men to feel that way, then you've got a problem in your marriage that can't be fixed by opening it up."

"You and Pete are best friends, but I always felt if you and I met first we would be the ones calling each other best friends. I need you in my corner, Julian."

"I am, Grace. I always will be."

"Believe me, then, when I say that I need this. I know it sounds crazy—"

"It doesn't sound crazy. A lot of couples have arrangements. But the timing for you and Pete is wrong. You're just adding another challenge to your marriage, which is already having problems. What do you think will happen?"

"I don't know, Julian."

"Yes, you do."

"So what if we end up separating? Pete and I won't certainly be the first."

"You can't start an open marriage with that attitude. It'll get messy—quick."

"You think that instead of behaving like a slut, I should be working on my relationship with Pete."

Julian frowned. "What?"

"Isn't that what you think?"

"That you and Pete should go to therapy? Yes. That you're behaving like a slut? I'd never think less of you for exploring your sexuality."

"No one in my family, or any of my friends, know. I can't tell them. They would never understand. Please, be with me on this."

Julian sighed. "You know what I think, but yes, I'm with you. No matter what happens."

She passed the boy in her arms to Julian so he now held both twins. "Thank you. We're lucky to have you."

He wanted to challenge Grace on what she had just said but he couldn't. Whatever mental stamina he had left, he had used it to argue with her about the open marriage. "Don't you have to be somewhere?"

She nodded as she reached for her purse. "I promise I won't be too late."

"It's OK if you are. I won't be sleeping much." He still couldn't believe Tatiana had disposed of his pills.

"Everything you need for Seth and Eli is in those bags. I've labeled their dinner and snacks. They don't need to eat for another hour, so a nap until then would be great. You know my number and if—"

"I got it. Just go, Grace. The boys will be fine."

After she kissed both her sons she turned to Julian. "I know. You're their dad, after all."

Grace left and Julian's eyes darted between the boys. Grace hadn't called either one by name, so he still didn't know which one was which. He called out the name Eli and both boys looked at him with guileless curiosity. He tried it again, now saying the name Seth, and he got giggles and incomprehensible babble from both boys.

"Sometimes the universe works in strange ways, don't you think?" Tatiana stood by the entrance of the living room. "You have two kids. Identical twins. When were you going to tell me that?"

"I can't deal with you right now."

"They like me. They're smiling at me."

"Leave." He didn't want to raise his voice in front of Seth and Eli.

Before disappearing down the hall, Tatiana winked at the boys.

Doing what he did every time they came over, Julian took the twins to his bedroom and made a makeshift bed for them on the floor by the large window. As he scattered their toys around them, he remembered that he had recently refilled his prescription. He rushed into his office and found the two new bottles inside his workbag. He didn't stop to think. Instead of one, he took two pills from each bottle.

He returned to the bedroom and lay down on the floor near the boys. Heavy, dark clouds hung low over the buildings, and the Chicago River had lost its beautiful turquoise color. It looked as gray as the sky above.

Julian watched Seth and Eli play for a while. He wanted to hug them, breathe in their scent, kiss their small toes, but his body became too heavy for him to move. He smiled when one of the boys draped himself over his chest. Then he closed his eyes.

• • •

Julian sat up, his heart racing. At first, he didn't know why he was on the floor with toys scattered around him, but then the intense lightning across the sky, followed by a loud crash of thunder, jarred him awake.

He didn't see Seth or Eli.

He got up and ran out of the bedroom. All the lights in the condo were off, but lightning illuminated his path. Julian checked each room, frantically searching for the boys. He called out their names, but there were no sounds that told him where they might be. He called out again, louder this time.

"In here."

Julian followed Tatiana's voice.

"Calm down," she said as soon as he rushed inside the guest bedroom. "They're already startled by the storm. Don't make them more afraid."

"What happened?" He kneeled by the bed. Seth and Eli snuggled colorful baby blankets beside Tatiana. Under the dim glow from the standing lamp, their eyes looked as green as his own. "Why did you take them?" His heart beat so fast it made it difficult for him to speak. "I told you to stay away—"

"It's five in the morning."

Confused, he stared at Tatiana.

"Look at the clock." She tilted her head toward the nightstand. "You passed out and their mom never came to pick them up. You left the door of your bedroom open and they were crawling all over the place, crying. They needed to be fed and changed. They were alone. Frightened."

The anger Julian felt toward himself for endangering Seth and Eli was so powerful and consuming he sagged forward. Already on his knees, he had to hold on to the bed.

He should get up and search for his phone, to see if Grace had texted or called, but he didn't trust his legs to support him.

"This one is Eli." Tatiana pointed at the boy closer to her. "And that one is Seth. It's written on the tags of their shirts," she explained, taking hold of his hand and placing it inside the collar so he could feel the tags. "They liked me when they first saw me, but now it's a full-fledged crush." Tatiana blew a kiss at Seth and he gave her a wide smile.

With adrenaline still coursing through his body, Julian said the first thing that came to his mind. "It's your hair." He caressed the back of the boy's small neck. Tatiana no longer held his hand and he was glad she had been the one to let go. He didn't know if he would have found the strength to do so. "It's wild. It catches their attention."

"Why is it so hard for you to admit that your sons like me? It proves they have good taste. Something for you to be happy about."

Julian felt the warmth of Eli's small body against his palm. His heartbeat slowed as the panic over the twins' safety subsided.

"Except for Grace, no one knows I'm their biological father. Pete doesn't know, and neither does Meredith. You can't repeat what you heard earlier."

Tatiana watched Julian caress his son's forehead. "You don't trust me."

"I barely know you."

"I've been living in your home for almost two months. You

know more about me than you ever did about Sofia. And yet, I get the impression you trusted her."

He had grown to trust Sofia, but she had lied to him from the day she approached him at the coffee shop. "Did you know about us?"

"Not until the night she died. When are you going to ask me to tell you everything I know about her? We have twenty-two years to cover."

"Not yet." He didn't feel ready.

The storm had died down, but every few minutes, lightning crossed the sky and a white flash peeked through the side of the curtains.

"I recognized you as soon as I saw you at the club," she said.

"I was sixteen and you were eight the last time we saw each other. Did you remember me that well?"

"Years ago I looked up your birth name. I couldn't find anything. Then I thought of all those times you said you'd change your last name to Reeve. You were obsessed with the Superman movie and the guy that played him. That's when I came across a Julian Reeve, Child Psychologist and Associate Professor here in Chicago. The hospital had your picture up on the website. You were standing with a kid and a scary-looking clown." Tatiana's voice slowly faded out, as if she were lost in a memory. "I remember being impressed with the number of research papers you had written on abnormal child psychology. I guess fucked-up kids is your thing."

He decided it was best not to tell her that she and Sofia were the reason behind his career choice.

"I found out which classes you were teaching at Feinberg," she said. "I went there. I wanted to make sure it was really you. I watched you walk to your car after you were done giving a lecture. Not long after, I saw you at The Raven Room and I avoided you then. Fast-forward a few years and there you were, with Meredith, watching me fuck my husband. I'll never forget how you looked at me."

Julian realized he had been holding his breath "How did I look at you?"

"Like you always did." She stroked Eli's temple with her fingertips. "Like you're looking at me now."

Julian lowered his eyes to the floor.

"I saw the new pill bottles." Tatiana's voice lost its soft quality. "While Pete and Grace are out there, fucking other people, too afraid to put an end to their bad marriage, Seth and Eli are here, with you. Act this way again, endanger them, and you and my sister will suddenly be reunited."

CHAPTER 15

Julian arrived at The Raven Room earlier than he thought he would.

He paused, taking in the vibe of the club. He never ventured more than a couple of steps inside before taking in the scene around him: identifying the genre of music being played, smelling which aromas mingled with the defining scent of the club. The time he took to observe his surroundings, short as it was, always revealed to him what he might expect from the night ahead.

Before he moved into the crowd, Julian flexed his toes inside his black leather shoes. He felt the silky touch of his dress socks against the soles of his feet. He gave the left sleeve of his suit a brisk tug, then the right, making sure the crisp, high thread count white dress shirt didn't poke too far past the cuffs of his jacket. He glanced at the new timepiece on his wrist. On his drive to the club, he realized he had forgotten his watch at home and tonight, because he had an appointment he couldn't be late for, he needed to keep track of time.

That forced him to stop at a small Chinese gift shop on South Wentworth Avenue and purchase an analog watch in the only style they had. With its circular white face set against a silver-tone case and black synthetic leather strap, he liked the watch, as long as he forced himself to ignore the colorful Hello Kitty graphics.

Noting the time, Julian tucked the watch under his shirt cuff. If he stayed away from the lower floor, which he intended to, he had thirty minutes to watch strangers have sex, or sit by the bar and drink more than he should. Neither sounded appealing to him.

He caught a glimpse of his reflection in the large vintage mirror. He looked confident and in control—the magic of a good suit.

As he reached the second floor, a woman in black lingerie ran into his arms. Half of his whiskey landed on her breasts.

"We're playing a game," she said, flustered and out of breath. "Want to join?" She wiped the whiskey off her skin and brought her fingers to her lips, sucking on them with a smile.

"Sure." Julian sounded more resigned than excited. He yearned for a distraction from what he had come to the club to do.

"Yes!" she shouted, taking his glass away. She reached for his hand.

Julian let her lead him into the Basilisk, the smallest room in the club. There were several people lounging around, draped over large leather couches and chairs, smoking hookahs. The flavored tobacco enveloped him.

"The rules are simple." The woman covered Julian's eyes with a blindfold. "You move around the room. You belong to the first person you touch."

The lighting, coming from several electrical lamps made to look like gas flames on old light fixtures, didn't permeate the thick fabric of the blindfold. Julian found himself thrown into complete darkness.

"One more thing," she said, loud enough for everyone around them to hear.

"Before we start, you need to choose the sexual act."

"Oral sex," he replied.

"Receiving or giving?"

"Receiving."

Before he knew it he was spun around, her hands moving on his waist and, as fast as she had started, she stopped.

"Off you go," she said with a laugh. "May the Basilisk offer you great pleasure."

With hesitation, Julian started to move around the room. He heard laughter, encouragements, voices telling him to move here or there, promises of great oral sex, descriptions, in graphic detail, of what would be done to him.

He didn't pay attention to any of it. Instead, he took refuge in the darkness offered to him by the blindfold, in the strong tobacco scent scorching his lungs. With Sofia forever gone, his relationship with Meredith collapsing, and an emotionally unstable Tatiana making him confront his past, he wanted to evade the sorrow that consumed him.

Julian's legs touched the edge of one of the couches and he reached out, his hand coming in contact with an arm. He didn't move. He felt a glimmer of anticipation.

"Sit down," he heard a masculine voice say.

Julian didn't hesitate. He lowered himself onto the sofa. While he couldn't see who had just kneeled at his feet, the sound of someone unzipping his suit pants, the sensation of an unknown person reaching inside his boxer briefs and pulling out his cock, carried a message that spoke to Julian's basic nature. He had felt a man's hands on his body before. The touch carried a weight, a hardness that commanded Julian to surrender himself to the pleasure of it.

Julian didn't have an erection, but the man at his feet showed no discouragement. He forced Julian's legs further apart and licked the sensitive head of his member, which grew exposed as Julian's arousal heightened. As soon as Julian felt the man's moist lips close on him, Julian let his hands rest on the couch. Pleasure spread through him and he dug his fingers into the soft leather. The tempo of the music had slowed and the man's movements matched the rhythm of the sounds reverberating through the space.

The man took him deep into his mouth and a wave of satisfaction shot up Julian's spine, forcing him to arch his back. As he thrust further, the man's throat accepted more of his erection. His hips shot off the couch and a pair of strong hands pulled him even closer to open lips. Julian felt stubble rub below his cock, and the discomfort of it, mixed with the softness of an eager mouth, intensified his release. His loud moan resembled a cry.

Julian's body shuddered when he felt warm breath fan his temple.

"You have a gorgeous cock." Julian heard the smile in the man's voice. "And the prettiest watch I've seen."

Julian remained seated, his head resting on the back of the couch. He took a series of deep breaths. His body still shook.

Julian removed the blindfold, but the man was gone. The spectators, too. They were already focused on a new game. Zipping up his suit pants, Julian got to his feet and left the room.

Checking his watch, he took the second staircase to the third floor. It was time. Instead of entering the only room on that level, the Black Dragon, Julian made his way to the bathroom. He found it empty. Like the rest of the club, no detail had been overlooked. Invisible speakers filled the space with mellow jazz tunes, and vases with fresh cut white peonies sat on the large vanity, which was made of the same marble with dramatic gray veining as the floor. The wainscoting, together with the royal blue wallpaper and its gold details, contributed to the regal ambience. An elaborate vintage-looking chandelier—an art piece—made of filament amber light bulbs, hung from the ceiling. No person stood in that bathroom and didn't feel a little bit richer, a little bit more beautiful.

Julian approached the larger private stall at the opposite end of the bathroom. He pulled out his key and pressed it against an unmarked spot on the tiled wall adjacent to the door. As soon as he did, the wood door unlocked. Julian turned the handle, opened the large door, and he entered the stall. With no toilet, it turned out to be an empty space. After closing the door behind him, he scanned the key again on the wall inside the stall, and a hidden door slid open. He climbed a set of narrow, rusty metal stairs, until he found himself above ground.

The smell hit him first—cooked meat, roasted skin, and boiled fish—a mix of scents so strong that Julian held his breath. And the heat. He started to sweat almost immediately. The relentless commotion of a small, hectic, twenty-four hour kitchen swirled around him.

No one paid attention to Julian as he passed through. He had to dodge several sharp elbows. If he lingered, the odor of fried food would cling to him and nothing short of throwing his clothes in the washer and showering would make it go away.

Julian walked down a poorly lit serpentine corridor with patched-up walls that had once been painted white. He stopped when he reached a closed office door at the end of the hall. Although he appeared in control, Julian felt nervous. Without a surface to drum his fingers on—something he did every time anxiety consumed him—he ran his fingers through his hair instead.

Julian checked his watch. Right on time. As soon as he knocked, he was told to enter.

"You're always punctual." From behind the desk, Vincent spoke in perfect Mandarin. "It's the reason I like you."

He had been in that office often throughout the years, and even though they weren't equals, Julian knew he held more power than the man smiling at him liked to admit.

"I want to place an order," Julian replied in Mandarin. He hoped his discomfort wasn't obvious. He had received instructions when he booked the appointment, but he had never done this before.

Vincent smiled. "What's the special occasion?"

"It's a private party."

"How many?"

"One."

"When do you want it delivered?"

"As soon as possible."

"Flawless parties take time to organize."

"OK. When the timing is right. But before the end of the month."

"You know the menu. What dishes would you like?"

Julian glanced at the cheap desk. There were no papers, no computer, no picture frames. Besides the desk and the two rickety chairs they sat on, the room looked bare. There were also no windows. Only a large, exposed fluorescent light tube on the ceiling. Both he and Vincent looked out of place.

"The house special. I want a receipt."

"This order will be added to your profile."

Julian nodded.

The smell of food filled the room and, being less pungent than in the kitchen, Julian caught himself salivating.

"Guest of honor?"

Julian reached inside his pant pocket and pulled out a tissue. He then removed a small piece of paper from his coat pocket, making sure the tissue worked as a barrier between his fingers and the paper.

He placed it in the middle of the table and returned the tissue to his pocket. "Picture and details."

Vincent covered the paper with his hand and pulled it toward him. Without looking at it, he slid it inside his own pocket. "Thank you for your business."

Julian got up and exited the room without looking back. He had just ordered Steven Thompson's death.

CHAPTER 16

"Ballsy of you to show up at my office."

Julian took in the impressive sight of Peter. While Julian continued to age faster than everyone else around him, in the last few months Peter seemed to have shed several years. Besides his new slimmer body, Peter had shaved off his blond beard. Clean-shaven, sporting his Ivy League style, he was the quintessential vision of success.

"You made me wait three hours in your waiting room," Julian said.

"I should have had you escorted out of the building."

"I wouldn't have left quietly and you know it. Doubt your patients would have appreciated the show."

"Are you here so I don't tell the cops you were the one who beat Tatiana Thompson?"

"I didn't touch her," Julian replied, his voice clipped.

"That's not what you implied that night. Why did you lead me to believe she was Alana or Sofia or whoever the fuck you were seeing? Why the lies, man?"

"I wasn't aware of Alana's identity. Or that she had a twin. Or that she and Tatiana were the same twins I told you about years ago."

"Did you come here and wait all this time to ask for my forgiveness, then?"

"I have nothing to apologize for."

"Jesus Christ, not only are you a sick fuck, you're also an arrogant fuck."

Julian had a specific reason to seek out Peter: Grace and Peter's actions worried him. If they continued to use their new sexual freedom as a distraction from the problems affecting their marriage, they would end up divorcing. Julian believed that Peter and Grace could still salvage their relationship and offer Seth and Eli everything he couldn't.

"Grace was at my place. She told me you've opened up your marriage."

"And what's that to you?" Peter threw his pen across the desk. It landed on the floor. "Grace needs to learn how to keep her mouth shut."

"Grace can say whatever she wants. She doesn't need your permission."

"We're talking about my marriage. It's pretty personal stuff."

"Cheating on your wife is pretty personal stuff. You shared that with me."

Julian didn't plan to divulge to Grace her husband's unfaithfulness, but Peter didn't know that.

"This open marriage experiment will blow up in your face," Julian continued. "You and Grace need to get into therapy."

"Let me get this straight—you have no family of your own, you go to sex clubs, you're into that whole BDSM scene that gives me the creeps and you're telling me how I should handle my marriage?" Peter laughed. "You're in no position to open your mouth, man."

"I'm trying to protect Seth and Eli."

"They're not yours to protect."

Julian ground his teeth together to the point that his jaw hurt. "Grace is unhappy. That's what led her to want an open marriage. If you weren't too busy taking advantage of your hall pass, you'd see that."

"Has she told you she's unhappy? Because she hasn't said anything to me. And Seth and Eli have everything they need. They always come first. Even when Grace and I are sleeping with other people."

Not the night Grace forgot to pick them up and I was too fucked up on benzos to take care of them, Julian thought. To be fair, that incident hadn't been Peter's fault, but he wasn't about to criticize Grace or reveal how irresponsibly he himself had acted.

"Listen, I'm not here to pass judgment on your decision to have an open marriage," Julian said. "I just know you two are doing it for the wrong reasons. You and Grace need to address the state of your relationship first. Do it for Seth and Eli. C'mon, Pete, how long have we been friends? Twenty, twenty-one years? Can't we get past what happened that night and focus on the well-being of your wife and children?"

"You've got a problem with how I choose to live my life? I've got a problem with how you choose to live yours. What happened that night just drove it home for me."

"My sexual life should have no weight on our friendship."

"And what about Grace's and mine?"

"If you didn't have Seth and Eli we probably wouldn't be having this conversation," Julian said.

"I won't tell Grace what you're into, and if she wishes to hang out with you and take the boys, I'll allow it. I'm doing this for her though. I know how much she likes you."

Julian tensed up at the word *allow*. "You're so certain that if Grace found out she wouldn't understand."

"Go ahead then, tell her. Who's stopping you?"

At that moment, Julian hated Peter. They both knew that if Grace found out about Julian's connection with The Raven Room, she might not want him to spend time with Seth and Eli. Julian resented that Peter had the power to prevent him from seeing his own biological children.

Julian decided he would have more to gain if he kept his true emotions toward Peter to himself. "Do you remember our trip to Prague?" he asked.

"During the summer of our junior year? Yeah."

"We ended up at that sketchy-looking motel with those two Italian girls we met at the nude beach."

Peter's expression softened. "You didn't know who they were when we ran into them at the bar later that day."

"To my defense they looked different with their clothes on."

"I recognized them."

"Then that guy stole your wallet and I chased him down for five blocks."

"And you got beaten up so bad we thought you'd go blind in one eye."

"But I got your wallet back."

"Why did you do it? I didn't care about the money."

"I know. You paid for my plane ticket."

Peter couldn't hold back a smile.

"You had a picture of your family in your wallet," Julian said. "It was the only one you had of you and your grandfather. I wasn't going to allow anyone to take it away from you."

Peter came to sit beside Julian. With his shoulders slumped, he stared at his own feet.

"I've always had your back, Pete. That's what I'm trying to do right now."

Someone knocked on the door and they both looked up. A nurse peeked in. "Sorry, Doctor Morin, you're running an hour behind. The patients have started to complain."

Peter's new amenable demeanor vanished. "We're done here. Walk Dr. Reeve out and bring in my next patient."

Julian remained seated. "Listen to me, Pete."

Peter returned behind his desk and started to type. He ignored Julian.

The nurse opened the door further and pointed toward the hallway. She gave him a nervous smile. "This way, Dr. Reeve."

Julian had just stepped outside of the office when Peter spoke, "I'm sorry about what happened to Sofia."

The sympathy in Peter's voice lingered between them.

"I hope Tatiana is OK," he added.

As Julian left, he realized that, regardless of his anger toward Peter, he missed the friendship they once had.

CHAPTER 17

As Meredith walked toward her parked car after a quick manicure at her favorite spa on West Division Street, she threw her head back and felt the late afternoon sun on her face. So far, the summer had consisted of a few sunny moments between overcast skies that only cleared after strong thunderstorms.

The lack of sun hadn't made the days or nights any cooler—the heat persisted. Sunny or not, warm weather made Meredith happy, but the pleasure she took from it failed to make her content. She still didn't know who, if anyone, could be following her, and the sensation that someone watched her every move persisted. These days, because of how anxious she felt, she preferred to stay at home rather than venture out.

Meredith entered the aboveground parking lot, and searched for her car keys in her tote. Unable to find them amongst her laptop and schoolbooks, she groaned with frustration. She suddenly became aware of the sound of approaching footsteps. She looked up and noticed a man standing thirty feet away, at the entrance of the parking lot, staring at her. People passed him on the sidewalk and his attention did not waver. He focused solely on her.

Meredith held his stare. He looked unmemorable—a middle-aged Caucasian man, with no striking features, clad in a pair of jeans and a t-shirt. Emboldened by the fact they were in a public place with pedestrians nearby, she started to walk toward him.

"What do you want?" she demanded, leaving a few feet of space between the two of them. She didn't dare get too close.

He didn't reply and, as she waited for a response, Meredith tried to memorize as many details about him as she could: his graying hair, his brown eyes, the fact that she would still be taller than him even if she weren't wearing high-heel sandals.

Before she could ask him again, the man turned and started to walk down the street. Too stunned to act, Meredith watched him disappear around the corner.

All of a sudden, a wave of vulnerability washed over her. Determined to get to a safe place as fast as she could, Meredith struggled to locate her keys as she hurried to her car. With her heart pounding against her ribcage, she locked herself inside. It took her several tries to successfully insert the key in the ignition— her hands shook and she felt lightheaded. Now, with the engine running, she grasped the steering wheel. She didn't know who the man was, but clearly someone wanted to scare her.

At that moment, she heard her phone buzz and reached for it. Colton had just texted her, wondering where she was. They had planned to get together and she was running late. She quickly replied, letting him know she would meet him at his place. After what had just happened, she didn't want to have a conversation about the investigation in public.

As Meredith pulled her car out of the parking lot, she nervously surveyed her surroundings. The man was nowhere in sight.

She checked the rearview mirror every few seconds as she drove to Colton's house. She parked the car on his street—her heart still racing with fear—and quickly walked toward his home, scanning both sides of the street.

"I thought you wanted to go to Burt's Place for pizza," Colton said, scowling at her from his La-Z-Boy.

Meredith smelled his cologne from across the living room. His clothes looked freshly pressed.

"I changed my mind." She sat on the couch across from him. The air conditioning unit in the window behind her blew cool air on the nape of her neck. She welcomed its low humming sound, which muffled the noise from the football game playing on the television.

"You love pizza."

"Not hungry."

"Are you OK?"

Meredith wondered if she appeared as overwrought as she felt. "Got a bunch of papers to write, that's all. They're due by the end of the week." She lit a cigarette and slid the ashtray on the coffee table closer to her. She hoped a hit of nicotine would help settle her nerves. "Have you had a chance to look at Sofia's toxicology report?" She stared at the familiar mark of her bright red lipstick on the cigarette. "How about Thompson? Was he in Chicago at the time Lena was murdered?"

"Sofia's toxicology report shows she was clean. No drugs. And when in comes to Lena's death, Thompson was in New York for a conference that whole week. That rules him out."

Meredith tried to keep her mind away from what had happened at the parking lot. "I need you to find out something for me." She reached for a forgotten napkin on the coffee table and wrote on it. "Who owns the building at this address? The name on the property deed?"

Colton took the napkin from her. "Why? What does it have to do with the murders?"

"Get the name and we'll talk about it."

Colton passed her a pile of papers.

"What's this?" She thumbed through it, discovering a series of police reports and crime scene photos.

"Three more women. All found dead, on their beds, posed the same way as Lena and Sofia. All—besides Sofia who was clean and died from a hit to the head—were ruled accidental overdoses. The first one is from two and a half years ago. Lena was the fourth, then Sofia."

If she didn't know the women in the photographs were dead, she would've assumed they were asleep. They all looked so peaceful.

"All of them died during the last week of January," Colton added. "Thompson has attended the same marketing conference in New York for the last two years, so he either killed Sofia but not the other women, or someone else killed them all and somehow Sofia's murder didn't go as planned."

Meredith remained absorbed in the photographs. She held Lena's the longest.

"But whoever killed Sofia must have at least known about the others," Colton said.

Meredith flipped through the files once more. "Where did you find all of this?"

"Sung's office."

She had to put out her cigarette. Her hands started to shake again.

"I went to see her and when I walked into her office she was looking at something. She quickly threw it inside one of her desk drawers and that tipped me off. Whatever it was, she didn't want me to see it." It was Colton's turn to light a cigarette. "While I was still there she realized she was late for a meeting so we walked out together. But I snuck back in and had a look. Knew right away it was important so I photocopied it and put the originals back in the drawer." Colton pointed at the documents in her lap. "It's all there."

Pam's connection to Thompson had made Meredith uncomfortable from the beginning. But this was proof that Pam was hiding something and Meredith now suspected her stepmother was just as corrupt as the people that Meredith and her father often criticized.

No matter what Meredith uncovered about the murders, it wouldn't make a difference. She couldn't go to Pam or the police with any details and expect them to carry out a proper investigation. The murders of five women would go unpunished, and if there were to be any arrests in Sofia's death, Meredith worried an innocent person would end up paying for a crime they didn't commit.

Meredith placed the pile of papers back on the coffee table. Hugging her legs close to her chest, she slowly inhaled through her nose and exhaled through her mouth, repeatedly, hoping to calm her anxiety.

"Fuck, Meredith, are you OK?"

She heard the concern in Colton's voice.

"I just need to sit here for a bit."

She wanted someone to hold her, but Colton didn't move from his La-Z-Boy.

• • •

Meredith didn't know how long she sat there, with the air conditioning caressing the back of her neck. She couldn't stop seeing the faces of the dead women.

"Come to bed with me."

She felt Colton touch her.

"Don't." It was late, but she didn't want to drive home alone.

One of his hands found her breast and the other slid between her legs.

"I said don't." She pushed him away.

"What's wrong with you? You've been on this couch for like an hour."

"Colton, no."

"Are you pissed because of what I showed you? Forget about those women—"

"Leave me alone."

"So you're going to stay down here all night?"

"I'm not in the mood to fuck you and yes, I'm staying right here." She rolled over, her back to him.

She heard an angry Colton stomp up the stairs. Suddenly, without a second thought, Meredith stood up, grabbed the photographs and police reports still on the coffee table, and rushed out the door. The man who had approached her earlier might be waiting for her outside, but her need to get out of that house grew stronger than her sense of self-preservation.

As Meredith drove toward Near North Side, she kept a close eye on the cars around her. White-knuckling the steering wheel, she took particular notice of anyone who drove behind her. Rather than diminishing, the trepidation that had taken hold of her since her encounter in the parking lot swelled inside of her, threatening to engulf her at any second. She feared losing herself to panic.

By the time she parked in the visitor area of Julian's building and got into the elevator, her legs had gone numb. She forced herself to walk down the hall, grab her key, and unlock the door. All the lights were off. Meredith didn't look for Tatiana in the guest bedroom. Instead, she walked down the hall, past the silent kitchen and living room, toward Julian's empty bedroom.

Suppressing a sob, Meredith lay down on the unmade bed. She hugged one of the pillows and pressed her face into it, hoping to draw comfort from it. The pillow smelled like Julian, a mix of his aftershave and the scent of his body.

She didn't know how long she had been crying when she felt a pair of strong hands on her back.

"Meredith?"

She didn't move and continued to clutch the pillow. The sensation of Julian's hands on her body calmed her. Only he could make her feel safe. The realization made her cry harder.

"Meredith, what's wrong? What happened?"

Her breath came in and out in short gasps. She tried to speak but her throat felt too tight for any words to come out. The bed dipped under her and she welcomed the warmth of Julian's body molding itself to hers, cradling her from behind.

"Talk to me, Meredith." His arms came around her, embraced her, and she felt her hair being brushed aside and lips grazing the skin below her ear. That was her favorite way for him to hold her.

She struggled to speak. "I just want to be here."

Meredith kept her eyes shut but let go of the pillow. She closed her hands on Julian's arms, which cradled her tightly. The shivers racking her body lessened and her sobs morphed into silent tears. Her heart no longer threatened to rip through her chest.

They held each other in the dark for a long time.

CHAPTER 18

"You want to finish the piece and have it published."

Meredith savored the taste of her fine vintage Bordeaux. "That's exactly what I said. That's why I called you."

"And here I was thinking it was because you wanted me," Isaac said.

"That would make you delusional, not optimistic."

"Ouch." He placed his hand over his chest. "Remind me to protect my heart from you, merciless woman."

"I've been called worse."

"I'm sure you have."

"If you and I are working together—" Meredith paused, shaking her head. "We really shouldn't."

"Because we're two adults who are attracted to each other? Because we are both honest enough to admit to it and take it for what it is?" Isaac reached for her wine glass and touched the red smudge left by her lipstick with the pad of his thumb. "But if you tell me, right now, you don't want anything sexual to happen between us, then I'll stop."

Meredith stared at the way his finger caressed the rim of her wine glass, where her lips had just been. She raised her eyes to him and smiled.

"You're smart. Driven. Successful. I admire you." Meredith touched the other side of her wine glass, her fingers not far from his. She then circled the edge of the glass with her fingers, until they touched his, and caressed the space between his thumb and index finger.

"Why did you change your mind about the piece?" he asked.

They were at The Office, the speakeasy-style bar below The Aviary in West Loop. They shared a table in one of the softly lit nooks. The atmosphere was intimate, and with fewer than twenty people around them, Meredith and Isaac didn't have to struggle to hear each other.

"I found out there are others. So far five women have been murdered."

Isaac sighed. "And this conversation just became really depressing."

"Maybe there are more victims. I'm not sure. Only the last one was ruled a homicide. The others were considered accidental deaths." Meredith thought of the folder Colton had found hidden on Pam's desk. "The women were poor, uneducated, with hardly any friends or family. They were living their lives unnoticed, and whoever is killing them knows this. For a while, I thought I'd uncover information on the murders, share it with the police. But they're covering it up, Isaac. That's why I need to write the piece. It's the only way people will know about these women. I hope they'll demand justice."

"It's easy for the police to shove these deaths under the rug. The general public isn't aware of the existence of the club. You found out because of the man who took you there, and I came across it thanks to Glendon. Within the police force, anyone who knows what's going on is either corrupt or too afraid to do anything about it. It's easier to look the other way."

Meredith didn't believe fear would stop Pam.

"How about the man who took you to the club? Did you tell him you've decided to pursue the piece?"

Isaac's question made Meredith order another glass of wine.

"Not yet. He was romantically involved with the last woman that got killed. Now is not a good time. The piece is no longer about him. It has nothing to do with him, actually. It's about these women and the club. But once it's done and ready to go out, I'll tell him. When do you need it by?"

"In two months. Plenty of time. We'll find Glendon's journals."

"What if we don't?"

"Do you have enough material to make it a good piece?"

"If those journals hold the information you believe they do, they'll certainly help."

"All of Glendon's files are still in storage. I'm sure no one remembers they're still there. I'll bring them to my place and we can go through them together."

"Is there a lot?" Meredith asked. "You said he worked there for more than fifteen years."

"Only a few boxes, but I could be wrong. The man was a pack rat."

"Have you told anyone about me and the piece?"

Isaac reached for his Barley Wine. "I haven't. You?"

"Besides my professor? My stepmother. But that was a while ago." Meredith couldn't mention Pam without feeling resentment.

"How did you find out about these murders?"

She paused. "Different sources. I'd rather not say."

"You don't have to. Not to me or anyone else. Are they reliable?"

"I know what I've seen with my own eyes. And yes, they are reliable." Meredith decided to bring up something that had been bothering her. "Why didn't you tell me you knew my father?"

Isaac didn't hesitate. "It wasn't important and it still isn't."

"Is he the reason you're interested in the piece? Why you've been trying to help my career?"

"No, Meredith. This"—he pointed at her and then himself—"has nothing to do with your father. Did you two talk about me?"

"Recently we had lunch and he mentioned an acquaintance of his saw us together. I wish you had told me."

"It didn't occur to me that you'd care. I enjoy spending time with you, and your piece has value to me. Can we focus on that?" Isaac asked.

Meredith wanted to work with Isaac, enough to believe him

when he assured her that her father wasn't the reason why he had shown interested in her work.

"Yes, let's do that," she replied.

"Good." He sounded relieved. "Be smart, Meredith. Finish the piece. Do your best. But don't take unnecessary risks, got it?"

"I have no desire to get hurt."

"Maybe if you told the man who took you to the club about the piece he could help you gather information. Perhaps he saw Lena or the other women there."

"Maybe." She had no plans to involve Julian in her research. She had yet to find out who owned the necklace she had discovered in Julian's drawer.

They finished their drinks, and Meredith wondered if maybe they already had too much alcohol. She certainly felt it.

"My place, your place, or we each grab a cab home." He reached inside his wallet and pulled out his credit card.

"I'm paying for the check," Meredith said, opening her purse.

"I'm not letting you pay for it." Isaac glanced at the total and made a face. "It's bloody expensive."

"I can afford it." It was her father's money, but she didn't dwell on it. "And this isn't a date, so in reality we should be splitting the check. But you can make it up to me."

"In that case you have to come to my place."

"OK."

Isaac raised an eyebrow. "That's all I had to do?"

"What?"

"Let you pay for the check?"

"I want to sleep with you. All you have to do is want to sleep with me, too." The bartender returned with the card and Meredith signed the receipt.

"You know I do."

"Be forewarned, it'll backfire on you," Meredith said as they walked, side by side, out of The Office.

"I can't see how that's possible." Isaac wrapped his arm around her waist and Meredith leaned closer to him.

"Tomorrow morning you'll wake up and won't be able to remember the last time you enjoyed yourself so much." She smelled the alcohol on his breath. "But then you'll have a realization—I'm not yours."

They were standing on the edge of the sidewalk, trying to flag down a taxi, and his laughter carried down the street.

"I'll want you to be mine, huh?" he asked.

"We always want the best toy in the store."

A taxi pulled over and Isaac opened the door for her. As she was getting into the cab, he brought his lips to her ear. "I always get what I want," he whispered.

• • •

"Is your place always this pristine?" Meredith sauntered, barefoot, across Isaac's industrial loft. She enjoyed the feeling of the smooth concrete against the soles of her feet.

"I was hoping you'd agree to come back to my place." Isaac opened one of the windows and soft city sounds filled the small loft. "I tidied up a bit."

As Meredith climbed onto his bed she pointed to the neatly stacked pile of magazines and newspapers on his night table. "You're a literary guy. I like it."

"More of a words guy. I haven't read a novel in forever."

"That's a shame."

"Are you a literary girl?"

"When I'm not busy writing about dead women."

He lay down beside her. "Can I kiss you?"

Why was he asking her if he could kiss her? No one had ever asked her that before and she felt awkward answering. Instead, she leaned toward him and initiated the kiss. As soon as their lips touched and her tongue caressed his, she knew that Isaac would be the type of lover she rarely sought out—cautious, a bit uncertain, an over-thinker. It surprised her, since up until now he had been flirting boldly.

She took hold of Isaac's hand and directed it to her breast, hoping the gesture would encourage him to be more assertive. She wanted to feel his touch under her dress, his fingers tugging on her nipples. His just-out-of-the-shower scent—clean and fresh—together with the heat of his body, made her want to rip the clothes off of him, lick every inch of him.

"Should I turn off the light?" Isaac asked, breaking the kiss.

"No. I like it on."

They continued to kiss, but his hands refused to venture further. She craved more of him and, unbuttoning his shirt, she caressed his chest and stomach. She fondled him over his jeans.

"Is this OK?" His hands had finally found her naked breasts.

Frustrated, Meredith nodded. "If there's anything you do that I'm not into I'll let you know."

She got off the bed and started to undress, slowly. After pulling the straps off her shoulders, her silk dress slid down her torso, past her hips, and pooled at her feet. Her matching bra and panties came off next. Seeing Isaac ready for her compelled Meredith to touch herself. She wanted to show him how his arousal fed hers.

Approaching the bed, she grabbed his hand and placed it on her core, guided his fingers inside of her. "You make me wet."

She got on her knees and unzipped his jeans after unbuckling his belt.

"You don't have to do this." He had propped himself on his elbows to watch her pleasure him.

"I know. I want to."

She took him deep into her mouth, all the way, and she only pulled back when she needed air. She did this several times, enjoying the heaviness of him on her tongue and how well he filled her throat.

"Stop, stop, please stop. I'm gonna come if you don't."

"Finish in my mouth. You can fuck my pussy in the next round."

"I can't get hard again so soon."

"I'm in no rush."

"I'd rather have your pussy."

Putting her annoyance aside, Meredith got to her feet and wiped the saliva off her chin. "Where do you keep your condoms?"

"In the bathroom. I'll be right back."

Meredith got a good view of Isaac's ass he undressed and then rushed across the loft. He had the body of a sprinter—strong legs, impressive upper back muscles, and broad shoulders. He was probably one the most attractive men she had seen naked, if not the most attractive, but while he knew how to use his brain to lure women into his bed, he didn't know how to use his body to keep them there.

He returned, already wearing a condom and Meredith had to look away so not to laugh. While she did believe in safe sex, she didn't want to stare at a condom any longer than necessary.

Isaac crawled on top of her and nudged her legs apart with his. She wanted him to slow down but suspected more foreplay wouldn't suddenly make the experience enjoyable.

He entered her and then stopped. "Does this feel OK?" He waited for her reply.

"Uh-huh." He did feel good but each of his questions took her out of the moment. "Just fuck me, Isaac."

Responding to her demand, he began to thrust. Seconds later, he let out a soft moan by her ear. He then stopped moving.

"Are you done?" she asked, unsure.

He rolled off of her and she lay there, staring at the white ceiling, his fast breathing a stark contrast to her steady heartbeat.

"Meredith?"

He moved her hair off her face and they locked eyes.

"That wasn't very good, was it?"

Truth without tact is cruelness and Meredith had no right to treat Isaac poorly.

"You have a gorgeous body and your cock feels incredible." She gave him the warmest smile she could muster. "Maybe we're just not compatible in bed. That's OK."

"I'm sorry, Meredith." Isaac fell back onto the bed. "Jesus, everything about you is so damn sexy and I fucking blew it."

"No you didn't. It happens to everybody. At least once."

"Wow, you're actually nice."

Suddenly, they both chuckled and the serious tone of their conversation dissipated.

"Is it OK if I hang out for a bit?" She wasn't just being considerate. Isaac made her laugh and she enjoyed his company.

"Of course. I want you to."

"What would you like to do now?"

"Drink?"

"Yes, please."

• • •

Meredith rolled over and her face landed against a stubbly chin. Startled, she opened her eyes and realized she was not alone. Cursing, she quickly sat up, the whole room spinning around her.

"You're brave. I'm afraid to move. Feels like my skull has been invaded by garden gnomes and they're gnawing on my brain."

Meredith glanced at Isaac over her shoulder. "Garden gnomes?"

"I've always had a fear of garden gnomes."

She wanted to laugh but she was too hungover. "Now I know your weakness."

"If you ever use that knowledge against me I'll have to do horrible things to you."

Meredith realized that they were both naked, on top of the covers. She let her face fall into her hands. "How much did we drink last night?"

"We finished off all of my bourbon."

"I remember us drinking but then"—Meredith frowned—"it all goes black. That's never happened to me before." She moved her head too quickly and that made her feel sicker. She took a couple of deep breaths and willed herself to push through the dizziness.

"At one point you tried tying me to the bed and that's when

I started getting scared." Isaac sat up beside her and she glared at him. "That was a joke," he added, straight-faced.

"I still haven't located my sense of humor. Or my memory."

They sat on the bed in silence. Meredith exhaled with relief when he didn't kiss her. She didn't feel sexy. She hid her face against his chest and Isaac rested his cheek on top of her head.

"Do you remember what we talked about when we were pounding back the bourbon?"

His question jolted her. "No. Why?"

He didn't reply, and Meredith's head started to hurt more. She got up and put on her underwear. She found her wrinkly dress under the bed and slipped it over her head.

"I would offer you coffee but I suspect you'll say no." Isaac watched her from the bed.

"I need to go home, shower, and start my day. I have a piece to write, remember?"

Meredith got a glimpse of her reflection in the wall mirror by the entrance door and almost gasped. Embarrassment over her disheveled appearance made her turn away from the mirror.

"Meredith?" Isaac called out from across his loft. "This Julian...be careful, OK?"

Meredith almost dropped her purse. She stood, mouth agape, staring at Isaac.

"I don't know if you're the best toy in the store but you're for sure the coolest," he continued. "If anything happens to you, I'll make sure he regrets it."

CHAPTER 19

"Are these it?"

Meredith and Isaac stood in the corner of his living room with barely enough space to move, staring at twenty cardboard boxes.

"How can one person have enough stuff at his desk to fill so many boxes?" She shook her head with amazement.

"Most of these are books, but I imagine there's a lot of garbage in there. I told you the man was crazy."

"And we're looking for his journals? Which we hope are filled with information on a sex club shrouded in secrecy?"

"We have to give it a shot." Isaac reached for one of the boxes. "If those journals are here you should at least read what's in them."

Meredith sighed, rubbing her forehead. "Are they labeled? Organized in any specific order? By year, maybe?" She suspected she knew the answer but hoped she was wrong. She didn't want to go through all of those bulging cardboard boxes.

"No shortcuts, I'm afraid. We'll have to go through them all. One by one."

"These damn journals better be in there. And they better be worth it."

"I had to sneak these boxes out of storage, put them in my car, and haul them up four flights of stairs. And, I had to do all of that more than once, because as you can see, there's a hell of a lot of them. So how about you say: *Thank you, Isaac, for all your hard work. Let's get to it.*"

She almost told him to fuck off but she reconsidered before the words crossed her lips. "I'm sorry. I'm not being a team player.

I've been in a foul mood since our drunken night last week. Too much going on."

Isaac started going through a box. "The draft you sent got me thinking that we should publish the piece sooner than we had discussed."

"Why? How soon?"

"September."

"That's a month away. I need more time."

"Think about it. Glendon packed up and went to wrestle crocodiles—"

"He didn't go wrestle crocodiles," Meredith interjected.

"He went somewhere, let's just say that. Assuming the research in his journals goes back ten, fifteen years, that's an excellent foundation for your piece. You talk about what was happening with The Raven Room at that time, and then, because you've been to the club, you layer in what the place is like now, the type of people you've seen there, what they do. Next, you bring up the deaths of the women, how they were killed, how they're connected to The Raven Room. You link it to the police cover-up of the murders. That's all you need. That's your piece, right there."

"You're assuming we'll find the journals. What if we don't? Or what if we do, but they're just the ramblings of a mad man?"

"You know the exact location of the club. Ideally, we'd know the history of it, but if we can find out who owns the property, that's already something. It might lead to more information."

"I need more time," she insisted.

"You don't, Meredith."

The box slipped from her hands and its contents spilled on to the floor. She cursed.

"Just remember, we're in this together," he said.

Meredith looked down at the papers scattered around her feet. She recognized the potential value of the journals, but she was having a hard time finding the motivation to dig through endless stacks of dusty boxes. Walking toward the window she stared at the dark street below her. It had been a beautiful day earlier but now it was raining hard. She couldn't remember a wetter summer.

"That night…what did I say to you?" she asked, her back to the room. "I don't remember any of it."

"You were drunk. We both were."

"I've never been so drunk that I can't recall several hours of my life. You seem to remember more than I do so I want you to tell me—what did I say that night?"

"A lot of it was impossible to make sense out of, and don't forget, I wasn't sober myself."

Isaac moved several boxes around. He then picked up the papers she had dropped on the floor. Watching him organize the room instead of answering her question increased her trepidation.

"Julian Reeve. You talked about him."

Great, she thought, he knew his last name as well. If he hadn't already, Isaac could now find out a great deal of information on Julian. "What did I say about him?"

"That he took you to the club. Sounds like you really like it there. And what happened to Sofia. You also mentioned Tatiana. And how, recently, you two have grown closer."

Isaac had used the word *recently,* which meant that he knew they were at least in contact with Tatiana, if not aware of her whereabouts. "What else?" she pressed.

"You talked about Thompson and Tatiana. What he did to her."

"Why did you tell me to be careful with Julian?"

"The necklace. You found it inside one of Julian's drawers. There's a chance it might be Lena's. You also told me why Julian goes to The Raven Room. The cutting."

What hadn't she shared with Isaac? Meredith wondered. "If I ask you to keep everything I told you to yourself, will you? I need to know."

"As long as nothing happens to you," he replied.

She wanted to trust him, but she suspected the two of them

had a personality trait in common—no qualms about lying when it suited their needs. She felt Isaac had it in him to betray her.

"Why would Glendon leave behind his journals?" she asked, changing the subject. She opened a new box. "When you told me about the conversation he had with you about the club, it sounded like he was consumed by it."

"Maybe he didn't. Maybe he was forced to."

"He's not wrestling crocodiles?"

"Full of sunshine, aren't you?"

"I thought I was doing pretty good, considering."

"Were you close with Sofia?" Isaac asked. "How have you been holding up?"

The questions caught her off-guard. No one had asked her how she felt about Sofia's death. In comparison to Julian, who, for the second time, had lost one of the only people he appeared to have ever loved and Tatiana, who mourned her twin sister, the only family member she had left, Meredith considered her own feelings unimportant. "I only met her once."

"How did you meet her?"

"At Julian's."

"Is Tatiana OK? It sounded like she was in bad shape after what her husband did to her."

Meredith didn't want to reveal more about Tatiana than she already had. She focused on the only person who she didn't mind being vocal about. "Thompson is the kind of man that needs to hurt women."

"Just like your friend, Julian."

"Excuse me?"

"You don't have to protect him from me."

"I'm not."

"I saw the look in your face when I said he was just like Thompson."

"He's not just like Thompson."

"Are you sure of that?"

Meredith glared at Isaac.

"How did you get him to take you to the club?"

"What do you think?" Her voice was filled with scorn. "I used my best asset—my pussy."

Isaac threw the papers in his hand back into the box and approached Meredith. Refusing to acknowledge him, she continued to flip through a stack of yellow-stained paper.

"Being nosy is in my DNA," he said. "Like it's in yours. We can't turn it off. Whatever type of relationship you have with Julian is your business and not anyone else's. I'm a straight-up vanilla guy. It seems to me that a lot of men out there use their so-called fantasies and kinks as an excuse for abusive and violent behavior and that should never be tolerated."

"How about the straight-up vanilla guys who manipulate, beat up, and destroy a girl's self-worth? I guess being vanilla is their cover."

Before Isaac returned his attention to a box full of papers, he smiled. "Remind me to get you pissed off more often. You reveal how smart you really are." He closed the box and moved on to the next one. "It's hot."

Even though he meant it as compliment, it didn't feel like a compliment to her.

"So, do you think Thompson's involved in the murders?" Isaac added.

"I did for a while. But he was out of town when most of them took place," Meredith explained. "Have you ever found yourself losing someone who you believed would always be part of your life?" she asked, changing the subject once more. She thought of Julian.

"My ex-wife."

The knowledge that Isaac had once been married caught her by surprise. "How long were you married?"

"Six years. The last two years were just fighting against the idea that we might not be right for each other. Hurt like hell. But our divorce was one of the best things that ever happened to both of us."

"What's her name?"

He grinned.

"What?"

"You're a true journalist at heart." Isaac carried one of the boxes across the room. "Simone." He stacked it on top of the ones they had already gone through. "Her name is Simone."

"That's a strong name."

"She's a strong woman."

"Do you ever miss her?"

"At times. When I look back I don't miss the things I imagined I would, like the sex, the weekend-long trips outside of the city, or our late night political debates. I miss her for who she is. Completely separate from anything that we did together."

"If you still miss her then why was the divorce one of the best things that happened to you?"

"We're both happier now. Simple as that."

"You do seem happy," Meredith said as she picked up a pile of books at the bottom of the box. A photograph fell out from inside one of them. She kneeled down and forced her hand between the stacked boxes to reach it.

"What is it?" Isaac asked with curiosity.

Meredith grabbed the photograph and, after looking at it briefly, passed it to him. "Any idea who this is?"

"I'm afraid not." Isaac flipped the photograph. "There's a name on the back, Rebecca, and a date."

"Could be Glendon's daughter."

Meredith took the photograph from Isaac. The girl in the photo, not more than five or six years old, wore pink flannel pajamas, and her hair was in disarray as she ran, with an expression of pure joy, toward her Christmas presents.

Meredith slid the photograph into her back pocket then checked the time on her phone. "I've got to go. Got plans." She and Colton were getting together at his place.

"What? I was hoping to blow your mind by ordering us dinner from my favorite Greek restaurant. And then you'd stay the night."

Meredith didn't want to have sex with Isaac again. She liked him but henceforth she would be sure to keep their relationship platonic.

"Next time," Meredith said, walking toward the door.

"I'm holding you to it."

"You don't have to. Have you looked around? We went through four boxes." Paper and books littered Isaac's living room. "Tomorrow, same time?"

"Just ring the bell. You'll find me, and the best Greek food you'll ever eat, right here."

"And seventeen cardboard boxes?"

He winked at her. "It'll be worth it."

CHAPTER 20

Almost two in the morning and here I am, Meredith thought, sitting in a small, decrepit diner in Mount Greenwood.

She had been drinking coffee since she arrived three hours ago, and now she stared into her empty mug. She had her laptop with her and, at first, she had tried to do some work on the article. But after writing and deleting the same few words at least four times, she had given up. She felt too exhausted.

"Want a top off?" The waitress showed Meredith a pot of freshly brewed coffee.

"Thanks, I'm good."

Meredith pulled the hood of her sweater over her head and wished she could block out the Tim McGraw song playing in the background. While the temperature reached eighty degrees outside, the large air conditioner above the entrance door worked at full blast. Every hair on her body stood straight up. She shivered and, sinking further into the worn-out vinyl booth, wrapped her arms around her torso. She considered stepping outside to smoke a cigarette but if she got up from that booth she wouldn't come back. That wasn't an option. She had already wasted three hours and she refused to walk away empty handed.

She and Isaac had finished going through the boxes and they hadn't found the journals. With Colton's help, she had discovered Glendon had a son, Liam, his only family member still living in Chicago. Earlier in the day, Meredith had called the diner where Liam worked and, after a brief phone conversation, he had agreed to speak to her after his shift ended.

Meredith closed her eyes and dozed off. She was startled

awake by the presence of a stocky young man in a stained kitchen uniform standing next to her table.

"Liam?" she asked, sitting up straighter.

"You must be the one who called—a friend of one of my dad's old coworkers?"

He didn't sit down, and Meredith worried he might have changed his mind about talking to her. After having waited so long, the idea jarred her wide-awake.

"Ten minutes. Just give me ten minutes," Meredith said. "Please."

He stared at her for another long moment.

"Ten minutes," she repeated.

He sat down across from her. "What do you want?" He sounded worn out.

Meredith fumbled inside her purse. "I wanted to give this back to you."

She slid the photograph she had found in one of Glendon's books across the table toward Liam. Besides telling her where she might find Liam, Colton had confirmed that Rebecca, the little girl in the photograph, was Glendon's daughter. According to her file, she would be twenty-six years old now, but had been missing since shortly after she'd turned eighteen.

"My friend and I found this photograph inside an old book that belonged to your dad. I wanted to give it back to you."

Liam picked up the photograph and stared at it, his expression unchanging. Meredith noticed how short his nails were. His cuticles looked darker than the skin of his fingers.

"That's it? You wanted to give me an old photograph of my sister?" he asked.

"I'd have given it to your dad if I knew where I could find him."

"He's dead."

Taken by surprise, she leaned forward, narrowing the distance between them. "He is? What happened?"

"He took off and then one day I got a call from some folks in North Dakota saying he killed himself."

She didn't understand why Colton hadn't come across that information. "No one at the newspaper knows what happened to him."

Liam shrugged. "Didn't think to let 'em know, I guess. It's not like he'd been much use for a while, anyways."

"Your dad was a good reporter." She had no idea if that were true but it felt like the right thing to say.

"Not after my sister started acting up, and for sure not after she took off."

"Rebecca?"

Liam didn't reply.

She shouldn't expect Liam, a complete stranger, to speak to her about his family. Meredith needed to draw the information out of him but she couldn't rely on her charm alone to achieve that.

Liam passed the photograph back to Meredith. "I have no use for this."

Meredith glanced at it but didn't take it.

"You didn't come here to give me that photograph back. What do you want?"

She didn't see the point of trying to come up with an excuse. "Your father was believed to be an expert on the subject I'm covering for an article. I was hoping you knew where I could find him. But, you already answered that question." Meredith pointed at the photograph on the table. "If you don't want it, can I keep it?"

"If you had met my sister you wouldn't want it. She only brought hurt to everyone who went near her."

Meredith took the photograph and put it back into her purse. "Do you know if your dad kept his files anywhere else besides the office?"

"What's your article about?"

Now Meredith had to lie. "Personal finance. How young families can save up so one day they can send their kids to college. Same type of stuff your father used to write."

"And you need his old files for that?"

"I want to reference some of the research studies he covered.

I can read his articles but his notes, the information that was left out, is just as useful to me."

"There are a couple of boxes of his stuff left in the house," Liam said.

"Can I have a look at them?"

"Will you give me a ride home? My shift went long and I missed my ride. Don't want to take the bus."

Being alone in a car with a man who was essentially a stranger, in the middle of the night, driving to an unknown place, should have frightened her more than it did.

Meredith grabbed her purse and her laptop. "My car is parked right out front."

They didn't speak much during their drive, and by the time they reached Liam's home on South St. Louis Avenue, it was past three thirty in the morning.

"I'm sorry about your father," she said as she turned off the engine. No cars drove by. She could barely make out the contours of Liam's face in the dim light of the poorly lit street.

"They never found his body. Just his tent, his things, and the note he left. He was camping. He always liked being in nature. When my sister and I were kids, he always tried to take us."

Meredith felt uneasy with the fact that Glendon's body had never been found. "What did the note say? That he planned to kill himself?"

Liam nodded.

In that instant, Meredith wondered how she would feel if she suddenly lost her father. "I don't have siblings," she said. "My mom died when I was a kid. My grandparents are long gone. I only have my dad. If anything happened to him…I can't imagine it."

Liam remained quiet. He didn't try to leave the car.

"The less people you have to care about the easier it is," he finally said, matter of factly. "As least I imagine it would be."

She picked up on Liam's resentment. "Your sister never came back, did she?"

A car drove by and its headlights gave Meredith the chance to get a glimpse of Liam's somber expression.

"She was trouble," he replied. "On and off of the streets for years—drugs, hooking. When we finally stopped hearing from her, I thought it'd give my dad the chance to get his act together but it only made it worse."

"You never wonder what happened to your sister? Where she might be?"

"I'm better off without her around."

Liam got out the car and moved toward his house. Glancing at her surroundings to make sure no one had followed her, Meredith walked behind him.

"His stuff is in my sister's old room," Liam said, turning on the light. "Down the corridor, last door in the left. Just don't make any noise. My girlfriend and daughter are asleep."

As Meredith made her way to the room, the old hardwood floor creaked and she silently cursed to herself.

Mismatched pieces of furniture filled the bedroom. She gravitated toward the large pile of paper spilling out of a couple of boxes on top of a single bed frame. Not wanting to overstay her welcome, she started to search through the paper as fast as she could. Isaac had described the journals as being black leather bound, and Meredith kept an eye out for anything that fit that description.

Continuing to forage through the last two boxes, she came across another photograph of Rebecca. She looked about eighteen years old in this one and Meredith guessed it had been taken around the time she had disappeared. She resembled her brother with her long, dark curly hair and blue eyes.

Meredith put the photograph aside and continued to explore inside the box. She was about to reach the bottom when she came across a stack of three black notebooks held together by a rubber band. Adrenaline coursed through her. She opened the top one and instantly knew these were the journals they had been looking for. Glendon's name was jotted on the back of the front cover and, as Meredith leafed through it, page after page revealed neat handwriting from beginning to end. Additional notes filled the blank edge of the pages.

Having found what she came for, Meredith put the new photograph of Rebecca inside her purse and slid the journals under her arm. She quietly left the room and peeked inside of the living room. When she saw Liam sitting on a reading chair, fast asleep, she exhaled in relief. She had grown up hearing her father say that life was all about taking advantage of good opportunities. She now had a chance to leave without having to answer any questions.

She turned away from Liam and was about to quietly sneak out the front door when she came face-to-face with a toddler.

"Hi." The little girl looked up at Meredith.

Meredith stared at her with both panic and surprise. "Hi," she whispered back.

"Her name is Becca," Liam said from his chair.

Meredith held the journals closer to her body. "I'm on my way out. Sorry if I woke her."

"Did you find what you were looking for?"

Meredith had yet to turn around. She hoped Liam stayed in his chair.

The little girl took a step closer to Meredith, who almost automatically took a step back.

Liam chuckled. "She doesn't bite."

Meredith forced herself to smile at the little girl. "I'm just not very good with kids."

Liam came up to them and Meredith held her breath. She wished she had a big enough purse to hide the journals. As he picked up his daughter, he saw the journals peeking from under Meredith's arm. She faced him, waiting for him to ask her about it. If he didn't press her to see them she could say they were some of his father's financial research but if he did, he would catch her in a lie.

"You named her after your sister," Meredith said, hoping to take his attention away from the journals. "Maybe she'll return someday."

Liam kissed his daughter's cheek. "Rebecca's dead." He glanced at the journals. "I don't want those back."

He stepped aside and Meredith rushed out.

Liam might know the truth about the journals, she thought. When he had said that Rebecca had died, he could have been telling her what he knew, and not what he believed. Regardless, she had heard him loud and clear—he didn't want to see Meredith again.

CHAPTER 21

"You went to his home?" Isaac held one of the journals in his hand. "What if Liam was a rapist? A murderer?"

"I got the journals. That's what's important."

They sat on the floor of Isaac's living room, surrounded by papers. It had been a couple of days since she had found the journals, but Isaac had been on the East Coast for work, making this their first chance to meet.

He flipped through the now yellowed pages. "Is there anything in here you can use?"

"The Raven Room is the legacy of the Everleigh Club, a famous Chicago gentlemen's club owned and operated by the Everleigh sisters, Minna and Ada, that existed from around 1900 to 1911. Have you heard of it?"

"It was a brothel, right?"

"Yeah. Apparently *Tribune* reporters were among the clients."

Isaac smirked. "I need to do a better job of enjoying my down time."

"The Everleigh was extremely luxurious and selective," Meredith continued. "I did some research on it and I read it's considered the only brothel in American history that enhanced, rather than diminished, a man's reputation. It closed because of prostitution reform but the men who frequented were spending between two hundred to a thousand dollars per visit. Do you have an idea of how much money that was in the nineteen hundreds?" Meredith asked. "According to Glendon's notes, one of the Everleigh's butterflies, which was the name they used for the club's prostitutes, knew that even though the prostitution reform might have led to the closure of Everleigh, the demand was still there. Mary Tang, an immigrant from China, had worked at the Everleigh Club for years and learned the business from the sisters. Knowing she couldn't run a brothel out in the open, she took everything underground and founded her own club—The Raven Room."

"The club has been around since then?"

"Looks like it. She managed to secure most of the Everleigh's powerful clientele, and because The Raven Room always existed outside of the law, it's been part of every kind of activity organized crime can profit from: bootlegging during Prohibition, labor and gang racketeering, gambling during the Depression." Meredith reached for one of the other journals. "And now drug trafficking. The Raven Room keeps adapting and evolving. It's what organized crime does. It never disappears."

"So who owns it?"

"That's the section I'm looking for," Meredith replied, her eyes on the journal. "Glendon wrote that the club is managed by an organization," she tapped the page with her finger and showed it to Isaac. "The Wusun. I researched the word and it literally means grandchildren or descendants of the raven. It's not clear if they just manage the club, or if they own it, too. But I thought, how about the building, right?" Meredith said, with a hint of excitement in her voice. "The Raven Room occupies four levels below ground but there's a restaurant that operates above ground. Someone owns the building and I'm trying to find out who they are."

Isaac gave Meredith a pensive stare. "This is a lot to wrap your head around."

"Oh, but there's more. Here," she passed him a newspaper clipping that had been inside of one of the journals. "A *Tribune* article written by a reporter named Miles Leonard in 1964. It says that Michael Belfer, the son of David Belfer, who was the owner of South Works, mentioned at a party that he and his father were members of an underground club that controlled Chicago." She passed him another newspaper clipping. "That's Miles Leonard's obituary. He died in a car crash a week after the article was published."

"Damn, these people don't fuck around."

"It gets scarier." She showed him another newspaper clipping. "The same day Miles Leonard died, a large fire broke out at the Emperor Hotel in Chinatown. It burned to the ground. Glendon believed it was the location of The Raven Room at the time. Either someone found out and tried to destroy the club, which I find unlikely, or the people who managed it decided it was safer to relocate and not leave anything behind."

"Well, I guess Miles didn't die in vain. At least he inconvenienced the motherfuckers. So where is the club now?"

"Still in Chinatown," Meredith replied, her attention on two folded pieces of paper. "I found these in one of the journals. It's a couple of police reports from about ten years ago. Drug busts. One makes note that the dealer was under the influence of a designer drug at the time of his arrest—its street name Dali. He kept saying Dali had come from the Wusun."

"What else you got in there?"

"There are ten pages of rules the members have to abide by. A lot of these have question marks and side notes, so I don't think Glendon was completely certain of their accuracy." Meredith's eyes scanned through the beginning of the list. "Amongst the members, the membership is called a key, so instead of members they are keyholders. There are two different types of keys, a 78 key and a 22 key. The first one gives you access to this area." Meredith showed him a drawing of the layout of the club in one of the pages. "The top three floors. A 22 key gives you access to all of those floors, plus this area." She pointed to the lower area of the drawing. "The Raven Room."

"Keyholders are allowed guests, right? You've gone to the club."

"Yes, but guests are not allowed on the lowest level."

"Why do you think that is?"

"To create further exclusivity within an already exclusive crowd? To charge more money?" Meredith recalled what Tatiana had told her when they had visited the club together. "Maybe they offer a selection of unusual sex services to the ones with a 22 key?"

She leafed through the journal. "Glendon wrote that the club hires sex workers, both male and female. The women who died must have worked at the club."

"When you were there, did you ever meet anyone who you knew, or suspected, to be a sex worker?"

Meredith shook her head. "No. Perhaps if I spent some time watching everyone closely I would have. Even then, I'm not sure I could tell who is a member and who is a sex worker. It would be great if I managed to speak with one of them for the piece."

"What are these letters?" Isaac asked, his finger moving across the page. "They look like abbreviations."

"Each room at the club has a name. All animals." She circled the letters BD beside the top floor. "It stands for The Black Dragon." She circled the letters RR at the opposite end of the drawing. "The Raven Room."

"How does one get a membership to the club? Does Glendon mention that in the journals?"

"For a 78 key you need to be invited by three members. Then vetted by the Wusun. For a 22 key, he mentions that there's a different process but there are no details."

Isaac seemed to be lost in thought.

"What's on your mind?" she asked.

"As much as I want to publish your article, everything I've just heard makes me think it's a really bad idea."

"I told you it was dangerous. I told you people died."

"A crime organization over a century old runs The Raven Room. Powerful people are committed to protecting it. The police won't go near it. Don't you think this goes beyond what we both thought?"

"You believed it was only vulnerable women who'd been murdered. Now that you know Miles Leonard and Glendon might have also been killed, you're hesitating."

"Aren't you wondering how Glendon got all that information?" Isaac asked. "It's detailed. Someone knew what he was up to. And what made him look into The Raven Room in the first place?"

"I have a theory. When I spoke to Glendon's son, Liam, he told me about his sister, Rebecca, who went missing when she was eighteen. She'd been on and off the streets, working as a prostitute, using drugs. It's possible she got involved with the club. Glendon started to look into what might have happened to his daughter and somehow learned about the existence of The Raven Room. He was doing research, possibly to expose them."

"Do you believe he committed suicide?"

"I don't know…I'm starting to think this organization is capable of anything."

"Fuck." Isaac stood up and paced back and forth. "Who else, besides your professor and I, knows you're writing this piece?"

"My stepmother."

"I'm more worried about your professor. Call her right now and tell her not to mention your piece or The Raven Room to anyone. Tell her that if she does, her kids could get hurt."

"Have you lost your mind, Isaac? I can't tell her that. And if she did mention—"

"If you don't call her, I will, Meredith."

"It's Saturday. She's not in the office and this is not exactly the type of stuff you tell someone over voicemail. I'll speak to her on Monday. She's known about the piece for months. One more day won't make a difference."

"You and I will speak to her, together."

"I told you I would do it," Meredith said, raising her voice.

"Your stepmother."

"What about her?"

"Can you trust her?"

Meredith didn't reply.

"Can you trust her?" Isaac pressed.

She met his eyes and his expression changed. "Your own family would put you in danger?" he asked.

"You're worried they're going to put *you* in danger."

"It's your name on the piece, not mine."

"Exactly. And I'm going ahead with it. If you won't publish it, someone else will. What's it going to be?" She hoped what Isaac lacked in courage he made up in ambition.

He continued to pace in agitated contemplation. Eventually he came to sit beside her.

"I still want the finished article by next month, Meredith."

"Remind me to threaten you more often. You show how smart you really are."

She didn't mean it as a compliment and he knew it.

CHAPTER 22

When her mother first showed Meredith the Chagall Windows at the Art Institute of Chicago, she had been six years old and the cool blue glow shining through the vibrant and luminescent multicolored glass, made her feel like a mermaid swimming in the sea.

Now, she had come to seek comfort in a childhood memory that had always brought her joy. The simple, rough shapes—squares, rectangles, triangles—together formed a beautiful world. Whenever her life felt beyond her control, Meredith always found peace staring at its simplicity.

But today, Meredith no longer felt like a mermaid.

It frightened her how fast all her close relationships were deteriorating. Without Julian, Pam, and her father, she was left with many acquaintances and a small group of friends that she would never call family or confidants. Colton and Isaac had entered her life because of her desire to know more about The Raven Room. As for her connection to Tatiana, the tragic circumstances of Tatiana's situation had forced the two of them to develop a relationship she didn't know how to categorize. The Raven Room had taken over Meredith's life in every way, and even though she knew it was all her doing, she didn't like it.

She moved closer to the Chagall Windows but she didn't feel any happier or more serene than when she had arrived. On the contrary, now she also missed her mother more keenly.

Meredith's stomach growled, a reminder that she had forgotten to eat lunch.

She glanced at her phone to check the time and was surprised to see it was almost five o'clock. Glad she had picked the end of the day to visit the Art Institute—being surrounded by large crowds, unaware of who might be watching her, made her nervous—she started to make her way toward the exit facing Michigan Avenue. Going home to order some food and work on her article sounded like the best option for the evening.

She entered the spacious Alsdorf Galleries and was about to pass the large statue of the Seated Buddha in the center of the room when she heard hushed voices coming from her left. She glanced at the two people standing close to the wall.

The man's silver hair made her stop. Upon a second glance, Meredith realized it was Steven Thompson. In a controlled, low voice he spoke to the woman standing close to him.

Meredith quickly stepped to the opposite side of the statue. She peeked around it to get a look at the woman with Thompson and, suddenly, she froze. From her new angle, she recognized her stepmother.

At that point, Thompson, his arm in a cast, wrapped his other arm around Pam. They hugged, holding onto each other as if they weren't in a public place. He kissed her hair and she hid her face in the curve of his neck.

Meredith had been aware that Pam and Thompson had known each other since college, but she had no idea how close they were. Meredith was certain that her father also didn't know.

Afraid she would be seen, and thankful she wore flats and not high heels, Meredith snuck out of the gallery. When she reached the grand staircase, she picked up her pace until she made it outside. She called Tatiana, even before she got to her parked car.

"I need to see you."

"You sound out of breath."

"It's about your husband and my stepmother."

"Just get over here," Tatiana said before abruptly hanging up.

As soon as Meredith entered the condo, Tatiana rushed her toward the guest bedroom.

"What did you find out about Steven and your stepmom?" Tatiana sounded apprehensive.

"I was on my way out of the Art Institute when I saw them in one of the galleries. They were talking. I watched them for a while. I couldn't hear what they were saying. They looked like they were concerned about being seen…but then they hugged each other. He kissed her hair." Meredith replayed the scene in her head. "It was intimate. Friends don't act like that."

"Are you sure they didn't see you?"

Meredith nodded. "Do you think—"

"They're sleeping together?" Tatiana finished for Meredith. "Maybe. I don't care. Listen to me." Tatiana cradled Meredith's face between her hands. "She's the detective investigating my sister's murder. Steven dislikes Julian, and everything I've heard about your stepmom tells me she shares my husband's feelings. That's not good."

"Do you think they would incriminate Julian?" Meredith asked. "I wasn't with him the whole night and yes, I admit, there have been moments when I wondered, but I know Julian would never hurt your sister. He didn't kill her. Neither Thompson or my stepmom can change that."

Tatiana sat on the bed with a heavy sigh.

"Lena and your sister aren't the only ones. Three other women have been murdered," Meredith continued. "My stepmother knows that but she hasn't done anything about it. I saw the files."

Tatiana now stared at the floor, lost in thought.

"Whoever killed Sofia didn't kill the others."

"Meredith, what are you talking about?"

"There are too many differences. Sofia is the only one that didn't have drugs in her system. She didn't die from an overdose. She wasn't involved with The Raven Room."

"And these four other women were?"

"I don't know that for sure, but from reading their files I found out that all of them have had run-ins with the police before. They were poor, uneducated, without close family…it's not a far stretch to think they could have been involved in the sex industry. The club hires sex workers."

"Who told you that? Julian?"

Meredith hesitated, unsure if she should mention Glendon's journals. "Yes."

"What's wrong with him? He's going to get both of you into serious trouble."

"Don't you want to know who killed those women?"

"No. I don't."

Perplexed, Meredith stared at Tatiana. "Why?"

"Because I'm trying to stay alive. And you need to be careful, too. The more you know, the worse off you are. Your dad might be a federal judge and your stepmom a detective, but they won't always be able to protect you."

"My stepmom—" Meredith started to say, but then stopped herself.

"What about her?"

"I used to admire her, you know? This strong woman who fights for what she believes is right and is good at what she does. Doesn't take shit from anyone. She let me down."

"Every time someone disappoints you it hurts less and less," Tatiana said, her voice softer. "I promise."

Meredith heard a noise coming from inside the condo. "What's that?" she asked, looking at the closed bedroom door. "Julian?"

"You should thank me."

Confused, Meredith waited for her to continue.

"He's tapering off the benzos. He's on medical detox."

"How did you get him to do that?"

"You can use someone's weaknesses to destroy them or help them. I used Julian's biggest weakness to help him."

"You're scaring me, Tatiana. What did you do?"

"Have you met Seth and Eli, Grace's twin boys?"

"What do they have to do with this?"

"They're beautiful."

"I've never met them."

Tatiana seemed to consider what to say next. "All I did was

take something away from Julian, watch him understand how it would feel to lose it, and then give it back to him."

"He's himself again?"

"You mean an addict? Julian will always be dependent on something." Tatiana reached out for Meredith's hand. "Stay the night. I don't want to be alone."

Meredith nodded. She didn't want to be alone either. "I need to eat something. I'm starving. I haven't eaten all day."

"I'll grab us something. There's lots of food in the house. More than I could ever possibly eat. I guess Julian gave up trying to starve me to death."

With Tatiana now in the kitchen, Meredith ran a bath in the en suite bathroom. The bathtub was only half full when she undressed and got in. As the tub continued to fill, she laid back and water rose to touch her hairline. She tilted her head further back until her face became submerged, and then she screamed as loud as she could.

When Tatiana joined Meredith in the bathroom, she sat with black mascara running down her cheeks.

"Come eat," Tatiana said.

"Get in the tub with me."

"Not starving anymore?"

Tatiana pulled the oversized t-shirt she wore over her head. She dropped it on the floor. Next, she slid out of her underwear. Meredith recognized them as the black panties she had bought for her.

She climbed into the bathtub and shifted closer to Meredith, their legs intertwined, sitting face-to-face. Tatiana pressed her palm to the middle of Meredith's chest, between her breasts. "Why are you doing all of this?" Tatiana asked. "Forget about the murders. Steven and your stepmom? They aren't getting in your way so you should keep your distance. It's not on you to seek justice for Sofia's death, to be here for me. If I were you I'd be miles away. I wouldn't get tangled up in something that isn't my business."

"I'm not you," Meredith replied, scooping water in her hand and then letting it drip over Tatiana's head.

"You're smarter."

"Not by a long shot. I have something to tell you." She had decided to disclose the existence of her article—she needed a friend in Tatiana. "But you can't repeat it to Julian. I'll talk to him when the timing is right."

"What is it?"

"I'm writing a piece on the deaths of those women and how they're connected to The Raven Room. I'm going to reveal that the police know about the murders but they're taking no action."

Tatiana remained silent.

"Say something," she pressed.

"That's crazy, Meredith."

"I just need proof that those four women worked at the club."

"Why would you do that?"

"Write the piece? Because women are being murdered and no one is paying attention."

"Your stepmom is."

"She's covering it up. And there's clearly something going on between her and your husband. He's a member of the club. I can't trust her."

"He's only a member because of me. Julian is a member. You trust us."

"Are you defending your husband and my stepmom?"

"I'm asking you to think this through."

"I know it's dangerous but it's the right thing to do, Tatiana. Don't you want justice for your sister?"

"Nothing will bring her back."

"You refused to answer this question before—did you see who murdered Sofia?"

"I didn't. I told you, when I got to the New Jackson Hotel she was dead already. I didn't spend more than ten minutes in that place."

"But you know it wasn't your husband."

"I do."

"How?"

"He stayed at the club. He didn't go to the New Jackson with me."

Meredith shared with Tatiana the potentially damning evidence against Julian that she had found in his bathroom drawer, a necklace that was, according to Samantha Williams, almost identical to the one Lena always wore—gold with a small cross. Samantha had seen Lena wear the necklace the day before she died, but, when the police had discovered Lena's body, the necklace was nowhere to be found. She told Tatiana how she had been trying to locate Samantha to show her the necklace and to find out if it was the same one.

"The necklace, regardless if it actually belonged to Lena, puts Julian in a bad spot," Tatiana said. "If Steven and your stepmom share a goal, I doubt it's to see Julian walk away untouched. All they have to do is convince Samantha to say that this necklace belonged to her friend and Julian will be in serious trouble. I'm sure your stepmom won't let the tidbit of my mom ending up with a bullet in her head go unnoticed. There has always been doubt about whether Sofia was really the one who pulled the trigger."

Tatiana's comment jarred Meredith. "You said you saw Sofia pull the trigger."

"I was eight years old. I was scared out of my mind. What I remember holds little weight. Make sure no one knows you have that necklace," Tatiana insisted. "Cease looking for Samantha. She shouldn't know you have it either. Who else have you told about the necklace?"

"Just you."

"Please, Meredith, stop with the article."

"Does this mean that you won't help me find out if those women worked at the club?"

"I'm sorry, Meredith."

"Why won't you?"

"Because I don't know how to access that information."

"How about Vincent? I know he works at the club. What's his role?"

"Forget about Vincent, OK?"

Meredith leaned back, resting her head on the edge of the bathtub. "Please don't share anything I just told you with anyone."

"Of course not." Tatiana kissed Meredith's collarbone. "I can still smell it…you always smell so good. Body lotion? Perfume? What is it?" She pressed her nose closer to Meredith's skin.

"Chanel No. 5. Every day, any day, always." Meredith closed her eyes as she spoke. "I started to wear it because it reminded me of my mother. It was her scent. When I was a little girl I used to sit on the bathroom counter and watch her put on makeup. I loved watching her do it. She always hummed a song under her breath. I thought she looked beautiful even without it, but as she layered the makeup on her cheeks and around her eyes, she would come to life and suddenly look so confident. At the end, she would always put a few drops of perfume on her wrists and on the sides of her neck. And then she would wink and put a few drops on me too. It was our ritual. It made me feel special. Now the perfume is just part of who I am."

"Do you look like her?"

"Not at all. I always carry a picture of her with me. Do you want to see?" Meredith reached out of the tub and searched for her wallet inside of her purse. She passed Tatiana a photo that had seen better days. The corners were bent and, at some point, it had been folded in half. "That's us when I was five or six on a family trip to New York City. I think that was taken in Central Park."

Tatiana stared at the photo. "What happened to your mom?"

"She died when I was nine. Breast cancer. The thing I remember most from that time is my father disappearing for a while, then coming home for a day or so, crying when he thought no one could hear him, and then disappearing again. My nanny basically raised me for well over a year."

"He must have loved your mom very much."

"He never got over her death."

"He remarried."

"Yeah."

"But you don't think he loves Pam."

"No, I don't know. I'm pretty sure he loves her. But it's a different kind of love. Sometimes I wonder if it's because she's like the opposite of my mother, and so when they are together he never has to think about her."

"That's sad." Tatiana returned the photo to Meredith. "You weren't kidding when you said you didn't look like your mom."

"I have her eyes but I'm the spitting image of my father. According to him, I've also got my mother's personality. I always took that as a compliment but now I wonder."

They both laughed.

"You and your mom have that girl-next-door charm down pat, though. Rich, girl-next-door," Tatiana added.

"I splurge on perfume and beauty products because I can't do it on clothes, shoes, and bags, at least not yet."

Tatiana frowned. "You lost me there."

"I'm twenty-three. If I walk around on a pair of Manolos and holding a Birkin bag what kind of message would I be sending? That I'm a rich girl that knows how to spend either her parents' or her boyfriend's money. That's not how I want people to perceive me. One day I'll buy everything I want. But until then, I spend money on things that make me feel pampered but which cannot be seen. Understated, Tatiana. That's the secret."

"I'm Russian. I don't do understated. And everything you just said is bullshit. I've seen you wear a Burberry raincoat." She reached out of the bathtub and picked up one of Meredith's flats. "These are Alexander McQueen." Next, she reached for Meredith's shoulder bag and held it up. "Don't make me search the inside of it for the brand tag."

"It's Céline."

Tatiana stared at Meredith, wide-eyed. When Meredith didn't reply, Tatiana dropped the bag on the floor.

"It's still understated," Meredith said, defensively.

"You're privileged, spoiled, and—"

"You still like me," Meredith said, cutting Tatiana off. She grinned.

"Do I have a choice?"

• • •

With Tatiana asleep beside her, Meredith got up and grabbed Glendon's journals from her large purse. With a set of copies back home, she felt she should hide the originals in a second location, yet somewhere she could easily access them.

Careful not to make any noise, Meredith tiptoed to the living room. She scanned the built-in shelves that covered an entire wall. Finding hardcover books would be easy—Julian preferred to read philosophy and classic literature and most of those works were published to look beautiful on a shelf, leaving her a vast selection of hardcover books to choose from. She needed to find three that looked unremarkable, that wouldn't tempt a casual browser to leaf through them. Narrowing her attention to the top shelf, she spotted a few books that might be perfect—difficult to reach and written in Hungarian.

Lifting a lounge chair that proved to be heavier than she had anticipated, she struggled to bring it closer to the shelf. She couldn't drag it and risk waking either Tatiana or Julian. She exhaled with relief when she managed to rest the chair down quietly.

Climbing on the chair, Meredith pulled three of the Hungarian hardcover books off the top shelf. She removed the books from their jackets, replacing each one with one of Glendon's journals. She then returned the covers, with their new contents, into the space the books once held. She stepped down from the chair, took a few steps back, and turned her gaze to the bookshelf—no one would ever be able to tell the difference.

Moving the chair back, Meredith returned to the bedroom and hid the three books inside her purse. When she turned around, she found Tatiana looking at her from the bed.

"Where did you go?"

"The kitchen. I needed water." Meredith got under the covers with Tatiana.

"How long have you been awake?"

"Not long. I woke up and saw you."

"Do you want me to turn off the nightstand lamp?"

Tatiana shook her head. "I don't think I'll fall back asleep."

"Are you OK?" Meredith hoped Tatiana hadn't seen her hide the journals.

"Most of the time I can't sleep. I think I did earlier because you're here."

"What's your plan, Tatiana? You can't hide in Julian's home forever."

"I don't have a plan."

"You need one."

"Before my sister's death, I hoped to leave Chicago. Go to school."

"That sounds like a great plan to me."

"I don't have enough money. And you're forgetting Steven."

"I know if I talk to my dad he'll do whatever he can to help you divorce your husband. You have me. You have Julian. You're not alone. I'll help you apply to college."

"I didn't even graduate from high school."

"So you'll get your GED."

Tatiana moved closer to Meredith and kissed her. "You're a good person, Meredith."

She smiled in response. "I thought I was privileged and spoiled."

"Yes. But don't forget that I like you."

Meredith caressed Tatiana's hair, continuing her touch down to Tatiana's naked breasts. "I like you too," she whispered.

They kissed and Tatiana moved her hand under the covers. When Meredith felt Tatiana's fingers in her, she thought—*we are in this bed together not because we like each other but because we are both lonely.*

"You're wet."

Meredith moaned in response.

Tatiana rested her other hand over Meredith's mouth. "Sh."

Swaying her hips, Meredith made sure the heel of Tatiana's hand remained pressed firmly against her body.

"Ride my hand. Let me make you come," Tatiana commanded.

Meredith buried her face in Tatiana's hair, still damp from their bath, and opened her mouth in a silent cry. Tatiana's hair carried the scent of the shampoo Meredith had bought for her.

Meredith's orgasm hit her, lurching her body forward against Tatiana, who wrapped her arm around Meredith and held her as tightly as she could. She kept her fingers inside Meredith and as her hand moved in circles, it triggered renewed pleasure for Meredith. Spasms rocked her and she lost control of her body.

As the spasms subsided, the first thought that entered Meredith's mind was that she could barely move and that she felt very wet—wetter than she had ever felt in her life. With her face still in Tatiana's hair, Meredith started to laugh.

Soon they were both laughing, hard.

"Did I pee myself?" Meredith asked, trying to find her breath. They were speaking in hushed tones, so close to each other they whispered into each other's mouth.

Her question made Tatiana lose herself in another fit of laughter.

"Seriously, did I?" she asked again, feeling the wet sheets.

"Meredith, don't be crazy. You squirted all over the bed, that's all it is."

"But it's never happened before." There was wonder in her voice. "I didn't think I could."

"Now you know better."

"I don't want to sleep on this wet spot."

"You're not stealing my side of the bed," Tatiana said, unable to stop laughing.

"Can you?"

"What?"

"Come like that."

"Sometimes."

As they kissed Meredith rolled onto her back, bringing Tatiana with her.

"You have the nicest tits, full and heavy." Tatiana squeezed them with her open hand. Before Meredith could react, Tatiana licked her erect nipple. Meredith wanted to feel her mouth on her whole body, but for now, the sensation of Tatiana sucking on her breasts proved to be erotic enough to bring Meredith to the brink of another orgasm. The sharp bite of Tatiana's teeth on her nipple made Meredith cry out.

Tatiana raised her head and smiled at Meredith. "Your body was made to fuck."

Holding Tatiana by the hair, Meredith brought her face closer. They kissed, in earnest now, and in the same way Meredith had initiated the kiss, she closed her fingers on Tatiana's hair and pulled hard, making Tatiana's head jerk back.

Meredith took in the sight of a flushed Tatiana. "I'm so attracted to you." She buried three of her fingers in her own mouth and moved them in and out several times, slowly, covering them with her saliva. They continued to stare into each other's eyes and Meredith felt hypnotized by Tatiana's expression.

Meredith placed her fingers between Tatiana's open legs and started to stroke her.

"I like that you have hair on your pussy. It's sexy." She smiled when she felt Tatiana's arousal coat her fingers.

Offering more of herself to Meredith's touch, Tatiana bent her knees and brought them closer to her chest, on each side of Meredith's body.

"How close are you?" Meredith licked Tatiana's skin, from her stomach to her lower abdomen. "My fingers are drenched."

"Put your mouth on my pussy," Tatiana demanded, her whole body undulating.

As Meredith complied, it only took a few short seconds for Tatiana to come undone, panting, her knees still pressed to her chest.

With the aftermath of her orgasm still rolling through her, Tatiana sat up and kissed Meredith. "I can taste myself on your mouth."

"Get on your hands and knees," Meredith ordered.

Being with a woman as slight as Tatiana made Meredith feel strong, powerful. At that moment, arousal seeped out of her body. Without thinking twice, Meredith dabbed her fingers with it, knelt behind Tatiana, and buried them deep inside her, mixing her own arousal with Tatiana's.

She got a loud groan in response. "Spread your legs wider."

Tatiana did as asked but Meredith wasn't satisfied. "Wider," she instructed, keeping her fingers in Tatiana.

As soon as she moved her legs further apart, Meredith caressed Tatiana's body.

"You look so hot," Meredith said in awe.

Using her forearms for support, Tatiana had rested her cheek on the bed. The sounds coming from Tatiana were beautiful to Meredith. She pressed her face between Tatiana's open legs, licking her from front to back several times. Getting Tatiana's arousal in her mouth, Meredith concentrated on the tight, small opening displayed to her. The tip of Meredith's tongue entered Tatiana, whose mix of words and whimpers conveyed how much pleasure Tatiana felt.

Meredith looked up and was suddenly faced with Julian's green eyes on her and Tatiana. He stood by the bedroom door.

Having Julian's gaze on them didn't make Meredith want to move away. Instead, as a new wave of arousal washed over Meredith, it encouraged her to continue pleasuring Tatiana.

He reached inside his sweatpants and pulled out his erection. He started to stroke himself.

Suddenly, Tatiana seized up, and her knees slid further apart on the bed. Her orgasm brought with it loud sobs and, at that precise moment, Meredith saw that Julian found release as well. The proof of it now coated the backs of his fingers.

She wrapped her arms around Tatiana and kissed the side of her neck. When Meredith looked up again, Julian still watched them.

CHAPTER 23

Ten minutes at The Empty Bottle, a small dive bar in the Ukrainian Village, and Meredith already regretted her decision to be there. She didn't feel like drinking, and the band playing made her head hurt. It was her birthday and her roommate Tess had convinced her that they should go out for a few drinks. Meredith disliked celebrating it—her mother had passed away on her ninth birthday—and, whenever possible, she avoided sharing her birthday date.

Meredith glanced at the crowd. While she stood, hands in her pockets, everyone around her danced. And Tess was late, which didn't surprise her. Tess never arrived anywhere on time.

A woman in a leather jacket and heavy makeup leaned in closer to her. "They're good, right?" she asked.

"Sure."

Meredith felt her mobile phone vibrate in her pocket. She checked the display—an unlisted number. She hesitated then decided to answer. It was too loud in the bar for a phone call and, since she stood too far from the exit, she turned toward the bathroom. The bar had three single unisex stalls. With its door ajar, one was clearly unoccupied. Meredith answered the phone as she opened the door further.

"Hello—"

She didn't have time to react.

A hand covered her mouth as she was pushed inside the stall from behind. She tried to scream, but then she was shoved against the wall and all her breath left her lungs.

"Shut up." A threatening man's voice rung out as she heard the door slam shut behind them.

As Meredith continued to scream and struggle, the man slammed her once more against the wall. Her calls for help morphed into a cry of pain.

"Listen to me, Meredith."

Hearing her own name made her go still. He knew who she was.

"Good, don't move and listen. Stop investigating. Do not publish your article."

Her breathing came out in loud pants. The panic flooding her body urged her to flee but she forced herself to focus on the low voice by her ear. She didn't recognize it.

"You're going to tell Croswell that you're done. Do you understand?"

The man closed his other hand on her hair, close to her scalp. He pulled hard and Meredith whimpered.

"If you continue, the people you care about will suffer. Your father, Reeve, Tatiana—they will be the ones who face the consequences of your actions. Remember that."

All of a sudden, the man was gone, and Meredith slumped to the floor. Shaking, she used the wall for support as she got back to her feet and quickly locked the bathroom door.

The shivers rocking her body made it impossible for her to remain upright. Only a few seconds ago she believed she was about become the sixth dead woman in Pam's folder.

Meredith's cell phone screen had shattered after being knocked from her hand. Still, she was able to call her roommate.

"Where are you?" she asked as soon as Tess picked up.

"Sorry I'm late, M. I'm on my way. I should—"

"Don't bother. I'm leaving. Can you stay with me on the phone for a bit?"

"What's the matter?"

It took everything in her to calm herself. She didn't want Tess to know what had happened. "I just want to have someone on the line as I walk to my car."

"OK, cool. I'm here. But why are you leaving?"

Meredith rushed to the exit, pushing through people until she finally made it outside and into the muggy night. Concerned that the man might still be watching her, she quickly scanned her surroundings.

"Are you there?" she asked Tess.

"Yeah, I'm here. You didn't answer my question. Why are you leaving? Are you sure everything is OK?"

Meredith reached her car, which was parked on the street. She checked the back seat before getting in.

"Uh-huh." Even at night, the intense heat inside the car made it hard for her to breathe, but she didn't turn on the AC. She locked the doors. "I'm in my car. Are you home?"

"No. I told you, I'm on my way to The Empty Bottle."

"I gotta go."

She hung up and, before she drove away, dialed Julian's number.

"Can you meet me at my place in ten minutes?" she asked when she heard his voice on the other end. "We need to talk."

She drove to her apartment, both hands on the steering wheel, her eyes fixed on the road.

When she parked in front of her building, Julian stood by the front steps with a small box in his hand.

As she approached him, she tried to curb her nervousness.

He kissed her. She couldn't remember the last time they had kissed. It made the conversation they were about to have much more difficult.

"Let's go in." She wanted to remain in his arms but if she did she wouldn't find the courage to speak.

When they were inside the apartment, Julian watched her with concern as she turned on all the lights. She sat on the couch and lit a cigarette. When he joined her, he passed her the small box he had been holding.

"Happy Birthday, Meredith."

She stared at the beautifully wrapped box. "I was at this bar and"—she took a puff of her cigarette—"this guy assaulted me."

"What?" Julian moved closer to her. "I'm taking you to the hospital."

"I'm fine. I don't need to go to the hospital."

"Were you raped?"

His calm tone sounded forced to her.

"No, he didn't touch me like that."

"Did he rob you? Take anything from you?"

She shook her head in response.

"Did he harm you?"

"He shoved me against the wall."

"What did he want? Did he speak to you?"

Meredith covered her eyes with her hands.

"What did he say?" Julian insisted.

"He threatened me."

"About what, Meredith?"

He moved her hands away from her face. He held them in his.

She wanted to tell him—*stop, don't kiss me, don't hold me, don't touch me; I can't hurt you when you're trying to comfort me*—but she couldn't bring herself to say any of that, nor could she pull her hands away.

"I've been hiding something from you." The expression on Julian's face made her pause. He looked stricken. She forced herself to continue. "When I found out you were a member of The Raven Room I got the idea of writing an article about it." She waited for him to say something. When he didn't, she carried on, "An article about you taking me to the club and my experiences there. To me, it was a perfect way to launch my career—a peek inside of a members-only sex club, which caters to the wealthiest in Chicago. A club that most don't know exists. But after Sofia's death, I decided not to go ahead with it. It felt wrong to betray you like that."

Julian leaned back on the couch, his face tilted toward the ceiling. Instead of spending time trying to decipher his thoughts, Meredith knew she needed to finish. "Lena and Sofia's deaths made me see that, while I didn't want to write the article anymore, I needed to find out why they were killed and who had done it.

With access to the club and with more information on Lena and Sofia than the police, I could actually make a difference. I figured I'd gather the information and then hand it over to Pam. But then I found out that there were three other women…and the police had covered up their deaths, which meant I couldn't take what I'd find to them. So that led me back to writing an article. I'll share everything I know with the public and hope, once the club and the murders are exposed, it'll make a big enough stir that people will demand justice. The *Tribune* already said it wants to publish it."

"You're investigating the deaths of those women? Sofia's?"

"Investigating is a heavy word, but yeah, I'm trying to find out as much as I can."

Julian stared at her. "There's something else, isn't there? Please, Meredith, you and I have reached the point that only honesty will do."

She didn't hold back—she told him everything she had learned regarding Lena and Sofia's deaths: the similarities and differences between the two murders, how she had seen Thompson and her stepmom together at the Art Institute, Owen Glendon's journals and how she believed his daughter might have also been a victim.

Meredith showed Julian the pictures of the four dead women. He picked up the photographs one by one. He studied them for a while. "Where did you get these photos from?"

"My stepmother." Meredith wouldn't involve Colton. "I need to ask you"—she pulled the gold necklace with the cross from inside her wallet—"who does this belong to?"

Julian's eyes widened. Tatiana had advised her not to ask Julian about the necklace, but Meredith couldn't continue to keep that from him.

"Where did you find that?" His tone was cautious but she also heard indignation.

"In one of your bathroom drawers. I found it when I was looking for a brush the morning Pam and Colton showed up at your place."

"And you took it?"

"I was worried that if the police searched your home they would come across it…I thought it was safer with me."

"Why would the police care about a necklace they found in one of my drawers?"

"Lena's friend told me she always wore a gold necklace with a cross on it. She had seen Lena the day before she was murdered and she had it on her. But when they found her body, the necklace was missing. I was worried the police would think this necklace belonged to Lena."

Julian flexed his hands into fists, and had he been any other man she would have put as much distance between them as possible.

"Give me back the necklace," he demanded. "Now."

"First, tell me who it belongs to."

"I don't have to tell you anything." He extended his hand toward her. "Give it back."

"Tell me the truth, Julian."

He gestured to the photos. "You think I did this, don't you?"

"If I did, we wouldn't be having this conversation."

"You had no right to take that necklace from me." Resentment distorted his features. "And you have no right to demand I answer your question before you give it back."

"I want us to be honest with each other."

Julian punched the coffee table and Meredith gasped. The gift box on her lap fell to the floor. She had never seen him so irate. "Don't you fucking give me that bullshit excuse. You don't trust me." Julian rose to his feet. "The necklace, Meredith."

She pulled back and clasped the necklace to her chest. "Why won't you tell me?"

All of a sudden, Julian closed the distance between the two of them and ripped the necklace from Meredith's hands.

Startled, she didn't try to stop him when he stormed out of her apartment. The unwrapped gift box stood, forgotten, on the floor.

CHAPTER 24

Julian stepped into the 12th District police station. He disliked everything about the place—the dirty white walls needing a fresh coat of paint, the faint musty scent that mixed with the smell of strong chemicals used to wash the floors, the smug expression on the faces of the cops who came and went through the main doors.

He had called Pam that morning to set up the meeting, but as he walked down the hall toward the closed door of her office, he paused. His palms were sweaty. Returning to the station brought him memories of the time right after Sofia's death. During the days he had been in a jail cell, he had felt fear and confusion, but stronger than that had been the overwhelming sense of loss. The recollection reinforced his decision to speak to Pam. Even though the man had threatened the ones closest to Meredith and not her directly, she was the one in danger. He had to put his anger regarding the necklace aside and do anything in his power to protect her.

Julian didn't knock. He opened the door and stepped inside. "I want to keep this brief," he said, standing across from Pam's desk.

After everything he had learned from Meredith the night before, he had considered what to do next. He didn't know if Meredith had decided to give up her article. He feared she wouldn't be able to and would find herself further embroiled in her amateur crime investigation.

"If you hadn't mentioned Meredith I would have had you thrown out the door." Pam leaned back on her chair, her arms crossed over her chest. "It must be important for you to show up here."

"Meredith is planning to publish an article."

Pam didn't look as surprised as Julian expected her to.

"You know about it," he said.

"I'd hoped she had given up on the idea."

His previous dislike of Pam paled in comparison to the new hatred he felt toward her. In that moment, he vowed to destroy what she clearly loved the most—her career.

"She has information that she says she got from you," he said. "Information that she'll put in her article."

"What information?"

"About four women who were found dead in their beds," he continued, making sure he kept his voice low. "Sofia might have been the fifth, but her death was ruled a homicide and, according to Meredith, hers differs from the deaths of the other women. She showed me photographs. There were police reports too, but I didn't get to see those. Meredith said the four women were killed by drug overdoses but that you covered it up and ruled their deaths accidental." Julian paused, watching Pam closely. "Have you done that?"

Pam rushed toward Julian. "Shut up." She pointed a finger at him, only a few inches away from his face. Pam was shorter than him but it made no difference. Her rage turned her into an imposing force. "We don't operate like The Raven Room."

Julian was surprised she had openly mentioned the club. "You're out of your depth here, Sung. I don't give a fuck what you and your lackeys are up to but you have to stop involving Meredith in your investigation."

"She's got nothing to do with my investigation. I have no idea how she got her hands on those files."

"What have you been telling her?"

"Nothing!" Pam raised her voice, but after glancing at the door nervously, continued in a lower tone. "If you hadn't taken her to the club, none of this would have happened."

"The club is not in the business of killing women." Julian tried to control his anger but his tone remained biting.

"How do you expect me to stop her? She won't listen to me."

"I want Meredith out of Chicago."

"What else did she say to you?"

Julian remained silent.

"Fucking tell me."

"That you and Thompson are friends. Or maybe even more than friends. Which explains why you've been working so hard to pin Sofia's death on me."

Pam shook her head.

"Meredith has to leave Chicago," Julian insisted.

"Why don't you tell her that?" Pam asked. "You have a stronger hold on her than anyone. This is the worst thing that could happen. All I ever wanted was to protect her…and now this."

"You say you want to protect her—this is your chance. Use whatever means available to you to make sure she gets as far away as possible from Chicago and stays there." He watched Pam pace her office. "If they are actual homicides, I'm not the guy who killed them."

It was Pam's turn to sneer at Julian. "I know you didn't kill those women, Reeve. But I've seen what you do at the club. You're far from innocent."

Taken aback by Pam's statement, Julian didn't know if she spoke because she had something on him, or if it was an attempt to test him. "You have no idea what you're talking about."

"I bet Sofia and Tatiana do. Too bad one is dead and the other is missing."

Julian had to leave Pam's office. He was afraid of what he might do otherwise. "I'm not the only one who knows about the article. Meredith needs to be out of Chicago by the end of the week."

CHAPTER 25

"I'll go."

Grace stood in Julian's kitchen, getting ready to leave Seth and Eli. Julian worried Grace would somehow find out about Tatiana's presence but he also knew he could use Tatiana's help when dealing with Seth and Eli; his training as a child psychologist fell short when it came to entertaining and comforting two nineteen-month-old boys. Tatiana appeared to do just fine merely by smiling at them, which secretly irritated Julian.

"Good," Grace replied. "We're having dinner at Maggie's at seven. I've heard great things." She approached Julian and her hands came to rest on his shoulders. "It's time you and Pete put this squabble to rest."

"Does Pete know I'll be joining you?"

"Does it matter?"

"He doesn't know, does he?"

Grace hesitated. "Of course he does."

"Don't lie to me. Please, not you of all people."

"Pete knows you're coming." Grace gave him one of her usual sad smiles. "We both need you back in your lives."

"I'm already in your life. I'm babysitting Seth and Eli. What difference will it make if Pete and I are on good terms?"

"I want you to come over for holidays and birthdays and dinners. Like before. I want you to be part of our family."

He wanted to continue to see Seth and Eli. "I'll do my part."

"Thank you," she whispered as she hugged him.

Julian closed his eyes and allowed himself to relax, even if for just a brief instant. He was stunned to find out how much he craved another human being's touch. His own vulnerability disgusted him.

"How's the open marriage coming along?" Julian asked, now leaning against the kitchen counter. He put as much space as possible between him and Grace.

"I met this new guy at the gym. We're seeing each other again this weekend. It's exciting."

"Is he in an open relationship as well?"

"He's single."

"How does he feel about being involved with someone who has a husband and kids?"

"Well, I haven't told him yet."

"C'mon Grace, really? How would you feel if you were in his place and all of a sudden you found out he had a family and he didn't tell you?"

"We were working out when we met; I didn't have my wedding band on. Afterwards, I wanted to tell him, I really did, but it never felt like a good time. Then we had sex, and at that point I didn't know how to tell him. It felt like it was too late." Grace sighed. "It's not easy."

"No, it's not. But you have to be honest, from the beginning. Discreet, but always honest."

"When you met Sofia, how did you and Meredith make it work? You two never stopped seeing each other."

"We were honest." Sure, they both had kept secrets, Julian rationalized, but not when it came to their sexual life. "Who'll be watching Seth and Eli tonight while we go out for dinner?" he asked, changing the subject. It pained him to speak about Meredith.

"I've left a message with my babysitter. I've got a spa appointment with a couple of friends but I'll stop here afterwards to pick them up on my way home."

Julian heard a cry coming from outside the kitchen and, as he made his way toward the noise, he wondered what the boys had gotten themselves into.

They were inside a large playpen set up in the middle of the living room, and one of them wanted out. He wasn't interested in playing with his brother or any of the scattered toys around them.

Julian picked up Eli. "That's fine," he said to Grace, who was already getting ready to leave. "Don't worry about keeping the phone with you. Enjoy the spa. Just text me when you're on your way."

"Uh-huh," she said as she waved goodbye to the boys.

"It's Sunday morning. Where's Pete?"

"Tennis, I think," she answered already from the foyer.

As soon as the door closed, Tatiana entered the living room. "Dinner with Pete and Grace?"

"I don't have a choice."

"Sounds like an excuse to me."

Before Julian could reply, Eli giggled. Tatiana had the boys' full attention.

"Why are they so enthralled by you?"

"You were so certain it was my wild hair. Not so sure anymore?" Tatiana kneeled on the floor and reached for a toy. She held it in front of Seth, who was quick to grab it. Both she and Seth were now pulling on the toy in a friendly tug of war.

"Do you remember how close we used to be?" she asked. "From the first day you arrived at our home we trusted each other. For no reason at all. But I guess that's what kids do. Even messed-up ones like us."

Julian's happiest memories involved Tatiana. So did his most painful ones. He put Eli inside the playpen with his brother and went into the kitchen. He needed a strong cup of coffee.

"Why are you going to this dinner?" she asked, following him into the kitchen. "Are you doing it for Seth and Eli? Grace, maybe? I thought you were done with Pete."

Julian opened one of the cupboards, looking for a mug. "Pete has many faults. I know that better than most, but he has been there for me when I needed him. He's the one who came and took care of you when you were beaten within an inch of your life."

"That's not why you're doing it. Do you feel guilty for fucking his wife?"

"She wasn't his wife at the time." Julian filled the electric kettle with water and turned it on. "Not that it makes any difference," he admitted. "Even if they were broken up, she was still his longtime girlfriend. I knew he loved her."

"Why did they break up?"

Julian continued to move around the kitchen.

"C'mon, why?' she insisted. "There isn't a TV in this damn condo. Entertain me."

"He cheated on her."

She lifted herself onto the kitchen counter, sitting between the sink and the stove. "This is better than I expected. She slept with you to get back at him? I would've."

"Grace is not you."

"If she was, she would've dumped Pete for good and would be raising those kids with you paying child support and taking care of them half of the time."

Julian realized he needed something from the cupboard above Tatiana and couldn't reach it with her sitting there. "Can you grab the moka pot behind you? As soon as you open the cupboard you will see it. It's on the first shelf."

"What's a moka pot?" She opened the cupboard door. "Is this it?" She grabbed a stovetop coffee maker. "Since when is this a moka pot? You've really become fancy, haven't you?"

"If I had I wouldn't be making coffee in one of these, would I?" Impatient, he took it from her and filled the aluminum basket with ground coffee beans.

"Anyway, now you've got a playpen filled with toys in the middle of your living room. What's next?"

"I enjoy having Seth and Eli around. They help me...I need them."

"Do you now regret not claiming paternity when they were born?"

"Pete and Grace had a lot to offer them. I didn't."

"Had Pete not been part of the picture you wouldn't have left them without a dad, regardless if you had anything to offer them or not. You know what it's like to grow up without one."

Julian filled the moka pot with the boiling water from the kettle and placed it on one of the stovetop gas burners. He turned it on, keeping the lid of the pot open.

"Of course I would have been there for them," he said. "Not their fault I was too drunk to use a condom."

Julian served them both the freshly brewed coffee. He took pleasure feeling the heat of the mug seep into his palm.

"Thanks for getting groceries."

He took Tatiana's eagerness to chat as a sign that she felt lonely.

"I didn't think you had noticed," he said.

"Once all you have to eat for several days are Oreos and soy milk, you notice when there's something else in the house."

"I'm sorry I didn't do it sooner."

Tatiana shrugged. "Not your responsibility."

Before he could move, she put down her mug and jumped off the counter. She grasped the front of his t-shirt and she pulled him toward her. Julian felt the soles of her bare feet step onto the tops of his. Her hands ventured to his shoulders and down his arms. She kissed the spot on his chest, where she had bitten him.

While he struggled to understand Tatiana's intentions, if he didn't push her away he knew what he would want and need from her. For that reason alone, Tatiana remained the only person he truly feared.

"Please, Tatiana, don't."

She let go of him. Secretly, Julian wished she hadn't.

CHAPTER 26

Since the incident at The Empty Bottle two days ago, and her conversation with Julian, Meredith hadn't left her apartment. But this morning she needed to go for a run. She refused to live afraid.

Back home and on her way to her bedroom, she froze. She was suddenly face-to-face with a tall man standing by the bay window. Her instinct told her to rush out of the apartment, but then Tess stepped out of the kitchen.

"Hey, you," Tess said as she walked by Meredith. "I texted you, but your phone's dead. Your friend has been waiting for you." She reached for her car keys. "I've gotta go to work so I'm going to jet. Nice to meet you," Tess added, glancing at the man over her shoulder.

The man gave Tess a quick nod of acknowledgement. "Likewise."

Meredith didn't want to be left alone with him but she didn't ask Tess to stay. She wasn't sure how the man might react, and she couldn't risk her roommate's safety.

Tess closed the front door behind her and suddenly Meredith's heart started to beat so fast that she felt dizzy.

"What are you doing here?"

"My wife. I know she's with Julian but I can't go near him. That's why I need you to tell me how she's doing. Please, Meredith. I'm aware that you don't know me and I shouldn't be here in your home but it's been several months and I'm desperate. Right now you're the only person who can help me. I'm concerned for Tatiana's safety."

198

Meredith wanted Thompson out of her home. "You need to leave."

"Can we please sit?" he asked.

"No, we can't sit. I want you gone." Meredith took a step to the side. Even with his arm in a cast, he was bigger and stronger than her.

"Please, just hear me out. That's all I ask."

"Why don't you ask Pam to help you?"

"What do you know about Pamela and I?"

She had never heard anyone call her stepmother by Pamela. "Enough to know I shouldn't trust either of you."

"We are friends. Longtime friends. We don't always agree, but it doesn't change the fact that she's the only person I trust completely. You should trust her, too."

"That's interesting, because the only time I've heard her talk about you was to say how you're the mayor's lapdog. Hardly the type of compliment you want from a friend." It frustrated her that she had fallen into conversation with Thompson. "I don't want to talk to you. Leave."

"I'm not surprised Pamela said that. She's a woman of strong opinions."

"If you don't leave right now I'll call the police."

"I thought your phone was dead and"—Thompson looked around the room—"your friend Tess mentioned you don't have a landline."

"Are you trying to scare me?"

"I just want you to listen to me." Thompson sat on the couch. "Please, for Tatiana."

"Say what you have to say and then get out."

"Tatiana is not safe with Julian."

Meredith opened her mouth to interject but he stopped her.

"I'm not here to enlighten you as to who Julian is. That's not my concern and you look old enough to handle all the consequences your actions might bring you." His eyes ran down her body and Meredith wondered if he had seen her have sex at the club. "I'm worried about what will happen to her if she remains with him. You're Julian's lover and you've been to The Raven Room. By now you must know he has fetishes that are"—Thompson paused, searching for the right word—"difficult to satisfy outside of the club. Tatiana is no different from him. They won't stop each other, and knowing the history between them, I'm afraid that she will end up hurt. Seriously hurt."

Meredith couldn't face Thompson.

"I disgust you," he said.

"I saw the state you left your wife in."

"I was kicked out of the club shortly after Julian. Tatiana stayed behind. When I left her she was fine. I don't know what happened after that."

"You're lying. You started beating her in front of Julian."

"I slapped her," he replied, defensively. "I didn't beat her. Did Tatiana tell you that I did?"

"Get out."

"I left the club and I waited all night for Tatiana to get home. She never did. Then, I get a call from the police telling me they had found a woman, who might be my wife, dead at some hotel. I had to go identify the body. Can you imagine how I felt?"

"This is not about Tatiana coming home," he continued. "I don't know if we can or even should try to salvage our marriage. But she has to get out of that condo."

Meredith refused to answer.

Thompson reached inside his pocket, opened his wallet and pulled out a business card. He rested it on the coffee table. "This is my contact info. Please give everything I told you some thought. I'm not the enemy."

He stood up and stopped in front of Meredith. She raised her chin and faced him head on. She almost took a step back but she willed herself to hold her ground—at such close proximity the pale blue of his irises made her think, for a brief instant, that she was freefalling deep into his eyes and she couldn't stop it. Never before had she experienced such a feeling. She remained still, not by force, but because she found herself transfixed.

"It might be futile for me to ask you this—but can you please not mention my visit to your stepmother?"

Meredith didn't reply.

He gave her a crestfallen smile. "I didn't think so."

He had already opened the door when Meredith spoke, "You said you weren't here to enlighten me on who Julian is. I want you to tell me."

"You already know who he is. You just don't want to admit it. I'm sure, as you research your article, it will be impossible for you not to face it."

Meredith felt all the air being sucked out of her lungs. "Did Pam tell you about my piece?"

"You really should be more careful who you tell things to." Instead of hostility, she heard the concern in his voice.

Thompson left. Without a moment of hesitation, Meredith hurried out the back door, down the fire escape, and toward the Western station, determined to get to Julian's condo as fast she could.

CHAPTER 27

The sound of his phone beeping reminded Julian that Grace should be on her way to pick up the twins. As he read her text message, the crease in his brow deepened. Grace hadn't been able to get a hold of her regular babysitter and she wanted him to find someone to watch the boys at his condo while they went to dinner. She had included the address of the restaurant.

Cursing under his breath, Julian called Grace, but the phone went straight to voicemail.

"Grace, call me back as soon as you get this. I don't have anyone to watch the boys and I can't take them anywhere without car seats. You and I need to talk."

Tatiana leaned on the doorframe as she held a sleeping Eli. "If you're planning on tearing into her you know you have no ground to stand on, right?"

His frustration around Grace's uncharacteristic behavior also involved the concern that her actions were steering them into a dangerous situation—one that would bring them all more heartbreak. "Despite everything they're still my sons."

"Tell her that and you're in for a world of misery. As I said, Grace is their mom. You don't want to piss off the mom of your kids, who happens to be a lawyer and married to your best friend who, in turn, knows your secrets and who you also betrayed by fucking his wife and getting her pregnant. Grace likes you and you want to keep it that way. Didn't you learn anything from dealing with my mom?"

"Tatiana—"

"Shut up," she interrupted. "If you're dead set on going to this dinner, bite your tongue around Pete and act like nothing is wrong. Now is not the time to be making more enemies."

"I don't have anyone to watch the boys."

"I'll watch them."

"No one knows you're here. Remember?"

"No one needs to know I'm the one watching them. Lie. Say you got someone you know and trust from the hospital to come over. I doubt Grace or Pete will give it a second thought."

"Eli is passed out in your arms and I'm sure Seth is just as tired. They need to go home," he said.

Tatiana raised an eyebrow. "You've learned to tell them apart."

"There are differences between the two."

"Not that many. How do you know this is Eli?" Tatiana asked, glancing down at the sleeping boy in her arms.

"His complexion is lighter."

"You've learned to tell them apart by which of your sons is whiter. I guess that's better than not telling them apart."

"Only you would make it sound like that."

"Like what?"

"You know. Wrong."

"You should know how to tell your sons apart by something other than the color of their skin. Come here. I will show you how I know which one is which."

Julian hesitated, but he walked up to Tatiana.

"See here?" she asked, pointing to a small beauty mark above Eli's right eyebrow. "Seth doesn't have one."

Julian stroked Eli's dark curls and, without giving it a second thought, kissed the boy's beauty mark.

"And they have very different personalities," Tatiana added. "But I'll leave that for you to figure out."

"It took me forever to tell you and Sofia apart," Julian said, his mind filled with memories that always made him smile.

"Did you ever?"

"What?"

"Tell me and Sofia apart."

"After the first few months of living with you I did."

"We tricked you all the time, even after you thought you could tell us apart. It was kind of a game between us. It was fun."

Julian and Tatiana stood close together as she held Eli and he continued to caress his son's head.

"You wish I had been the one who had died that night, don't you?"

Her question astounded him.

"Even if you two hadn't been sleeping together you'd still wish I had been the one who got killed," Tatiana added. "She was your favorite."

"That's not true."

Tatiana stared him down, an expression of skepticism on her face. "Go get ready. I'll watch Seth and Eli."

She turned and walked away, leaving him alone in the living room.

As he showered and quickly got dressed, Julian went over in his mind what he would say when he saw Peter. After their conversation in Peter's office, Julian didn't think his friend would mention what he had seen the night Julian had called him over to his condo to take care of Tatiana. But he worried what Grace might say. He could no longer anticipate her actions.

As Julian made his way to leave, he stopped by the playpen in the living room. Both Seth and Eli were fast asleep.

"They won't wake up for a while," Tatiana said. "Probably the whole time you're gone."

"You know my number. Call me if—"

"Nothing's going to happen. Go to this dinner and come back. We'll all be here when you do."

Julian held his keys in his hand and he closed his fingers tightly around them. He felt the sharp edges dig into his flesh.

"I'm trusting you with Seth and Eli. This is me waving a white flag at you," he said.

"You and I have hurt each other. Because of that, there are things I can't ever say to you. Or give you." While her words were directed at Julian she continued to watch over the sleeping boys. "But I can say and give you one thing—I love your sons. That's my white flag."

CHAPTER 28

Meredith got off at Grand Station and hurried the four blocks to Julian's condo on North Wabash Avenue. Like any other summer Sunday afternoon, tourists filled the sidewalks. As she rushed through the crowds, Meredith called Tatiana's phone. She didn't answer and it eventually went to voicemail.

Thompson's description of the night's events differed from Tatiana's, and while she expected him to lie, the discrepancy bothered Meredith.

She had just walked by the Dunkin' Donuts across the street from the entrance to Julian's building when she heard a voice call her name.

"Meredith, get in the car."

She glanced at the blue car and saw Colton leaning toward the passenger window.

"Get in," he repeated.

"What the hell are you—"

"Meredith." He paused, quickly scanning their surroundings. "Get in the fucking car. I need to talk to you."

She opened the car door and sat in the passenger seat. "Is this about the name on the deed of the Chinatown building?" she asked, frustrated he had stopped her.

Colton drove down the street and turned right, parking as soon as he turned the corner.

"Colton, c'mon—"

"Ming-Yue Li," he said, interrupting her.

"What?"

"That's the name on the deed. Do you know how many Ming-

Yue Lis there are in Chicago?" Colton shook his head. "A lot. And it's a unisex name."

"And this couldn't have waited until later? I've to go—"

"Cozy up to Reeve?"

She had been frustrated before, but now she was livid. "What's it to you?"

"Speak of the devil." In the rearview mirror, Colton stared at the car that had just passed. He pulled out into traffic.

"What are you doing?" Meredith asked, raising her voice. "Where are we going?"

"That was Julian Reeve. I'm doing my job, which is to follow him."

"Let me out."

Colton kept his eyes on the road. "I thought you wanted to know what I was able to dig up."

The quicker Colton shared with her what he knew the faster she could go. "Fine. Tell me what you found."

"I told you, it's under the name Ming-Yue Li."

"Shouldn't there be an address or phone number associated with this person?"

Meredith spotted Julian's black Mercedes ahead of them. She worried he would see her.

"The phone number on the deed is for the restaurant in the building and the address is for a retail management company, registered to another address," Colton replied. "The name of the company is Ming-Yue Li, owned by Ming-Yue Li."

"You're saying the information on the deed is of a company who is registered under the same information?'

"You got it."

"Can you find more about this company?"

"First, you'll have to tell me why you asked me to look into this building. I've driven by it. It's just a shitty-looking building in Chinatown."

"I know I promised, but I can't tell you, I'm sorry."

"What the fuck, Meredith?"

"I don't want to lie to you."

"Why can't you tell me? What's going on?"

She would jump out of the car the next time they came across a red light, she decided.

"I just want you to be honest. Why is that so hard for you?"

"I'm being honest," she replied.

"You have a fucked-up idea of what honest means. You're using me."

Meredith felt her hair stick to her clammy neck. "You can be upset but I won't tolerate you yelling at me." Instead of shouting like Colton, she kept the tone of her voice low. "I've asked you to look into Thompson, share information about the murder investigation, find out who owns a building in Chinatown, but I didn't point a gun to your head. You did all of it willingly. Or better, you did it because you believe it would help your career. You've used me as much as I've used you, so shut your fucking mouth."

They were moving again as they continued to follow Julian.

"You do whatever the hell you want without giving a damn about how I feel," he said. "We only talk about this damn investigation. It pisses me off."

They stopped at another red light and Meredith took this as her opportunity to leave. "I don't have time for this bullshit," she said, opening the car door.

"Meredith, what the hell?"

She stepped out, holding the door open. "Listen, Colton, I don't want to fight right now. I thought you and I had an understanding."

"About what?"

"About us."

"You want me to tell you everything but when I ask one question, you clam up. Don't you think that would annoy any guy?"

Soon the traffic light would change to green and the drivers behind them would start honking. If Julian looked in his rearview mirror he would be able to see her.

"I came across something." Colton paused and shook his head. "I'll tell you what it is when you start telling me what you're up to."

"You're trying to corner me?" She slammed the car door shut but spoke through the rolled-down passenger window. "Won't work. Want to know why? You care a whole hell of a lot more about me than I care about you."

She turned onto the side street to her right. She needed to get into a cab and head back to Julian's condo.

Colton drove up to her. "Meredith, wait!"

"Your mark went that way." She pointed in the direction he had come from. She continued to walk away but Colton persisted.

"Reeve was at the New Jackson the night Sofia was killed," he said. "I got footage from the security camera on the building beside the hotel. He went in at 1:17 in the morning and came out thirty minutes later."

Meredith came to a halt and Colton pressed the brakes.

"He was there by himself," Colton continued. "You weren't with him."

Colton knew she had lied. Meredith faced him with defiance.

"It shows that Tatiana was also at the New Jackson. She got there after Reeve left, at 2:09 in the morning. Tatiana was at the hotel for over two hours. She left at 4:47. We know Sofia was killed sometime between midnight and five in the morning." Colton locked eyes with Meredith. "Both Tatiana and Reeve were there."

While Meredith had known all along that Julian had been at the New Jackson, what Colton was telling her further contradicted Tatiana's version of the events.

"How about Thompson?" she asked.

"No sign of him."

Meredith rushed toward the one-way street they had been on. Colton called after her but she didn't look back. Instead, she flagged down a cab and hopped inside.

CHAPTER 29

Julian saw Peter as soon as he entered Maggie's.

He took his time approaching. He still hadn't heard back from Grace and he had no idea when she might show up, if at all.

"I don't want to talk to you, man," Peter said as Julian sat down.

Before Julian could reply, the waiter stopped by and poured Julian some water.

"I promise I won't bring up the open marriage, Pete."

"Fuck you," he mumbled under his breath.

Julian spotted Grace waving at them. He sighed with relief.

"Sorry I'm late." She sat down at the table, a big smile on her face. "I hope you guys didn't order without me. Maybe we can get some platters to share?"

Julian reached for his water and Peter inched his chair away from him.

"What were you guys chatting about before I got here?" she continued, oblivious to their silence.

Peter cleared his throat. "I told you not to invite him."

"Don't you think this little spat of yours has lasted long enough?" Grace asked. "It's time you guys get over whatever this is."

"It's none of your fucking business," Peter said to Grace, his jaw clenched. "Stay out of it."

"Don't talk to me like that. I'm your wife. Whatever happens with you is my business."

"Who's watching the boys? I know our regular babysitter wasn't free tonight."

Grace observed Peter through narrowed eyes. "How do you know that?"

Peter started to speak but stammered, not being able to give Grace anything more than a couple of unintelligible words. For a man who had cheated on his wife multiple times, Peter was a horrible liar, Julian thought.

"You're fucking her, aren't you?" Grace asked with a nervous laugh. "You son of a bitch, even Seth and Eli's nanny is fair game to you. Could you be any more of a cliché?"

"I'm not fucking her. Listen—"

"Stop," she cut him off. "Stop with the lies. We have an agreement and you still go and cheat on me."

"I didn't cheat on you. We can have sex with other people, no?"

"Just because we both agreed that we can have sex with others you think fucking the nanny behind my back is OK?"

"What was I supposed to do? I didn't want to hurt you."

"How about not fucking her? Did you think of that? We're supposed to have a conversation about these things. Not just run off and do whatever the hell we want."

"You're not being fair. You've gone on sleepovers with different guys and I never pressed you for answers."

"Because it was convenient for you."

"You still haven't told me who's watching the boys."

"You weren't concerned about them when you took off for three straight days to fuck that slutty doctor you met at the conference." Grace stopped talking and took a steadying breath. She sipped her water. "Julian is watching them."

"He's sitting right here, so—"

"I have a friend from the hospital watching them," Julian rushed to say. "I trust her completely."

"I don't want him watching my sons."

"He's not watching your sons," Grace replied. "They're not yours."

Peter looked confused. Julian reached across the table and took hold of her hand. "Grace—"

"Seth and Eli are Julian's," she said, not letting him stop her.

"We slept together when you and I broke up, after I found out you cheated on me. He's their dad. Not you."

His stare fixated on Grace, Peter blanched.

"Have you had a chance to look at the menu?" the waiter approached and asked cheerfully.

"We need more time," Julian managed to say. His heart slammed so fast against his ribcage that he felt pain emanate from his chest and spread through his whole body.

"Is it true?"

Julian wanted to keep his eyes on the white tablecloth but he forced himself to face Peter. "It is."

"Jesus, man, I can't believe this is happening." Peter shook his head in disbelief. "I loved you like a brother."

Of all the possible emotions Julian expected to feel, shame was not one of them.

"I thought we told each other everything," Peter continued.

"I didn't want to hurt you." He found himself using the same words Peter had used earlier.

"Why?" Peter asked. "Why did you do it?"

"It just happened…we didn't plan it and it never happened again."

"Bullshit. I know you. You might have not planned it at the time, but you didn't fuck my wife and lie to me about it for over two years without ever thinking about it again. Tell me why you, my best friend, fucked my wife."

"Pete, I don't know." Julian wished he could stand up. He felt trapped.

"Don't lie to me, asshole. Tell me the truth."

"Enough," Grace interjected. Silent tears ran down her face. "We didn't do it to get back at you, if that's what you're thinking. But knowing what I know now, I wish I had. You deserve to suffer."

"Because I had sex with other women?" Like Grace, Peter was now crying. "I'm a good husband and father"—he paused and looked at Julian—"and friend. No one can tell me different."

"You are a good friend," Julian reassured him.

"Seth and Eli are my kids. You can't have them," Peter said, raising his voice.

"I'm not taking the boys away from you. You're their dad."

"I don't want you to have anything to do with them." Peter sounded determined.

"That's not your call." Grace held Julian's hand tightly. "I want Seth and Eli to grow up knowing that Julian is their biological father. I won't lie to my kids. Fight me on this and you'll never see them again."

Peter stood up and his chair fell backward, hitting the floor. The noise of it echoed throughout the restaurant. "I don't regret cheating on you. I just wish I had never felt guilty about it."

Peter stormed out and, as Julian picked up the overturned chair, the waiter rushed to the table and took care of it himself.

"I'm very sorry," Julian said to the waiter. He could feel the eyes of the entire restaurant on him and Grace. "We're leaving."

"Not yet." Grace dried her tears with the white napkin and then looked up at the waiter with a smile. "We'll have a bottle of your best Cabernet Sauvignon."

"Are you sure that's a good idea?" Julian asked as soon as the waiter walked away.

"A three hundred dollar bottle of wine is always a good idea. Especially when it's going on my soon-to-be-ex-husband's credit card."

The waiter brought them the bottle of wine with a hesitant smile.

"We love it." Grace didn't bother to taste the wine.

For a long while, Julian and Grace sat, side by side. She stared at her untouched glass of wine and he mulled over what would happen next.

"I wished we'd had a chance to talk about it before you told Pete," he finally said.

"Julian, we've been talking about it for the last two years."

"Will you be filing for divorce?"

"What do you think?"

"He loves Seth and Eli. He will do anything he can not to lose them."

"Do you want shared custody?"

"If I say I do, Pete won't let them go quietly. He knows things about me that, if they came out, it would hurt you and the boys."

"What things?"

Julian shook his head. "Not here."

"Don't be afraid of Peter."

"He's my oldest friend. That gives him a lot of power over me."

"This is not about him or you. It's about Seth and Eli."

"That's what I'm trying to tell you—whatever Pete decides to do with what he knows will affect Seth and Eli."

"You didn't answer my question. I need to know, right now, if you want shared custody of Seth and Eli."

"I'm not better than Pete, Grace."

"One of the things I've learned from all of this is that I can't raise two kids with a man I don't respect." She rested her hand on his cheek. "You and I aren't in love with each other but we do respect each other. That doesn't make you better than Pete, but it makes you better for Seth and Eli."

Julian took hold of her hand and brought it to his lips. "I don't want to let you down," he said, kissing the back of her fingers. "I'll tell you what Pete knows, and if you still feel the same way, we'll share custody of the boys."

"You will be a great—"

The sound of Julian's phone ringing made Grace pause.

"Sorry, I have to get this."

Seeing the word *Private* on his phone caused Julian to hold his breath. He hoped it wasn't Tatiana calling, but as soon as he answered and heard her voice he knew that something had happened. "OK," he said. "I'll be right there." He kept his voice impassive when she told him that Seth and Eli were fine but she needed him to return home at once.

"I have to go," he said already on his feet. "I need to go and check on something at the hospital."

"Can you keep Seth and Eli for the night? There's a lot Pete and I need to talk about."

"Sure, yeah, that's not a problem."

Julian said a hasty goodbye to Grace and rushed out of the restaurant.

CHAPTER 30

Meredith turned the key in the front door of Julian's condo. Stepping inside, she slammed the door so hard that she heard the painting on the wall rattle.

"Tatiana, where are you?" Meredith shouted. "Tatiana!"

"What's going on?" she asked, joining her.

"You said you went to the New Jackson Hotel, found Sofia dead, and you left." Meredith took a step closer to Tatiana. "I know that's not true. You were there for over two hours. Two whole hours. What happened in that hotel room?"

"I didn't lie to you." Tatiana didn't raise her voice, but her biting tone showed she was now as angry as Meredith. "I told you what happened. You didn't listen, though."

"What else did you lie to me about?" Meredith demanded. "Did you and Julian run into each other at the New Jackson? Was Sofia dead when he left? Was she dead when you left? Tell me the truth, Tatiana. Who beat you the night Sofia died?" Meredith was now yelling. "Was it really your husband?"

"What kind of question is that?"

"He was in my living room earlier today and he got me thinking—"

"You spoke with him?" Tatiana asked, her eyes wide.

"You didn't expect him to pay me a visit, did you?"

Tatiana closed her hands on Meredith's upper arms and shook her. "Are you stupid? I don't know what he told you but he's trying to mess with your head."

"I want the truth," Meredith replied.

"You speak to Steven once and suddenly you question everything I've told you?"

"Yes!"

Tatiana slapped Meredith across the face. Suddenly, they both had their hands on each other. They hit, scratched any body part they could get a hold of. Meredith pushed Tatiana to the ground but Tatiana held on to her and seconds later they were wrestling each other on the hardwood floor.

Abruptly, Meredith was pulled away from Tatiana.

"What the hell is going on here?" Julian grabbed Meredith, stopping her from lunging forward.

Tatiana got up and came toward Meredith. Julian put his other arm out, trying to keep them apart. "Enough! Have you both lost your minds?"

Meredith punched him in the crotch with her closed fist. Even though he still didn't let go of her, Julian grunted in pain.

He dragged her by the waist toward the foyer and, after managing to open the door with his free hand, pulled her into the hallway. Once they were out of his condo, he let her go.

"Why were you two fighting?"

"She lied—"

"You know what?" Julian said, cutting her off. "My house key. Give it back."

Julian's demand felt like a shot to the stomach. "I guess this is it, huh?" Meredith hoped she was able to keep her composure. "My purse is in your condo. Can you get it for me?"

Tatiana stood by the door, watching Meredith and Julian. Meredith refused to look at her.

Julian returned with her purse, and Meredith searched inside for the key. She passed it to him and he took it.

"The police know I wasn't with you when you were at the New Jackson." She didn't face Julian as she spoke. "They know I lied to protect you."

The elevator door opened and she stepped inside. At first she decided not to look in his direction, but she needed to see if he looked as crushed as she felt. Before Meredith could turn around, the doors closed and she missed her chance to look at Julian one last time.

CHAPTER 31

"Where are the boys?" Julian asked, now back inside the condo. "Why did you call me? Because of Meredith?"

The key Meredith had just returned to him felt heavy and cold in his palm.

"Your friend Pete was here. He just walked in. How many keys to your place have you given out?"

"Did he take Seth and Eli?"

"He said he was taking them home."

Blood rushed to his ears and no words came out of his mouth.

"Julian, Pete was here. He saw me."

"I forgot he had a key. I can't believe I forgot."

"What matters is that he knows."

"What did you tell him?"

"I didn't tell him anything. Julian?" Tatiana went up to him. "How bad is it that he knows? Will he go to the cops?"

"Pack your things." Julian ran into his bedroom and entered his closet. "You can't be here."

"You're throwing me out?" she asked, following him. "You know I don't have anywhere to go."

"I'm taking you to Hazel's." Julian came out with an envelope in his hand. He put it in his pocket. "We can't trust Pete. Grace told him the boys are mine."

He made his way to the bedroom where Tatiana was staying and started to open and close the dresser's drawers. "Where the hell are your things?" he asked when he found them empty.

"I'm not staying there."

"It's the only other place I can take you."

"I'm not going."

"Listen to me, Tatiana. If you don't do exactly what I say the police will find you here and there's nothing I can do to protect you. Your husband will eventually kill you and use the fact you've gone missing in the past as a cover-up. Please, Tatiana, let me get you out of here."

"I can't stay with Hazel."

"It's just for a couple of days until we can come up with a better plan."

Tatiana shook her head.

"Just for a couple of days," Julian repeated.

"You promise?" she asked, resolve in her voice.

"I promise. Now, get your things. We need to leave."

Tatiana grabbed a plastic bag from the nightstand table. "I'm ready."

"That's it?"

"I don't have anything else."

She wore one of his t-shirts and a faded pair of gray sweatpants. He pointed at her bare feet. "How about shoes?"

She shook her head.

Julian got one of his hoodies and passed it to her. "Put this on and cover your head. When we step out, look down. Make sure your face can't be seen by any of the security cameras."

As they walked out of the condo, Julian texted Grace with the news that Peter had picked up Seth and Eli. He told himself over and over again that the boys were safe, and if Peter did act on his anger, Julian would be the target, not the twins.

Julian and Tatiana got into the empty elevator and Julian scanned the key that gained him access to the garage. Tatiana kept her eyes on the floor. The sweatshirt was big and the hood covered her whole face.

"Why were you and Meredith fighting?"

"Ask her."

"Tatiana—"

"Ask her," she insisted, more forcefully this time.

Julian unlocked his car and opened the trunk. "It's the only safe way I can get you out of here."

She lay down on the floor of the trunk. "It's not my first time."

He closed the trunk and got behind the wheel. He checked his rearview mirror and saw a late nineties dark blue Ford sedan. Driving around the city while being followed by the police made it hard for him to concentrate. Now, with Tatiana hiding in the trunk, it became even harder. Sweat pooled on his lower back.

When he stopped at a red light on his way to Bridgeport, he checked the rearview mirror again. The unmarked police car still followed him. His phone beeped and he jumped in his seat. Grace had just replied to his message—she didn't know where Peter and the boys were.

He needed to calm down, Julian told himself as he wiped his brow. He raised the AC inside of the car. The driver behind him pressed the horn and Julian cursed, accelerating out of the intersection.

As Julian pulled into Hazel's garage, he glanced at the rearview mirror again and he saw the dark blue Ford sedan drive by. He turned off the engine and waited for the garage door to come down.

Inside, Julian maneuvered his body through the tight space between the car and the concrete wall. No sounds came from the house or the street beyond the old garage door. Julian unlocked the trunk.

"It's about time," Tatiana said as she climbed out.

"Pete didn't take the boys home. We don't know where they are."

"Do you think he'd hurt them?"

"No," he paused, trying to collect himself. "Of course not. Those boys mean the world to him."

"You need to take it easy, OK?" Tatiana spoke as if she feared he would break down in front of her. "They're safe."

"What if they're not?"

"Stop. Don't let your mind go there. Have you called Grace?"

"I texted her and she—" He stopped when he heard his phone beep. He hurriedly grabbed it from his pocket. "It's her again."

"What did she say?"

"They're home." Julian exhaled with relief. "They're all home."

"See? Everything's alright." Tatiana tried to sound reassuring, but Julian heard concern in her voice.

"I need to talk to you before I take you into the house." He took the envelope out of his pocket and, glad they couldn't see each other in the dark of the garage, put the envelope in her hand. "Here's ten thousand dollars in cash. If I call you on your cell phone or text you the word *busy* it means it's no longer safe for you to stay here. You get on the first bus out of Chicago and you lay low for a while. Use the money to survive."

He closed his fingers around hers, tightening her grasp on the envelope. "Take the money."

"Where did you get it from?"

"It doesn't matter. Take it."

Keeping his hands on hers, he felt her fold the envelope and put it in her pocket.

"The police followed us here," he continued. "When we go inside the house you stay away from the windows. Understand?"

"I'll be careful."

"Another thing, it might be hard for you, but don't antagonize Hazel. She becomes angry and it leads to screaming, crying fits. Think of it as a child having a tantrum. A really bad one. Whatever she says, whatever she asks, you keep that in mind."

"Do I have to see her?"

"It's her house. She spends a lot of time in bed but she still gets up and moves around. She's mentally sick, not crippled."

"Anything else?"

"She has a live-in caregiver, Carla. Do not tell her anything."

"Do you trust this Carla?"

"I trust her to take care of Hazel. I don't trust her not to mention to anyone that I brought over a woman who looks like she barely survived the streets of Chicago."

"I've been barely surviving you."

"Listen, I'm—"

"Is there anything else?" Tatiana asked. "I'm starving and my feet hurt. I'll do whatever you want me to do."

"You don't have to do anything. Just keep your mouth shut."

"Fine. But don't forget your promise to me—a couple of days."

"I never break my word."

He expected Tatiana to challenge him but she remained silent.

"Here, use the flashlight on my phone to see where you're stepping. This garage hasn't been cleaned in years." He passed his phone to her. "I'll follow you."

They started to make their way toward the door that would take them into the house.

"Maybe Hazel won't know who I am. We don't have to tell her."

"She appears to have an uncanny ability to remember the past. I didn't recognize you when I saw you but I suspect Hazel will."

They entered the house. "It's late. She'll be in bed," Julian said as he removed his shoes.

He turned on the kitchen light. As he was opening one of the cupboards, he saw Hazel's caregiver coming down the stairs.

"Hi Carla, how's Hazel?" he asked, noticing the surprised look she gave Tatiana, who stood in the middle of the kitchen, holding her plastic bag.

"She's in bed," Carla replied. "She had a good day. She asked for you, as usual."

"I'm sorry I didn't have a chance to come over earlier."

"It's not like it'll make that much of a difference for her, right?"

"Right," Julian answered with a sigh.

The loud ticking of the wall clock stood out in the now silent kitchen.

Carla smiled at Tatiana. "I'm Carla, Julian's mom's caregiver."

Tatiana hesitated. "I'm Julian's foster sister."

Carla's smile widened. "You're family then. Does Julian's mom know you?"

"She'll be staying here for a day or two." Julian jumped in.

He hoped he didn't look as nervous as Tatiana did. "Do you know where I can find some sheets for the bed in the spare bedroom?"

"I'll take care of that," Carla replied, already leaving the kitchen. "It looked like you were searching for food when I came down. I went grocery shopping today so there should be plenty."

Julian watched Carla walk up the stairs. When he could no longer hear her, he turned to Tatiana. "Foster sister?"

"Not a lie." Tatiana opened the fridge and peeked inside. "I didn't tell her my name. What do I say when she asks?"

"She won't. She's about to get a substantial raise."

Tatiana closed the fridge door. "There's nothing in there I can eat. I just want to shower."

"You can't afford to be a vegan now. Eat whatever you can get your hands on. I'm sure there's chicken or tuna. Have you looked at yourself?"

Tatiana pulled out a chair and sat down. "Are you telling me to abandon my morals?"

"I'm telling you to eat."

"Telling me to eat chicken or tuna is the same as telling me to abandon my morals."

"My god, Tatiana, I'm sure you won't go to hell for eating some defenseless animals."

"I don't believe in hell or heaven." She looked at Julian and frowned. "Don't look at me like I'm crazy. I know what I believe in—unless my beliefs change, of course."

"Any chance of your beliefs changing tonight?"

Tatiana left the table and Julian rested his forehead on one of the cupboard doors. He and Tatiana could not go back to fighting with each other the way they did after Sofia's death.

About fifteen minutes later, Tatiana returned from a shower and Julian slid a bowl down the table, toward her. "Vegetable soup. Came from a can, but it's vegan. Not a threat to your high morals."

She sat down, grabbed the spoon, and started to eat. "How bad is it with Pete?" she asked between mouthfuls.

"Bad. He knows too much and he's angry at me for what I did."

"What exactly does he know?"

"He knows about the club and what I do there."

"Everything you do there?"

"Pete is as vanilla as they come," Julian replied. "He thinks I'm into BDSM, edge-play. I never tried to correct him."

"How about the club? Does he know details, how it operates?"

"Of course not."

"But you told Meredith."

"I took her there. That was all."

"Do you think Pete would really go to the police?"

"Why wouldn't he?"

"He's your friend."

"Not anymore."

"You need to talk to him," Tatiana said as she chewed. "Make him see your side of the story. Tell him you're trying to protect me, how much you care. Does he know how you came to know Sofia and me? What happened then?"

Julian drummed his fingers on the tabletop. "Parts of it."

"Good. Remind him of it. Don't hold back on the details. Lay it on thick. Make him feel sorry for you, empathize with you. Telling him that you need him might be a good idea, too. Make yourself look vulnerable. It will make him feel powerful by comparison and that might be all he needs."

"I don't need to make myself look vulnerable." There was a hint of despair in Julian's voice. "I already am. Giving him more power over me when he's this furious is basically just asking him to destroy my life."

"How about Grace? Can she help you keep Pete quiet? No one likes a cheater."

"I don't want to involve her in any of this."

"Pete might have already done that for you."

The t-shirt she wore was absorbing the water that dripped

from her wet hair. It made it impossible for Julian not to notice the shape of her breasts.

"Stop!" Tatiana shouted, startling Julian. "Stop drumming your fingers on the table. You always do that when you're nervous. Drives me crazy."

Julian brought his hands together. "I do it without realizing. It's not on purpose."

"Just stop, OK?"

"Grace asked me if I wanted shared custody of the boys."

"And?"

The prospect of being a father to Seth and Eli gave Julian hope. He needed to hold on to that emotion. "I want to."

Tatiana smiled. "You'll have your own family."

"First, I have to tell her about the club and why I go there."

"Why would you do that?"

"Because Pete's going to tell her if he hasn't already, and it will be better if it comes from me. I can make sure she gets the truth and not some perverted tale Pete's built in his mind. Also, because she's the mother of my children. We'll be raising Seth and Eli together. She needs to know."

"No, she doesn't. *You* need Grace to know, which is different. Telling her will make you feel better but it will also force her to make your secrets her own. If Pete's already opened his mouth you can deny it—he has no proof—and, if everything else fails, you know the people who can help you manage Pete."

"You have a distorted way of looking at things, do you know that?"

"Don't tell her, Julian. You made that mistake with Meredith."

They grew silent. With only the stove light on, they sat in near darkness.

"When can I leave this house?" Tatiana asked.

"I said a couple of days. Not an hour or two."

"Maybe I can stay with Meredith?"

"Have you forgotten what happened earlier?"

"You should have stayed out of it," Tatiana said. "We would have figured it out."

"By hitting each other? I don't think so."

"Steven spoke with her."

Julian looked at Tatiana with alarm. "What? When?"

"He made Meredith doubt me. I can't believe she'd doubt me."

"Why didn't you—"

"Tatiana, you came to see me," Hazel said from the kitchen door, interrupting Julian. Her attention fell on Tatiana.

Between Hazel's mental state and Tatiana's temperament, Julian couldn't predict what might unfold next.

"You're looking better than I thought you would," Tatiana replied, her voice clipped.

"Must be all the rest I get." Hazel slowly made her way to the table, pulled out the empty chair and lowered herself into it. "I don't want to fall asleep. Not yet. Julian will come to see me."

Tatiana frowned at him. He gave a small shake of his head, warning her not to comment on what Hazel had just said.

"I see that you've eaten something." Hazel reached for the empty bowl in front of Tatiana. "That's not enough. No wonder you're skin and bones. There are burgers in the freezer. Carla picks them up at the butcher. I get these cravings for burgers, you know, not all the time but sometimes. They're good. Go make one."

"I only eat fruit and vegetables," Tatiana said.

"Not the last time you were here," Hazel replied.

Julian turned to Tatiana. "When were you here?"

"Who are you?" Hazel asked Julian. She sounded irritated by his interruption.

He didn't acknowledge Hazel's question. "When were you here?" he persisted.

"She just asked you who you were," Tatiana replied. "She doesn't know what she's saying."

He turned on his chair and took hold of Hazel's hand. "I'm a friend of your son, Julian. Remember me? I come to see you almost every day and bring you messages from him. I tell you how he's doing."

"Oh, yes, I remember," Hazel smiled. "Is he coming to see me?"

"Not tonight." Julian caressed her hand. "When was the last time Tatiana was here to see you? Julian would like to know."

He glanced at Tatiana from the corner of his eye. She muttered something under her breath but he ignored it.

"Julian was in med school...I don't remember what month it was but I know it was summer. He had gone up north with his friend, what's his name?" Hazel paused, "Pete, that's it," she continued. "Nice young man. They were at his cottage. Pretty place. Never been but I've seen pictures."

He was about to dismiss Hazel's story as mere delusion but Tatiana's dismayed expression encouraged him to pursue it. "What did she want?"

"Food, a place to stay. But what she really wanted was Julian. She came looking for him. I let her stay, you know." Hazel faced Tatiana, who in turn stared at her own nails. "I liked having you around. You had plans, goals, and that told me you were a girl after my own heart. I never touched the money you sent me. I gave you that money. It wasn't a loan. I still have it and I want to give it back to you."

Julian wanted to press Hazel for answers but she wasn't the person from whom he wanted to hear them. "Speak to me, Tatiana. What happened?"

"When I called the restaurant they told me you had left," Hazel persisted. "You didn't like it there?"

"Got a serving job in the Loop." Tatiana didn't raise her eyes from her nails. "Good tips."

"C'mon, Tatiana," Julian continued. "Tell me. I'll find out eventually. Hazel here can be very talkative when she feels like it, but I'd rather you to be the one to tell me."

"I got Hazel's address from a letter she had sent to my aunt." Tatiana started to scrape drops of dried soup from the tabletop with her fingers. "She wanted to know how Sofia and I were doing.

I had had enough of Lawrence so I got on a bus and showed up at her doorstep. I expected her to tell me to turn around and drag my sorry ass back to my aunt's. But, she didn't and for that, she had my immediate respect. That's when I found out she had adopted you. It sounded like you were doing really well for yourself."

Julian couldn't find his voice.

"And, that's the thing. When I got here I was sure I wouldn't be going anywhere until I saw you but, after talking to Hazel, I realized I needed to leave. You were no longer a druggie getting in shit with the cops and turning tricks for money. You had a good future ahead of you, all the things you and I never had."

Julian watched her as she continued to scrape the tabletop, even after the stain was gone.

"I wanted that for you," she said. "I still do."

Julian felt a tightening in his chest.

"I made a choice," she continued. "I packed up my things, said goodbye to Hazel, and took everything she offered me. That same day I rented an apartment here in Chicago. I stocked up my fridge, bought new clothes. I have no regrets."

"You shouldn't have regrets," Julian had to clear his throat before he could continue. "That was brave of you, though."

"It comes with being eighteen."

He let go of Hazel and approached Tatiana. He waited for her to look up at him. She took her time. At first, it was a suspicious glance through the corner of her eye but then she lifted her head and met his stare.

He kneeled beside Tatiana. He wrapped his arms around her shoulders and brought her closer to his chest. She didn't hug him back but she didn't try to push him away either.

"Thank you for coming back for me," he whispered into her ear.

CHAPTER 32

Vincent watched her sleeping peacefully, her body sprawled out between the sheets. It always impressed him how she could take up almost an entire king-sized bed.

He leaned down and caressed her hair. "I have to leave."

The woman opened her eyes and looked up at him. "Already? What time is it?"

"Four in the morning. I wasn't going to wake you, but I know you don't like it when I leave and don't say goodbye."

"I hate it."

"You should go back to sleep…or be with someone else. I don't want to tell you what to do."

"By now the place is probably empty. Anyway, I never book anyone else after I see you. Why don't you come back to bed?"

"I have work to do."

The woman reached for Vincent's hand and brought it to her lips. She kissed his palm. "You should quit. We could go somewhere together. I've been ready to leave Chicago since the day I got here."

There was a small part of Vincent that wanted to do just that—quit, go somewhere far away and forget the club with all its troubles, but he knew such a thing was impossible. "I love what I do."

"Liar."

Vincent smiled. "Yes, well, like they say, *no rest for the wicked.*" He turned his back on the woman and grabbed his black blazer from the chair.

The woman sat up on the bed. "Vincent?"

Already by the door, he turned.

"There's been talk…"

"About?"

"That some of us are disappearing…showing up dead. Is it true?"

Vincent could hear the fear in her voice. "We do everything within our power to protect all of you. I do everything within my power to protect you."

"What if that's not enough?"

"No one will hurt you here."

"I've heard someone's using the club to target us. People are freaking out, Vincent."

"You don't need to worry."

"I might be into satisfying rich people's fantasies. Sometimes I might even enjoy it, but I don't have a death wish. I'd have to leave."

"Where would you work?"

"I'd figure something out."

"Go back to working the streets?"

"Maybe work out of my place. Develop my own client list. I'm not the same person you met eight years ago, Vincent. I can do better now."

"Are you happy working for us?"

"I'm happy working for *you*."

"And you'll continue to be. I promise you."

Vincent left the room and headed straight to the bar upstairs. It was either too early or too late for a drink—depending on one's point of view—but he needed the booze to help collect his thoughts before the day ahead of him.

"An Old Fashioned," he said to Ben. The phone in his pocket started to vibrate, and even if he hadn't been standing in a member-frequented area where no cell phones were allowed, he would have ignored it. "How's it going?" he asked as Ben placed the glass in front of him.

"Tuesday night, you know."

Vincent glanced throughout the room. On weeknights, the

club resembled more of a social club than a sex club, especially the upper floors. Like Ben, he would rather be surrounded by elitists fucking than elitists discussing business.

"Two more hours and then you can tell them to go drink somewhere else. I'll make sure security helps get the point across."

Ben tried to suppress a yawn. "If we were open twenty-four hours I wonder if they'd ever go home."

"For some, this place is their home."

"That's a shame."

Vincent took his drink and, as he walked up to the third floor, the cigar smoke grew thicker. He wished he could ban the smoking of cigars throughout the club, but knew it wouldn't be well received by many of the members.

He entered the Black Dragon, which now stood empty. On the far end of the room, he unlocked a door that revealed a claustrophobic, badly lit corridor.

He kept his hand on the wall as he walked. He couldn't see the wallpaper but he remembered it clearly. When he was a kid, his mother had marched him down that corridor to visit his father. The lush green banana leaves on a gold background had captivated him. Once, his mother had caught him tracing one of the leaves with his fingers and she had asked him if he liked the wallpaper. Even before he could reply, she had told him, "It's from your grandmother's time. Your father hasn't ripped it off because it's a daily reminder of why he should hate his mother. Don't let your father know you like it."

Vincent had been his grandmother's favorite, the notorious Rose Cheng, who had managed the club until her death. Thanks to his aunt's defiant behavior, the generation-long tradition of having a woman run the club had been broken, and his father had found himself as the new club manager. Without daughters to pass it on to in his old age, his father appointed his youngest son, Vincent, to the position. Meanwhile, both Vincent's older brothers had been appointed to higher-ranking roles within the organization.

Ever since he had become the club manager, Vincent ran his

hand along the old wallpaper as he walked down the corridor—it was his daily reminder of why he should hate his father.

Vincent opened his office door and crouched down as his dog, Riley, rushed to greet him.

"How's my beautiful girl doing?" He placed his glass on the large mahogany desk and ran his fingers through her thick, healthy coat. She licked his face. Years ago, one of his brothers had left him with Riley, a mixed-breed puppy, after her owner had run into trouble with the organization. Vincent liked to think that Riley's previous owner would have felt some consolation in knowing his dog had met a better fate than him.

Vincent sat at his desk and Riley laid down by his feet. He pulled his phone from his pocket and saw he had two missed calls. They were from his boss, demanding answers. As he called the number back, he downed the rest of his drink.

"What took you so long to call me back?"

"I've been doing the rounds." It wasn't true. He paid others to keep an eye on the club's day-to-day operations.

"Where are we at on the workers' situation? How many?"

"So far, four female workers. In the last two years, all of them stopped showing up to work. But, the police aren't investigating their deaths."

"Why not?"

"They've all been deemed accidental overdoses."

"I don't know if I should be disgusted or happy at how incompetent the police are," the man said. "Still, this is bad. It gives us nothing to go on. What else you got?"

Vincent opened the envelope on his desk and looked at the police photographs of the four women. He had known them all. "Nothing. The police are a dead end. We can't rely on them for information. We'll have to do this ourselves."

"We offer those rich pervs everything. Now they also need to start killing off our workers?"

"We don't offer *everything*. Whoever is killing them has a fetish, a kink the club hasn't been able to fulfill."

"Happy workers means happy customers, and happy customers means a profitable business. Listen, I know once in a while accidents happen. When they do, we handle it. But this is different. It's not on our terms."

No. Happy customers who we can blackmail mean a very profitable business, Vincent thought to himself. "I believe this is the work of one person. Probably a man. I've gone through our records and hours of video surveillance, trying to find out which members these women have been with, who requested their services, who they might appeal to."

"And?"

"I've narrowed it down to twenty people."

"Twenty? What the fuck, Vincent? That's still too many."

"I'm working on narrowing it down further."

"You need to get control of this situation."

"I'm doing—"

"Vincent, don't make me take this to your brother."

He stood up and Riley jumped to her feet. She looked at him expectantly, her tail wagging. She wanted him to take her for a walk. "I'm handling it."

"Next time I talk to you I want to hear two things: the name of the fucker and that he's dead. Got me?"

"I'm doing—"

"Got me?"

"Yes," Vincent replied.

He ended the call and reached for Riley's leash. They both needed fresh air. "Let's go, girl."

Instead of exiting by the same door he had used earlier, he used the door at the opposite end of his office. After climbing a set of stairs, he and Riley emerged through a heavy metal door into the alley behind the restaurant.

His pre-dawn walks with Riley marked the only time Vincent almost enjoyed Chinatown. The streets, empty of people, loud noises, and overpowering scents, provided a calm space where his worries, for a brief moment, seemed far away and unimportant.

But this walk, unlike the others, did not provide the escape he needed. He had too much on his mind. He felt tense.

Vincent reached for his phone. "Get Nolan to meet me by Princeton and Alexander."

Born and raised in Chicago, at some point Vincent had thought about leaving, maybe for the California coast. Riley would have loved the ocean. But, fully aware of the responsibilities his birth placed on him, he knew both he and Riley would die in Chicago.

Vincent watched Nolan rush down the street. The man possessed the uncanny ability to look as if he belonged in whatever surroundings he found himself in, one of the reasons why he was good at his job. When he reached them, the three walked together toward the alley that ran from South Princeton to South Wentworth Avenue.

"We need to talk about the girl."

The man nodded. "I did exactly what you told me to do. She got the message."

Vincent had met Meredith. She was smart but also imprudent. "We might have to go all the away. Both with her and the *Tribune* guy."

"When?"

Vincent patted Riley between her ears. "I'll let you know."

"Is there a chance for, you know, some fun? She's smoking hot."

He stopped and faced the man. "If it happens, it goes down clean. If she has even a button undone I'll hold you responsible."

Nolan held his hands up in the air. "No worries. I understand."

As the three of them continued to walk together, Vincent focused on Riley, making sure she didn't eat any of the food scraps that littered the ground.

"It's not my place to ask, but shouldn't we just get it done now?" The man sounded impatient. "What are we waiting for? This isn't how we handle things."

"We handle things however I say we handle things."

After dismissing Nolan, Vincent and Riley returned to the club. Since their departure, the club had closed. With no background music and the fluorescent lights on, the club had lost its seductiveness. Only its unique scent remained.

"You got my message," Vincent said in Mandarin as he removed Riley's leash.

Julian's reply was also in Mandarin. "You wanted to see me?"

Throwing his blazer on a stool, Vincent joined Julian by the bar. "This meeting is a courtesy."

Julian did not bother to respond, merely shot Vincent a look of contempt.

"We need to discuss Meredith Dalton."

"What about her?"

"She's planning to publish an article on the club."

Vincent saw Julian's body stiffen.

"I'm giving you a chance to save her life."

"She's leaving Chicago."

Vincent chuckled. "She doesn't have to be in Chicago to publish her article. If you were anyone else, she'd already be dead. And so would you."

"When she started to pursue the article, she did it with no idea of the danger she was putting herself in. I was the one who brought her here. When I made her my guest, I was aware of the risks. I knew she was my responsibility. Harm me. Not Meredith"

Vincent smirked. Julian was trying to protect Meredith, which he had expected. He stood up and while Riley didn't move, she followed him with her eyes. "You think there's a chance you'll walk out of this unscathed? That's not how it works and you know it."

"I'm sure there's something we can do to fix this situation, to reach an agreement. I'll speak to Meredith. She will—"

"Julian," Vincent said, glancing at his watch. "It's seven thirty. You have twenty-four hours to convince me she's no longer a risk."

"How?"

"I don't care. Figure it out. After that, if I even get the slightest inkling she might be going ahead with her little story, she will be dead before she has a chance to type her next word. And as for you and your role in all this, you will never see your sons again."

CHAPTER 33

Under the late August heat, Meredith pressed the doorbell and waited. She felt nervous. Sweat dripped between her breasts and she fought the urge to slide her hand down the v-neck of her silk top and wipe it off.

No one came to the door and she pressed the doorbell again. The house stood in a peaceful, tree-lined street in the Lincoln Park neighborhood. She watched two young mothers pass, pushing strollers. The sight did nothing to calm her nerves.

Meredith had texted Tess with the address of her destination and, while at the time it had seemed like a silly precaution, now, as the door opened and Thompson stood in front of her, she was happy she had done it.

"Meredith." He stared at her with a mix of surprise and apprehension. "Why are you here?"

She couldn't blame him for looking taken aback. In her purse, she had his business card with his home address written on the back. She had his phone number, too, but hadn't called him to let him know she was coming. She had wanted to catch him by surprise, just like he had done to her.

"I'm here to finish the conversation you started." As she spoke, she didn't feel the confidence she tried to project.

"Come in."

Meredith took a deep breath and stepped inside.

Thompson had been barefoot when he greeted her at the door. He couldn't have looked more at ease in his jeans and white t-shirt, a strong contrast to the suit he had worn the day she discovered him sitting in her living room. He still had his arm in a cast and while she wanted to know what had happened, she didn't want to appear overly invested.

He offered her a choice of coffee or wine. Even though it was only two o'clock on a Saturday afternoon, Meredith went straight for the latter. It helped with the mantra she kept repeating in her head: *You got this. You totally got this, Meredith.*

"It's time I hear your side of the story. But, just so you know, I don't trust anything that comes out of your mouth," she said.

"You're straightforward. I appreciate that. And you're a curious young woman, aren't you?"

He wore a traditional-looking wedding band on his left hand and Meredith tried to remember if he'd had it on the day he stopped by her apartment.

"I'm assuming that's a rhetorical question," she replied, taking in her surroundings.

She hadn't known what to expect, but Thompson and Tatiana's home felt comfortable and lived-in. She wasn't fooled, though. Nothing under that roof had come from a garage sale. From the scuffed-up hardwood floor to the antique trunk in the corner, to the oatmeal curtains that so beautifully filtered the afternoon sun, there was only one price tag for all of it—expensive vintage. Remembering Tatiana's criticism of how much Meredith spent on herself, she wondered what she would find if she looked inside Tatiana's closet. By the décor of Tatiana's home and the understated, yet wealthy appearance of the man sitting in front of her, Meredith figured it would be wall-to-wall designer.

"You look nervous."

Meredith focused on Thompson. "Do you blame me?"

"You have nothing to fear. I came to you because I'm scared for my wife. Otherwise, I would have kept my distance."

"My father told me that you and Pam went to college together. That you were the one that introduced them."

"Yes. She was my girlfriend throughout undergrad."

After watching them at the Art Institute of Chicago this didn't surprise her. "Are you two sleeping together?"

"Set on protecting your father from his cheating, power-hungry wife?"

Meredith remained silent.

"We're not," Thompson clarified.

"Do Pam and Tatiana know each other?"

"As far I know, they've never met."

"Is Pam aware that you and Tatiana frequent The Raven Room?"

Thompson hesitated. "Yes."

"Does Pam go to the club as well?"

"Have you seen her there? Have you seen anyone you know there?"

"It's a big place. Tatiana and Julian didn't run into each other up until the day I went with him."

"That's because Tatiana avoided him."

"How did you and Tatiana get a membership?"

"I obtained access to the club because of Tatiana. And before you ask, I don't know how she came to know about the club or how she got a membership. That's something she always refused to share with me. I'm sure you have experienced the same with Julian."

"He and I haven't been married for ten years."

"You'd be amazed at the things you are willing to do, or overlook, to make the person you love happy."

"Is hitting them one of those things?"

"I have a temper. I'm not proud of it. I was lucky enough to grow up in an affluent home. Unfortunately, mixed with such affluence was the lesson that it's normal for a husband to hit his wife."

Meredith almost laughed. "Sounds like an excuse."

"Not an excuse. Just an explanation."

"I don't understand why Tatiana would waste a decade of her life, her youth, on you."

"Do you understand what true commitment is, Meredith? Loyalty?"

"Don't patronize me." His words made her think of Julian, but she was quick to put any thoughts of him aside. She took a sip of her wine. "Tell me how you two met."

"At the time she was waitressing at Balzac's, in the Loop. It's since closed, but I used to go there every Friday night, after leaving the office. I'd go by myself to think. I had just gotten divorced from my first wife. We weren't married long but it didn't make the breakup any easier. Before I went through it myself I would always roll my eyes when I'd hear someone say that going though a divorce is similar to going through the death of a loved one." Thompson's expression changed and his voice lost its lighthearted tone. "Nothing changes your attitude about something faster than experiencing it yourself."

"Let me guess, you then fucked the young waitress to alleviate your sorrow over your failed marriage?"

"Tatiana and I did end up fucking, but it took us a year to get there. We became friends. I would go as far as to say she became my best friend. She was pretty, but her personality is what set her apart. She was captivating." He smiled. "She *is* captivating."

"Now you think your wife is hiding with Julian and you want to make sure she's OK."

"Yes. I want to see her, talk to her. Julian is not the man you think he is."

"You don't know what I think of him."

"I'm going to show you something that, hopefully, will motivate you to do the right thing." Thompson fetched a laptop that was on the coffee table. "It infuriates me that I can't do anything with it."

A video began to play on the screen, showing two people in what looked like a bedroom. From the angle of the image, Meredith figured the camera must have be mounted on the wall, close to the ceiling, giving the watcher almost a bird's-eye view of the bed in the center of the room. It didn't take Meredith long to recognize the naked man. His large tattoo, which ran along his left arm, confirmed that it was indeed Julian. A younger-looking Julian.

"What's this?" she asked.

Thompson raised the volume on the laptop. "Just watch."

The young woman who was with Julian on the bed rolled over and Meredith got to see her face for the first time. The realization of who she was didn't hit Meredith right away. It crept in slowly, flooding her mind with a mixture of surprise and dismay. Rebecca Glendon. She looked almost exactly like she did in the picture Meredith had found at her brother's house. On white sheets that almost glowed under the lighting's deep red hue, Julian moved behind Rebecca and Meredith heard the loud moan that escaped the young woman's lips when Julian entered her. Meredith couldn't look away. She knew exactly how Rebecca felt in that moment, to have all her senses heightened by the intense and swift sensation of taking all of him—of Julian, deep and unyielding, inside of her.

The sex unfolding on the screen intensified. Closing his hand on the front of her neck, Julian pulled Rebecca toward him, her back pressed to his chest. They continued to move together, with Julian's free hand squeezing her breasts, then moving toward her stomach and continuing past her navel. Rebecca spread her legs wider in response. Fully open to Julian's thrusts and his fingers, she started to pant.

The video began to have an effect on Meredith. Her body's response didn't surprise her. She felt her arousal seeping into the fabric of her lace underwear, and even if she weren't completely engrossed by the footage, she wouldn't have dared to look at Thompson. She felt his body only a few inches from hers; she smelled his cologne mixed with the warmth of his skin and the aroma of the red wine. For a brief second, she knew that if he touched her she wouldn't rebut him. That realization scared her more than anything else since arriving in his house. What did that say about her, Meredith wondered.

At that point, Julian started to speak, explicit words, demands, pleas, so many of which Julian and Meredith had also said to each other to intensify each other's pleasure, to make each other lose control. Meredith was about to stop the video when she heard Julian say one word that made her snap out of her erotic trance—

Tatia. He called Rebecca *Tatia.* And he repeated it over and over again. Rebecca didn't hesitate or stop him to ask why he called her by the name. She continued to match Julian's movements with eagerness. Seemingly out of nowhere, Julian held a knife and he caressed Rebecca's skin with the blade, over and over again, starting at her neck and then moving to her collarbone.

Simultaneously afraid and enthralled, Meredith watched on. Every time she heard Julian say Tatia's name Meredith's heart beat faster. Julian's hand, the one holding the knife, returned to the side of Rebecca's neck, and with no warning, blood started to ooze from a cut along the young woman's collarbone, drip down her torso, and fall on the sheets. As Meredith gasped, Rebecca put both of her hands to her neck. Her eyes were wide open, fixated on empty space. She didn't scream. She didn't try to move away. Julian continued to thrust in and out of her and Meredith watched him orgasm as more blood covered the young woman's body and soaked the bed. Meredith tasted the metallic tang of it in her own mouth. She almost gagged. Rebecca appeared lifeless as Julian held her in his arms. Meredith waited for Julian to do something, maybe scream, maybe try to help the young woman, but instead he just continued to hold Rebecca.

The video came to an abrupt end. Meredith didn't speak and neither did Thompson. He eventually took the laptop away from her.

"Do you understand now why I'm worried for my wife? He'll kill her."

Meredith covered her face with her hands. "What do you want from me?"

"My wife."

"Have you showed this video to the police?"

"I can't. If I did I would be as good as dead."

"I don't believe you."

"The organization protects Julian. I'm sure no one since has laid eyes on the woman we saw on that video. They are experts at disposing of their trash."

Meredith reached for her wine and gulped it down. She needed it. Her throat felt so dry it hurt.

"I'm leaving." She stood up so fast that she was surprised she didn't stagger. Her fingers found her purse and she held it tightly.

"Meredith—"

"I want nothing to do with you," she said, not letting him continue. "Stay the hell away from me."

As she started to walk toward the front door her vision became blurry with tears. Suddenly, Meredith heard a loud, sharp cracking sound coming from behind her. She turned and saw Thompson standing, a hand pressed to his stomach. Red bloomed on his t-shirt. He had been shot. As she rushed up to him, she glanced around but didn't see anyone else.

Thompson slumped to the floor. She kneeled by him, putting pressure on his stomach.

"You'll be OK." If she didn't call an ambulance right away, Thompson would die. "You'll be OK," she repeated over and over again.

He gripped her arms.

"I need to call 9-1-1," she said, her voice rushed. "I need to get help."

"Meredith—" He looked past her with terror in his eyes.

She turned around and before she could see who now stood behind her, she felt a sharp, deep pain in the side of her head. She tried to remain upright but her vision blurred. She didn't have a chance to cry out.

END OF BOOK TWO